SCOTT NADELSON

# Saving Stanley

## THE BRICKMAN STORIES

HAWTHORNE BOOKS & LITERARY ARTS
Portland, Oregon :: MMIV

Hawthorne Books & Literary Arts

P.O. Box 579
Portland, Oregon 97207
hawthornebooks.com

*Editorial*:
Michelle Piranio,
Portland, Oregon

*Form*:
Pinch, Portland, Oregon

Printed in China
through Print Vision, Inc.

Set in DTL Albertina.

9
8
7
6
5
4
3
2
1

Library of Congress Cataloging-in-Publication Data

Nadelson, Scott.
Saving Stanley:
The Brickman Stories/
Scott Nadelson
p. cm.
ISBN 0-9716915-2-5
(trade paperback)
1. Jewish families – Fiction.
2. Teenage boys – Fiction.
3. New Jersey – Fiction.
I. Title.

PS3614.A34 S28 2003
813´6
[
2002006845

"Kosher" was first published in *Carve Magazine* and *The Best of Carve, Vol. 3*. All other stories appear here in print for the first time.

For my mother, father, and brother.

I AM DEEPLY GRATEFUL TO LITERARY ARTS, INC., FOR A FELLOW-ship without which this book could not have been completed. I would also like to thank Rhonda Hughes & Kate Sage of Hawthorne Books, Jay Clarke, Meg Daly, Tracy Daugherty, Ehud Havazelet, and Marjorie Sandor for their encouragement and guidance.

SAVING STANLEY

# Saving Stanley

WHEN THE CAT WAS SICK AND SLOWLY DYING, HANNAH canceled vacation plans, dinner parties, hair appointments, a manicure. Arthur, her husband, was sympathetic, though she didn't expect him to understand. They'd planned a trip to San Antonio, where Arthur had a conference. Then it was on to Veracruz, four nights, five days, a private beach on the Gulf. The conference didn't interest Arthur in the least; it was only circumstantially related to his job, and any of the four technicians in his lab would have been thrilled to take his place. But it coincided with Hannah's spring break, so he'd written it into his budget early in the fall. He'd agreed on Mexico for her sake as well – sitting on a beach had never appealed to him, and after complaining for a few hours about the sand in his shoes and hair, the salt in his eyes, he'd spend the rest of the trip sitting by the pool reading a magazine or searching the city's back streets for a copy of the *International Herald-Tribune*.

She waited as long as she could before calling it off. Each day she fully expected the cat to recover, to stand up on his own, to nibble from the dish of food she changed every morning despite its never being touched. But five days before they were scheduled to leave, she had to concede that there'd been no change and wouldn't be in time for her to go. Arthur nodded and raised no fuss. The registration for the conference had already been paid, charged to his corporate expense account, so he would still go to San Antonio. She knew how much he hated dining and sightseeing on his own: he would spend four miserable evenings alone in a stuffy hotel room, straining to read the newspaper by a dim lamp, ordering overpriced and overcooked room-service food, stepping out only to refill his bucket of ice. He called the airlines, canceled the extra leg to Veracruz. He struggled to explain to the Mexican hotel clerk that no, he didn't want a larger room, no, he didn't want an extra room, no, he didn't want any room at all. He paid a fortune in penalties, but still not one word of grievance, and for that she was entirely grateful.

More than Arthur, it was her younger son, Daniel, who urged her to go away. The first time Arthur had suggested saving Mexico for another year, Daniel, seventeen now, a senior in high school, had sprung from the family room couch where he'd been watching TV and run into the kitchen. "You can't cancel your vacation!" he said in genuine outrage. "I'll be here. I can take care of Stanley."

Daniel was rarely cruel or combative, but he was wildly inconsistent and very often confused her—this she would admit to almost anyone. They didn't fight so much as simply miss some vital connection when they spoke. Her older son, Jared, had been different. They'd battled outright. All the way through his high school years, she and Jared had had screaming matches over all the predictable things: his curfews, his girlfriends, his clothes. Once they'd been arguing for close to an hour—over what she could no longer remember—and Jared, in frustration, slammed his fist on the kitchen counter and shouted, "You're the Devil!" For a moment she said nothing, but then burst out laughing. Jared smiled in embarrassment. For the rest of the week, every time they crossed paths—which was rare even while they were living under the same roof—she held her fingers like horns on the sides of her head. After that she knew everything between them would turn out fine. And it had. They now spoke on the phone once a week, and Jared always ended with, "Good talking to you, Mom." He was graduating from Rutgers in another two months and had already lined up a promising position with a financial firm in Manhattan. She'd always feared he'd end up in California or overseas, but now he would be no more than an hour away, closer if he decided to commute and pay a lower rent. Despite their difficulties, Hannah and Jared had always understood each other on some very basic, primal level— at family gatherings, relatives often commented on how much they looked alike, how they had the same eyes, the same slender fingers.

With Daniel, nothing was so straightforward. At times he seemed just like his father: subdued, sensitive, somewhat timid. But after twenty-three years of marriage, she could predict the first word out of Arthur's mouth when he came home for dinner, could, when he went away for a week, picture his form slumped in the family room armchair, hear the choked sputtering of his snore. Not so with Daniel; from day to day he was a mystery to her. For weeks at a time he could be a sweet, quiet kid, helping around the house without being asked, listening attentively to her stories about school and students or to Arthur's about the evil workings of the corporate world. And then, out of nowhere came a belligerence, an act of stupid defiance.

Last spring he'd read a book or two about the '60s and discovered Arthur's collection of Bob Dylan records. Though he'd never opened a newspaper or watched anything but sitcoms on TV, he suddenly claimed to be an activist of some sort. Any cause would do. For almost a year he refused to buy new sneakers, even as the treads on his Reeboks wore down to flaps of rubber and his toe poked through a hole in the leather. No matter how forcefully Hannah commanded him, he wouldn't go with her to a shoe store. She tried begging, even bribing, but it did no good. "Do you have any idea who makes these things?" he said. "Twelve-year-old kids getting paid two dollars a week. I can't be part of that."

This all started during the war in the Persian Gulf, and while his classmates pinned yellow ribbons to their collars, Daniel wore a black armband, a perfectly good belt he'd snipped in half. Hannah came home one day to find a message on the answering machine from Daniel's vice-principal. Her son, the man explained, had been shockingly disrespectful in the classroom. Daniel, it turned out, had called his calculus teacher "an oil baron's whore," for telling the class to show support for the war in Iraq. Then, when the teacher sent him to the vice-principal's office, he left politics aside and called the man simply, "fat motherfucker." A few days later there was a note in the mailbox from a neighbor Hannah barely knew: Daniel, it said, had attacked her as she was pouring leftover paint down a sewer drain. He'd kicked over the bucket onto the woman's treated lawn and shouted maniacally, "Fish-killer!" Hannah was lucky, the woman wrote, that she didn't call the police. Even more recently, Daniel was suspended from school for a week after stuffing into lockers what he called an "underground newspaper," a sloppily written, one-paragraph rant about his principal, who, he claimed, cared only about sports and test scores and, aside from football players and merit scholars, didn't know a single student's name. "It's my Constitutional right," he insisted after being caught and sent home. "We should get a lawyer," he kept telling Hannah, until she cut him off, whispering through clenched teeth, "Another word, and you can say goodbye to your car."

After each of these fits, he went through a period of pure slothfulness, weeks without doing any homework, playing sports, or even watching TV. He'd sit for hours on the porch with a rock 'n' roll magazine in his lap. Through the kitchen window Hannah would watch him for fifteen, twenty minutes, and never see him turn a page. Occasionally she would ask if something was wrong. He'd answer quickly, "Of course something's wrong. Do you realize how many people in this country don't have a place to sleep at night?"

It wasn't, as some of her students might have guessed, her strictness as a parent that made Daniel act the way he did. She was more lenient with him than she'd ever dreamed of being with Jared, hoping to avoid the anger and tension that had consumed the house during her older son's high school years. She'd let Daniel buy his own car with the money he made as a cashier at a local discount store. His weekend curfew was late and flexible, though he was usually home well before midnight. She tried not to ask too many questions about where he went or whom he was with. She only knew a few of his friends by name, fewer by sight. He spent plenty of time on the phone, but calls rarely came in for him. Other kids never came by the house. Lazy as he was, he'd managed to get through high school with reasonable grades and would graduate in June. Of course, he'd been late filling out his college applications. The only deadline he'd made was for the University of Delaware, and a month ago he'd accepted their offer for the coming fall. There was nothing wrong with Delaware. It was a fine enough school, but Hannah had hoped he would have chosen something smaller, more personal. When she imagined him at Delaware, she could only picture a surging crowd, Daniel a tiny speck distinguishable for a moment by the awful mass of hair he was trying to grow long, and then quickly obscured from sight.

There were times when she wondered whether he'd already been dragged into something dangerous – drugs, gambling, she almost didn't want to know. But then he'd suddenly become a sweet kid again, helping her plant flowers in the front yard, surprising his teachers with a streak of flawless schoolwork. With relief and fondness, she'd recall a happier time, Daniel as a bar mitzvah boy, smiling broadly, surrounded by a group of dancing, hysterical kids. The promise of those days was not yet lost, she told herself then. The best was yet to come.

But when she finally announced her decision to cancel the trip to Mexico, Daniel was furious. She shouldn't have been surprised. Long ago she should have resigned herself to simply being baffled.

"You don't trust me?" he said with a bitterness that seemed foreign to him and already slightly faltering, slipping into self-pity. "Aren't I responsible?"

"This has nothing to do with you," she said. If she left, Daniel would try to take care of Stanley, she knew. He'd follow her instructions for a day, maybe two, and then slowly find excuses not to. If the cat didn't want to eat, he'd tell himself, why should he eat? Hannah would come home to find the cat buried in the backyard. "Stanley's getting better. I can't just break his routine."

"You've got to go," he said. His voice now wasn't so much angry as desperate. His face reddened, and his eyes searched beyond Hannah's shoulders. "You can't give up everything for a cat."

"That cat," she snapped. "That cat's been around almost as long as you have."

He nodded slowly. "And soon I'll be gone, too."

"What's that supposed to mean?" Hannah said. "Stanley's not going anywhere." But Daniel had already turned away and was heading for his room.

SHE STILL WENT TO SCHOOL EVERY DAY, TAUGHT ALL HER classes, but rushed home during prep periods and lunch hours. Three times a day she cursed the traffic on Route 46, which left her barely fifteen minutes at home to run upstairs, coax the cat from his hiding place, scratch his head, and tell him in the high, cooing voice she'd used so often on her boys as infants that everything, everything would be just fine. She told no one at school what was wrong, but begged out of staff meetings and turned down invitations she ordinarily accepted without hesitation – late afternoon coffee with a Spanish teacher, a Saturday shopping excursion to the Secaucus outlet malls with the front-office secretaries. She canceled French Club meetings and didn't schedule any afternoon tutoring sessions. She had no energy to come up with excuses.

After a week, the school's principal stopped her as she hurried from the teacher's lounge. He was an amiable man, completely bald and soft all over, with a compassionate, feminine way of touching the tip of a single extended finger to her elbow as he spoke. "Hannah, dear," he said. "Is everything all right? Are there–" He hesitated a moment, pulled at his chubby knuckles, and went on: "Something's wrong at home?" She nodded and tried to answer, but only managed to suck in her lower lip, which trembled between her teeth. "Whatever I can do for you," he said. "If you need a day–"

She waved a hand, then wiped her eyes, checking her fingers for traces of mascara. "Thank you," she said. "It's…hard. My…I'm sorry."

At school she'd long had a reputation for being willful. "Such a strong woman," other teachers had whispered close enough for her to hear; she didn't want to know what they whispered when she was out of range. Despite her small size, her quiet demeanor, she came across as tough, almost fearless in the face of opposition. This was, to some extent, a facet of her personality, though she was often conscious of playing a role. She was in her late forties but only a junior member of the French faculty– she'd taken more than a decade off from teaching to raise her sons. Seven years at the school, not a veteran by any standard. Other teachers were pushy; plenty were loudmouths; many threw around the weight of their seniority. But in a meeting she knew how to command attention. She chose her words carefully, enunciating with almost painful deliberation. Her attitude was one of weariness with other teachers' pettiness. This was a school. This was serious business. Anyone who argued with her came off sounding defensive, childish. Occasionally she saw her manner as calculating, even duplicitous, and the act shamed her; but mostly it served her purpose.

Only once had she lost control of her composure in a conference room. During an endless debate over whether to bar students from smoking in the designated outdoor lounge – a corral, really, with a head-high chain-link fence and a view of the maintenance shed – a physics teacher on the verge of retirement, a man who still greased his hair on the sides and combed it to a ducktail in back, stood and shouted over the jumble of voices, "Why can't they smoke in the damn toilets? It was good enough for us, wasn't it?" She was on her feet so quickly her chair toppled over. The room went silent. The physics teacher took a step backward and blushed. "Do we really need more ignorance in here?" she cried. "Isn't there enough in our classrooms?"

She expected this to undermine her reputation. All the respect she'd gained erased by one unnecessary display of true feelings. But instead, the outburst put the finishing touches on her image—not only was she thoughtful and determined, but beneath her calm exterior bubbled an active fury.

She didn't believe her students were afraid of her, exactly—few of them cared enough about her class or their grades for that—but the majority knew better than to test her patience. When she grew tired of their rowdiness or hilarity, she simply set her jaw and crossed her arms. A switch was thrown: talking and laughter dropped off to a few scattered whispers, pencils, ignored for half an hour, began scratching across paper, hands rose to answer a question.

A month or so before the cat got sick, a senior girl in her fourth-year French class had spent twenty minutes trying to convince her to postpone a test. The girl, Alyssa Silver, was one of her best students; not a member of the French Club or even the type to turn in extra credit assignments, but always attentive and lighthearted. She had enough confidence in her prettiness and popularity to participate regularly in class without fearing ridicule. In three years she'd never, as far as Hannah could remember, scored below a B+ on even the most unexpected of surprise quizzes. But now she wanted to miss class on Friday. Her boyfriend's baseball team was playing an important game in south Jersey, and really, she explained, there was no reason not to put off the test until Monday. Hannah listened without speaking and afterward nodded. If the girl chose to miss class, she would, of course, have a week to take a make-up, the same as anyone else. "Don't you think that's fair enough?" Hannah asked, though even she knew her make-up tests were notorious for being twice as difficult as their originals. And why shouldn't they be? Why should any of these kids miss class and not suffer consequences? Why should this girl—just because she was pretty and popular enough to have a baseball-playing boyfriend—be privileged in the classroom as well as outside? Alyssa tried pleading, crying, even raising her regrettably nasal voice. In the end it was less righteousness than a threatening headache and boredom with the girl's whining that finally made Hannah lean back in her chair, cross her arms, and say, "We're finished now." Immediately she saw herself blurred through the girl's teary brown eyes, now red and swollen, and thought, *Hannah, you old bitch.* Guiltily, she clamped her teeth and stared Alyssa in the face until the girl had no choice but to walk away. Only at the classroom door did she call back over her shoulder, "My God, Mrs. Brickman. I'd hate to be your kid."

Now again, she expected all this to change. The respect she'd always secretly believed to be fragile and fleeting would disappear entirely at the first sight of her colorless cheeks free of make-up – she bothered with nothing now but lipstick and mascara – her hair showing gray at the roots, her chipped nails, her blouses and skirts, ordinarily meticulous, now slightly rumpled.

The changes that did come, however, she never could have anticipated. No one seemed to know how to treat her. Male teachers passing in the halls nodded to her deeply, nearly bowing. Small packages appeared on her desk: seashell-shaped soap, raspberry-filled chocolates, a miniature ceramic flower basket. One morning she found an elegant card, cream-colored, with embroidered white ribbons, propped against her picture frame housing a postcard from the Paris Opera House. It read simply, "We're here for you," and was signed by the entire foreign-languages faculty. Her colleagues, she knew, assumed the worst: her father was dying, her marriage falling apart. But her father, eighty-three, was an ox. She expected him to live another ten years, though his hearing was half-gone and his short-term memory more than half. And Arthur was still Arthur. Nothing between them had changed for years.

The way her students reacted surprised her even more. She braced herself for a surge of impudence, a rash of back talk and open dozing. But instead, her lessons were met with an unusual silence. Even the laziest students began turning in assignments on time. Entire classes chanted vocabulary lists in an unprecedented, somewhat eerie unison. The kids seemed disturbed by her distraction, some even frightened. True, on a few faces – on Alyssa Silver's face – she thought she could read a snickering, disdainful pleasure. And, she guessed, rumors were spreading gleefully from desk to desk, along the rows of rusted lockers, in the parking lot and smoking lounge, more creative than anything written in English or drama classes. Each new version of her story would be more tragic than the last. Her son was on heroin. Or her son had stolen a car to buy heroin. Even better, her son had killed another boy who owed him heroin. Or her daughter – she didn't have one, but they didn't know this; she made it a rule never to speak of her family in class – her fourteen-year-old daughter was pregnant. Pregnant, that is, by an uncle. Pregnant and run away to Los Angeles, where police found her dead body in a Dumpster behind a back-street brothel, wearing nothing but stockings, garters, and a see-through bra.

THIS, THEN, IS WHAT NONE OF THEM KNEW. WITHIN THIRTY seconds of the day's final bell, her books were shut, her lesson planner stuffed hastily into her bag. The cloth tote and her purse, one over each shoulder, beat a march against her back as she cut through halls swarming with kids, some lingering at their lockers, deciding, maybe, whether or not to bother bringing any books home, others making their slow way to sports practices, clubs, committees they could list on their college applications, most simply loitering, getting in her way. She pushed between a couple, a kissing statue. Neither body was moving in any semblance of passion – they just stood, pressed together at the waist and the face, barely breathing until she forced them apart. Behind her they gasped for air. She bumped her way through a cluster of teachers clogging the stairwell. A girl's voice called after her, "Good night, Mrs. Brickman," but she only raised an arm, not turning to find a face.

In a sprint across the parking lot, she found herself staring down a speeding black sports car with a sharply angled hood and ridiculous pop-up headlights. Its brakes screeched and its bumper stopped inches short of her knees. A squeaky voice on a kid twice the size of her husband called out, "Crazy bitch!" He took off his sunglasses and waved them at the road. Hannah put a hand on his hood, leaned forward, and said, "What's your name?"

"You ran out in front of me," the kid said quickly, already apologetic. "I could have killed you."

"Tell me your name," she said. "Tomorrow at lunch, you can come to my classroom. You can find out what a bitch I am. We'll see about crazy." Not a word from the kid, who slipped the sunglasses back over his ears. He gripped the steering wheel in both hands and stared somewhere past her legs, at an interesting spot on the pavement. "It's sunny out," she said. "You don't need headlights."

She honked and weaved her way along Route 46, slamming the heel of her hand against the dash at every intersection that forced her to a full stop, more than once accelerating through a yellow light clicking over to red. There was no need to hurry. This wasn't a prep period; she wouldn't have to turn around and hurry straight back to school. She'd have the whole night at home. What difference would a few minutes make? But the thought of being too late – a minute, thirty seconds after nothing more could be done – filled her with such an unaccountable dread she couldn't help tearing off the highway into a maze of residential streets, roaring around garbage and mail trucks, once nearly clipping a jogger. She couldn't slow down even as she reached her street, her own steep driveway. The car fishtailed around the mailbox, skidded onto the lawn, kicked up a clump of sod, and left steaming tire tracks on the cracked tar she had, until two weeks ago, constantly nagged Arthur to have resealed.

The stairs from the garage she took two at a time, shoes in hand. Without pausing she glanced into the family room to see if Daniel was pretending to do his homework. He went to the regional high school only a mile and a half from their house – to avoid torturing either herself or the boys, she'd made sure to teach in a school they would never attend – and no matter how fast she rushed home, he beat her by half an hour. When she came in he often sat on the family room couch with a book in his lap, though she knew he'd only turned off the TV a moment before, at the first rumble of the automatic garage door. But now the room was empty. Another set of stairs, and she was out of breath and had to pee, but kept running, past her own bedroom, past the boys' bathroom, past the closed door of Daniel's bedroom, behind which he would either be grinding his torso against the sheets she had to wash at least twice a week or else already asleep from the exhaustion. There were worse things he could be doing, she knew. It could be a girl underneath him rather than sheets, giving her grandchildren no one was ready for. Or else, God forbid, a boy beneath him, and no grandchildren, ever. There were too many worse things even to think about.

The room beside Daniel's had once been her older son's, but a year after Jared had gone away to college, she'd turned it into her gym. Jared's desk was gone, and his dresser, replaced by a treadmill and a rowing machine that squeaked relentlessly even though Arthur had oiled it in every spot imaginable. Where Jared had once piled his dirty clothes, stubbornly refusing, despite her daily scolding, to carry them the fifty feet to the bathroom hamper, now sat a weight bench upholstered in shiny red vinyl. In the center of the room was a bulky black StairMaster she'd sweated over every morning for the last two years and now hadn't switched on for nearly two weeks. It was on this she tossed her purse and tote bag.

Only Jared's bed remained. He no longer slept here during his infrequent visits – he preferred to stay in the guest room rather than trip over loose dumbbells on his way to the toilet in the middle of the night – but still she couldn't bring herself to get rid of it, no matter how much extra space it would give her gym. To Arthur she'd argued that they needed it for extra guests on holidays and special occasions. But from his placating expression she could tell even he sensed there was more to it than this. Often she peeked into the room before heading off to sleep. Every two weeks she automatically changed the unused sheets and creased the blanket. She did so without quite understanding what she was after. Did she secretly hope to lure Jared back home after graduation? Was it so hard to believe, after three and a half years, there was only one boy left in the house?

Now the bed was surrounded by newspapers and plastic garbage bags spread over the carpet. By one corner sat an open litter box, untouched for days, the grainy surface as even as when she'd first smoothed it with the plastic scoop. It was Jared's bed that Stanley, the orange tabby, had chosen for his burial cave. Stanley: she'd never gotten used to the name. Jared, at five years old, had named him after a favorite great-uncle. When

she'd suggested more traditional feline names – Frisky, Tiger, Rusty, Tom –
he'd insisted with tears. Stanley was Jared's cat, officially, a birthday present after a long dispute with Arthur over getting a dog. Hannah had always
had dogs as a child; Arthur grumbled about the smell and about who
would always be stuck walking outside on cold winter nights, waiting for
a stupid animal to turn the snow yellow. Jared had pouted and whimpered
even after they'd brought the cat home. For sixteen years no one but Hannah had fed Stanley or cleaned his litter box. And the cat had sensed where
he was most wanted: he spent evenings on her lap, slept by her feet every
night, woke her each morning with a soft tap on her left eyelid. Often he
followed her into the bathroom and rubbed against her legs as she sat on
the toilet or waited on the bath mat as she showered. The first time she
ran on her new treadmill he seemed to think it was hurting her and rushed
to her defense; he growled and swatted at the belt until a claw caught and
she had to switch off the machine before he was dragged underneath.

And then, three weeks ago, she'd brought him to the vet to have four
rotting teeth removed. The doctor had suggested anesthesia to spare him
unnecessary pain. There was a slight complication, a minor infection,
nothing serious. But Stanley mistook his grogginess from drugs for the
onslaught of death. The first day home he ate less than a quarter can of food,
half his regular amount. The next day it was half again, the third no more
than three bites. He was out of danger, the doctor assured her, but on the
fourth day Stanley crawled under Jared's bed and stayed there. He didn't
come running at the sound of a can opener or the shaking of a bag of
treats. For a short while he still came out to use the litter box, but now not
even that – when he managed to build up enough waste, he moved no more
than a few feet from where he lay, to a spot on the carpet she'd been too
late to cover with plastic. The vet told her there was little she could do. "Are
you going to explain to a cat he's being a hypochondriac?" He chuckled
and quickly cleared his throat. "Sometimes, at his age, they just decide
it's time to go."

She didn't believe a word of this. No one, not even a cat, would simply
decide to die. He was just confused by the anesthesia and the four sore
gaps in his mouth. Now she dropped to her knees beside the bed, lowered

herself onto her belly, and squirmed forward until her head poked beneath the low metal frame. There, in the far corner, Stanley lay curled with his back to her, facing the wall, the same as when she'd left him at lunchtime. His slack skin draped over meatless ribs, and his ear didn't flinch as she reached out to scratch it. He smelled of rotting trash sprinkled lightly with chloroseptic. For a moment she was sure – as she was every time she checked under the bed – that it was over. He'd already taken his last breath. She'd missed it.

But no: here came the painfully slow rise of his chest, the sighing exhale. His fur was oily, clumped and tangled almost everywhere. Everywhere except on his front paws, where the fur was brighter and straight, ruffled like a bird's wings after preening. The paws, more than anything, brought her running home every afternoon, made her drop to her knees and squirm under the bed. If it weren't for the paws, she might have considered giving up, might have, as Arthur had tentatively suggested, asked the vet to end Stanley's suffering. But at least once a day the cat lifted his head and gave a few careful licks. It was more than an act of hygiene, Hannah was certain; it was a sign of pride. Could this be an animal who wanted to end his life? All day at school she feared coming home to find the paws as matted and oily as the rest of his body. Each time she found them clean, and each time her relief was only partial: there was still tomorrow, the next day, the day after that. When she left him, it was always with the certainty that everything would change in her absence.

But now the paws were clean again, and she pushed farther under the bed, holding her breath against the sharp, ammoniac smell that wouldn't subside, no matter how many carpet cleaners she sprayed on the spot Stanley used for his toilet. In the voice that had so captured her boys' attention in their cribs and strollers, she said, "Who's my sweetie? Who's the best kitty?" and ran a knuckle along Stanley's jaw. His eyes stayed closed, but his whiskers flattened against his cheek. She slid a hand under his flank, and he let out a weak groan, barely kicking his back legs as she dragged him into the light.

She had only one chance, according to the vet. Keep the cat alive until his own desire to live took over. So this was the routine. She carried him from Jared's room to the bathroom, propped him on the counter, and pinned him down with an elbow on his knobby spine. Into an enormous plastic syringe, she spooned a pinkish paste from a can available only by prescription at animal hospitals. Highly nutritious, the doctor had said. Concentrated protein. A small stack of cans had cost as much as a week's grocery shopping or a monthly phone bill. By now her bladder ached, the toilet only a few feet from her, but she only shifted from one foot to the other. The end of the syringe she pushed into the seam of Stanley's loose lips, prying open the grayish gums and yellow teeth, deeply grooved and sometimes brown – these teeth that had caused so much trouble. Couldn't she have brushed them from the day she'd first brought him home as a kitten? At the time the thought of brushing a cat's teeth would have struck her as laughable – but now look what she would do for him. His jaws resisted a moment, no more, and then gave way. With the first squirt of food, always a shock, his eyes opened fully – still Stanley's eyes, olive green flecked with yellow, surprisingly clear and even more beautiful now that they stood out against the emaciated face, the matted fur, the sunken temples, the exposed, fragile shape of his skull – and this is when Hannah's own eyes began to water. Stanley shook his head, thrashed his tongue, tried to spit, and flakes of food splattered the sink, the mirror, the floor, the blouse she knew she should have changed before starting this. The food smelled somehow the way a mouthful of salt tastes, bitter and sour at the same time, drying out the tongue and throat, impossible to swallow. It reminded her of a summertime beach at low tide – especially the beach in New Haven where she'd grown up, where seaweed and the leftovers of a barbecue mixed together on the sand, heavily salted by the previous night's waves, steaming under the same sun, deceitfully strong behind a wall of haze, that had burned her shoulders and legs red and raw by the second week of June.

Stanley made an attempt at hissing that was closer to a cough. This, too, Hannah thought, was an attempt at dignity, and she was glad for it. The second squirt from the syringe was easier, and though food still flew, she was sure some of it made its way into the cat's stomach. And now Daniel appeared in the bathroom's doorway, not a step closer. His thick hair hung an inch shy of his shoulders in back and stuck up ridiculously, bubble-shaped, on top. One cheek was red and lined where he'd been sleeping on a crease in his sheet. Hannah wiped the corners of her eyes with a sleeve. In the mirror she saw flakes of pink food in her hair.

"How's he doing?" Daniel asked.

"Pet him while I finish."

He scratched Stanley just above the tail, but of course the cat's haunches didn't rise as they once eagerly would have. Stanley was completely limp now, not a hint of struggle left in him. Whatever food failed to go down his throat dribbled onto his chin. She pumped a third syringe, a fourth, and then loaded a fifth, one more than the vet had instructed – but the first had been a total loss.

"Mom, look at him," Daniel said. "He's exhausted. He's had enough, don't you think?"

"I'll show you what's enough!" she shouted. She wasn't surprised by her anger so much as by the senselessness of her words and the quivering in her voice. She hadn't wiped her eyes for minutes now and knew mascara must be streaking down her cheeks. But she wouldn't check the mirror. "Of course he's exhausted," she said. "He doesn't eat. He needs strength. Don't you want him to get better?" Daniel stared at the floor but kept stroking Stanley's spine. Stanley's eyes, enormous, green, pleading, wouldn't leave her face. "Soon he'll eat on his own again," she said, and plunged the syringe deep into the cat's throat.

IT WASN'T A FEELING OF HELPLESSNESS THAT KEPT HER AWAKE at night, staring at the ceiling, listening to Arthur snore. She could say this honestly. She hadn't truly felt helpless in years, not even for a moment. Not while diabetes had been killing her mother. At the time, she'd been too concerned about her father: all her efforts she put into keeping up his spirits, into convincing him that her mother would have wanted his life to be happy when she was gone. Only a week after the funeral did Hannah realize she hadn't yet begun to grieve. If anything, what kept her from sleeping now was knowing she wasn't helpless, that she had the power to change the future, that with enough exertion she could bring Stanley back to life.

There was a time when she might not have believed this. She'd only discovered it for herself seventeen years earlier, when, late in her third pregnancy – the second had been brief and ended in a sudden miscarriage – a doctor had rested his hand on her arm and said, "We have a problem." A month premature, Daniel was cut from her stomach, terribly underweight, his skin a sickly yellow-orange. The doctor explained his condition, the words no more than gibberish until Arthur translated: "something wrong with his blood." Then the doctor said, "Transfusions." At least one, maybe more. This she understood.

She was told the baby couldn't be brought to her. He was already being prepared for the procedure, his blood being matched. "We can't afford to waste a minute," the doctor said in a scolding, exasperated tone. If they didn't act fast, no matter how successful the transfusions, there was a strong possibility of brain damage. She insisted on watching, but when she tried to sit up in bed, she was immediately struck with a whirling dizziness. Arthur stayed with her. He'd seen the baby and now couldn't look her in the face. He touched her hair and said, "Whatever happens. Whatever... You've got Jared and me. We both love you."

She didn't want to think about Jared, who'd been excited at the prospect of a new brother, skeptical at the thought of a sister. He was with Arthur's mother, waiting to find out whom his parents would bring home. She would still have Jared, yes, but what good did it do to remind her? She would have Arthur, too – Arthur, who'd already resigned himself to this loss, to a long period of sorrow after which life would return to normal. His head was lowered, his shoulders already slumped in mourning. She had no extra energy for him now. Eyes closed, she concentrated on the blip of a machine somewhere beyond the curtain surrounding her bed and walked herself down the bright white corridor she'd been wheeled through the day before. Her memory was hazy from pain and drugs, but her imagination made up for what was missing. She pictured swinging doors opening onto stainless steel tables, carts spread with cloths and strangely shaped sterilized instruments. Framed between face masks and elastic white caps, several sets of eyes – some stern, others patient, a few nervous – glanced at her as she came near. A deep male voice barked orders, but no one else spoke. And there, crowded by doctors and nurses, criss-crossed by tubes, stuck with needles – where? his neck? his arm? straight into his tiny heart? this part she couldn't imagine – her baby boy screamed as loudly as his thin lungs would allow.

Here was the hardest part: to love someone, to truly love someone on whom she'd never set eyes. This was the only thing required of her. Only! If it could have been as easy as it sounded. She'd always believed in God; her mother had taken her to shul at least every other week as a girl and passed on a faith that included miracles and divine acts. But it didn't occur to her that God would have any part in this. What she did had little rela-tion to praying. It was physical; every muscle in her body tensed, her skin itched to the point of burning. Some organ throbbed deep beneath her ribs, ready to burst – her appendix, she guessed later, or maybe her spleen. More than prayer, it was a statement, a demand she forced through the hospital's white hallways, into every operating room she could imagine: my baby will not die.

She slept for more than a day. When she awoke, Arthur was still beside her, his eyes on the same spot near his feet. Only at that moment did she come close to despair. What could it mean if her efforts had done nothing, if everything had still been lost? Didn't what she want matter at all? But she was still alive, almost refreshed. She hadn't expended all of her energy. There was more she could have given. If the baby had died, she knew it could only be her fault, a shortcoming in her love.

Arthur's eyes caught hers. His face lifted, his mouth broke into a rare, toothy smile without the least self-consciousness or restraint. "You're back," he said. Her throat was too dry to answer, but he read her thoughts. "Yes. He's going to be fine. Four transfusions. Can you believe it? No brain damage."

Later that afternoon, she was taken to see Daniel. His head was minus-cule, his skin mottled and bruised near the temples, his eyelids nearly transparent. On his ankle was a bright pink wound: here was where the tubes had been attached, where blood had flowed in and out. Never could she have imagined it this way. It surprised her so much she laughed out loud. The love that flooded her now nearly took her from her feet, and she grabbed Arthur's arm to steady herself. Briefly, she wondered if it had even been love she'd felt before. Compared to this, she didn't see how it could have done any good at all. She bent to kiss Daniel's cheek, laughing and weeping at his screams.

THE EVENING BEFORE HIS FLIGHT TO SAN ANTONIO, AFTER he'd packed his suitcase, double-checked his itinerary, confirmed his reservation on the airport shuttle, Arthur stopped her on the stairs. She was hurrying to the kitchen with a filthy syringe and an empty aluminum can. "It's only a vacation," he said. "I don't care. You were the one who really needed it. But there's only so long…You've got to set a limit. Sometime you've got to let yourself stop."

He lowered his head and scratched his beard, still mostly dark, though strangely white on dime-sized patches just below his ears. She could already see their progression – in another year the patches would spread up to his temples and down to his cheeks. By the time he retired, seven or eight years from now, his entire head would be drained of color. He leaned away from her slightly, expecting the anger she knew was unreasonable but felt all the same. Did he really expect her to stop? Could she stop if she wanted to? In no way could she imagine tomorrow being any different from today. How could she go back to sitting in the teachers' lounge, sipping coffee and exchanging gossip? What would occupy her mind? She said as softly as she was able, "I'll know when it's time."

At dinner, Daniel didn't speak a word. He picked at the baked chicken Hannah had made in a rush – it wasn't breaded or seasoned and ordinarily would have embarrassed her – clinking his fork too hard and too often against his plate. Arthur didn't seem to notice. He scraped his chicken bones bare and reminded her where to find the emergency telephone numbers, in case, God forbid, something should happen to his plane. He recalled for her the names of the stockbroker, the accountant, the lawyer who kept his will. She nodded but tried not to listen. She was busy filling with indignation. What right did Daniel have to sulk, when Stanley was lying under the bed, clinging to his life? Before she could clear the dishes and serve a two-day-old fruit salad for dessert, he was gone from the table, the shoes she'd told him to take off in the laundry room pounding their way up the stairs.

Later, on her way to see the cat, she heard him on the telephone, his voice a low, urgent rumble behind the closed door of Arthur's office. Exactly how long she stayed with Stanley, face down on the floor with shoulders jammed uncomfortably under the bed frame, she couldn't be sure – there was no change; the cat lay motionless as she stroked his head and whispered, "Who's my kitty? Who's the best boy?"– but she was surprised to still hear Daniel's muttering as she finally headed to her room for the night. She opened the office door quietly. The recliner was spread its full length, but Daniel sat on the edge of the foot rest, hunched forward, elbows on his knees, the clump of hair that usually hung before his eyes now gripped in his fist. He spoke softly, with weariness. "I'm telling you. There's nothing I can do. It's not my fault. We'll figure something out."

"Night, honey," Hannah said. Daniel jumped to his feet and slapped a hand over the receiver. She knew she should have knocked and was ready for his anger. But instead his expression was full of guilt, not very different from the time he'd come home from school anticipating the phone call from his vice-principal, already memorizing an explanation of why he'd had no choice but to call his calculus teacher a fat motherfucker. "Is something wrong?" she asked.

"It's not long distance," he said. "It's just Alex."

"Okay."

"How's Stanley?"

"We have to be patient," she said. "He's getting stronger. Did you say goodbye to your father?"

"I can't believe you're not going," he said.

"You wouldn't want to take care of him by yourself. You couldn't – "

But now he was gesturing impatiently at the phone. "Do you mind?" he said and turned his back on her. Why did this hurt so much? After all, her older son had once called her the Devil. Yet now she had to fight to keep tears away. She remembered him again at thirteen years old, a child, she'd believed, truly filled with joy. Her troubles with Jared had then been at their height, and the sight of Daniel was always a relief to her – though he was often in trouble at school for some prank, most harmless, a few less so, she never actively worried about him. His excitement over the Mets winning the World Series seemed to last for months, all the way to his bar mitzvah the following spring. After Daniel read from the Torah, Arthur surprised him with a ball signed by all the players. The Mets were the theme of his reception, which went off perfectly. The DJ kept the volume low enough for people to talk. Twenty or so boys and girls from Daniel's Hebrew school danced for hours, pausing only to wolf down miniature hot dogs and pizza bagels waiters carried around on trays. Daniel stood the whole time at the edge of the dance floor, watching and laughing, his face bright red. Once, passing from the buffet table back to her seat, Hannah stopped beside him and asked why he, too, wasn't out on the floor. Without taking his eyes from the dancing kids, he said, "Thanks, Mom. This is the greatest party." She ran her fingers quickly through his hair, proud of the trouble she'd gone to and pleased that it had been recognized and appreciated.

When was the last time he'd thanked her for anything? When had he stopped appreciating all she did for him?

"Good night," she said again, and closed the door behind her.

IN THE MORNING, ARTHUR WOKE HER, KISSED HER QUICKLY on the forehead, the nose, once on each cheek, and was gone. As she stepped from the shower, she heard Daniel's car rolling out of the driveway – why so early she couldn't guess. Steam followed her from the bathroom to the closet, and through it she had trouble finding a dress she wanted to wear. It seemed more than just steam. The air in the house had changed. She was struck by a sudden certainty: she was now completely alone. Not only had Arthur and Daniel left her, but Stanley, too. She'd only clipped on her bra and pulled up one leg of pantyhose; the other dragged behind on the carpet as she ran down the hallway.

In Jared's room, something was different. A new smell, rancid and overwhelming. But when she discovered its source, wonderful. On a corner of newspaper, only two feet from the litter box, a soft, yellow-brown curl. It was no bigger than the slugs that suddenly appeared on the sidewalk after a storm, but still this was the first from Stanley in nearly a week. And more important, he'd come out from underneath the bed on his own. Not quite all the way to the box, but this was a start. And now, when she dropped to her knees and reached out to him, his ear actually flattened under her touch. No response from the rest of him, no other visible change: his eyes were closed, his paws clean, his flank a filthy rag. But the ear! She tore off the soiled corner of newspaper, folded it over, and held it for a moment in her open palm. It was a gift, a reward from Stanley for her dedication, her loyalty, her love. The new surge of hope pained her physically as she left the house, tightening her stomach, shortening her breath, even sparking a slight headache behind one eye. But already she began to consider a hair appointment for next week, a manicure the week after, a vacation sometime soon, soon.

At school, too, the air felt different. It was the Friday before spring break, and kids buzzed with a raucous, almost violent energy. Even the most uptight teachers made an attempt at relaxing, resting their feet on the coffee table in the lounge, pondering out loud whether to put aside lesson plans at the last minute in favor of games or class trips to the library. The principal came in wearing a green Hawaiian shirt and shorts far too tight for him, and he laughed his way down the hall with students who pointed at his back and dropped to the floor giggling. Most people were distracted enough to forget how they'd been treating Hannah for the last month. She pretended to forget with them. She indulged in the pastries one of the German teachers had brought for breakfast. With a burst of welcome impulse, she made a tentative date during the week off, for lunch and shopping with a secretary who prided herself on sniffing out bargains in even the most high-profile designer shops.

In her class she led a round of hangman in French, and then taught some of her favorite songs: "*La Julie jolie*," "*J'ai dansé avec l'amour*," and "*Ne me quitte pas*." The kids picked up the words more quickly than anything she'd taught all year and sang together with surprising emotion. The room filled with an air of forgiveness – it might have been New Year's Eve or Yom Kippur, all grievances generously buried, the slate wiped clean for everyone. Even Alyssa Silver smiled and laughed and looked Hannah in the eyes. She turned out to have a rich alto voice, stunningly clear, none of the nasal whining that made it so difficult to listen to her speak. At the end of class Hannah told her to sing to her boyfriend before he left for his baseball games, so he wouldn't forget her while he was gone. "Oh, he doesn't forget me," Alyssa said with a wink. "How could he?" Hannah felt suddenly ashamed of how she'd treated the girl since they'd argued, immediately dismissing her as a brat, judging her an enemy. Now her heart went out to Alyssa with affection and also with an unmistakable pang: she wished it were her own son the girl would sing to. She tried to imagine the two of them together, Daniel always at his best, sweet, accommodating, Alyssa never selfish. She put a hand on the girl's shoulder and said, "You enjoy your break, okay?"

She stayed at school through her prep period and lunch hour. The morning's hope had settled into a dull fear. She was as afraid to go home now as, for the past month, she had been to stay, afraid lest Stanley had regressed to the way he'd been yesterday and the day before. What would she do if his ear didn't flatten the next time she touched it? What if he went back to shitting under the bed? She didn't know if she had enough energy to start again.

At the end of the day she took her time clearing off her desk. She drove home slowly, the whole way on Route 46, no side streets or short cuts. She jerked complacently along with the stilted traffic. Still the ride seemed too quick; already here was her street, her driveway. She crept slowly past Daniel's car and into the garage, where she sat motionless, wrists hooked over the steering wheel, legs stretched as far as the dash would allow. How long had it been since she'd last sat like this, not doing something, not preparing to do something? Long before all this business with Stanley. She couldn't remember and took pleasure in not remembering, in not doing anything but taking in the garage as if she'd never seen it before. Had she? It all looked strange to her now: rusted bicycles leaning against cinder block walls, brooms missing most of their bristles – except for one with plenty of bristles but no handle – half a dozen snow shovels, two plastic sleds, a deflated soccer ball. Against one wall stood three ancient tires worn almost smooth, and directly opposite, on a high steel shelf, paint cans were stacked to the ceiling. Brown crust lined their rims and streaked down their sides. Most were probably empty or a quarter full, left over from the last time her father had stained the porch. How long ago had that been? Five years? Six? Underneath the shelf was a pile of kindling the boys had collected from the woods when Jared was no older than twelve, Daniel eight. She couldn't remember Arthur having built a fire the last three winters, but even sitting in the garage she could picture the ashes not yet cleaned from the hearth. Above Arthur's car, a slab of insulation had come loose from a heating duct and hung unevenly, ready to fall. On the outside it was a metallic gray, beneath a strawberry blonde nest of fibers that made her skin itch even to look at. Along its edge were strips of silver duct tape Arthur had once hoped would keep it in place, now crinkled and useless.

They'd been in the house eleven years, but the day they'd moved in might have been last week. The truck had arrived during a fierce storm, the dregs of a hurricane that had battered Florida and the Carolinas. Jared slid feet first over and over down the sopping front lawn, leaving streaks in the new sod that took two summers to regenerate. Daniel bawled at the howling wind. The movers tried to overcharge her, and she told them to put all the furniture back in the truck. But Arthur scrawled off an outrageous check and sent them away. When she protested, he told her she could sit on the floor if she liked, but he preferred chairs, a sofa, a bed.

She remembered this as if it were happening now, yes, but at the same time she was seeing the garage as it would be in another year, in five years, ten. The slab of insulation would crash to the floor or onto Arthur's car, sending up a cloud of dust and fiberglass. The steel shelf would sag under the weight of the paint cans. The collection of snow shovels and brooms would grow until she could barely pull her car into its space. She wanted to be troubled by all this, wanted the sight to propel her out of the car into a frenzy of cleaning. But more than anything she was struck still with pure amazement – not a finger would move. What, exactly, was she seeing? What was she supposed to make of it? She forced herself to say out loud, in a voice that sounded mechanical, not like hers at all, "When Arthur comes home, he'll take care of this."

Uneasily, she left the car and went in the door beside the rack of snow shovels. But inside she had the same trouble moving forward. The basement was no less chaotic than the garage. Toys no one had played with for half a decade overflowed a wooden chest too full to close. On the ping-pong table sat a single stack of yellowed newspapers. How they could have been there long enough to yellow, she had no idea. Arthur recycled the paper every week, stuffed bags full and stored them in the laundry room until Saturday morning, when he hauled them to the dump on his way to the library. They both passed this stack every morning and every afternoon on the way to and from their cars. It was impossible that they could have overlooked it for months, even years. But worse, just above the stack, in the joint of the ceiling and a closet door, huddled a spider's egg sack, white around the edges, translucent in the center, a cluster of black dots within. Already she saw the eggs hatching, larvae squirming – what did spider larvae look like? She pictured them white and fleshy like maggots or grubs, saw them growing their eight legs and scattering through closets and air vents, cupboards and drawers. Everything around her was in motion, the toys spilling from the chest, the stack of newspapers rising to the ceiling, the spiders scuttling boldly along the walls. Only Hannah remained frozen. It took enormous effort for her to put one foot in front of the other and make her way upstairs.

But even in the rooms where she spent most of her waking hours, she was bewildered by what she saw. Tiny cracks webbed from a pinhole in the plaster on the first floor landing. Rays of dust fanned out behind the flower vases in the foyer. Under the dining room table, a bright orange stain marred the Persian rug. She paid a Polish woman to clean every other week, but still, here were streaky footprints on the white tile floor, and there, between the kitchen and family room, a trail of burnt popcorn crumbs and kernels. These she could only have dropped herself – both Arthur and Daniel hated the feel of popcorn stuck between their teeth.

She followed the trail into the family room, but after the first step inside, stopped cold. The TV was on, tuned to a cartoon of soldiers and tanks, jets exploding and parachutes streaming to the ground. On the couch Daniel lay with his feet up, Stanley sprawled on his lap. She was seeing into a day four years ago, the cat healthy, Daniel in middle school, still excited by all the gifts from his bar mitzvah and euphoric over the Mets winning the World Series. Or maybe this was a vision of tomorrow, of next week, all her hopes realized, Stanley saved, well-groomed, eating again on his own. And Daniel? Seventeen and still watching cartoons?

She approached slowly and stood above them. Only then did she see Stanley's tangled fur, the curve of protruding ribs. The right day returned to her. It was Friday, the start of spring break. There was no need for Daniel to pretend to do his homework. He stared open-mouthed at the screen, his hair only slightly parted over his eyes. In the crook of one arm he held a box of cookies, and crumbs cascaded down his chest and collected in a fold of his T-shirt. Stanley's head pointed toward Daniel's feet, tail curled at his belt. Now she understood what she was seeing: Stanley downstairs for the first time in a month. She shuddered with excitement, but was also left with a lingering confusion and apprehension. Somehow this wasn't right. Shouldn't Stanley have been sitting in her lap? Wasn't she the one who'd kept him alive?

Daniel yawned, stretched his arms over his head. "What time's dinner?" he said.

"Did he," Hannah began, but found it difficult to breathe.

"Can we eat early? I've got to leave by seven."

"He came down by himself?" she managed.

Daniel looked at her suspiciously, as if she were trying to trick him. "Are you kidding?"

"He didn't?"

"I don't think he can walk," Daniel said. "I brought him down. He needed to get out of that room. It stinks in there."

Even this disappointment dawned on her slowly. She felt the disorientation that comes with waking in the middle of a dream or starting from an accidental nap on a busy day – so much to do, but where to start? "I've got to feed him," she said.

"I think he's comfortable."

"He's got to eat, doesn't he?"

She lifted the cat from Daniel's lap, barely an effort; Stanley was no heavier than her purse. He drooped over her arm, both sets of paws dangling by her waist. His heart beat steadily, surprisingly close to the skin of her palm. On the way up the stairs she caught glimpses of small rips in the floral wallpaper, which was frayed in almost every corner. She saw it all peeling away from the walls, strips falling about her head. How long she paused outside the bathroom she didn't know, didn't even realize she'd paused, puzzling over scratches in the wooden molding around the door. She might have stayed there for hours, forever, if Daniel hadn't come down the hall, carrying the syringe and a can of food. When she glanced down, Stanley was staring up at her searchingly.

AS SOON AS HE FINISHED DINNER, WHILE HANNAH WAS STILL drinking her tea, Daniel excused himself under his breath and left the table. Five minutes later he came back wearing fresh jeans and a new T-shirt—this one black, with a frenzied, sweaty guitar player across the chest. His hair wasn't combed, but it seemed that he'd run his fingers through the front to make it hang evenly over his face. "Alex is picking me up," he said before she could ask.

She tried to sound casual. "You guys have some big plans?"

"Not really."

"Going somewhere fun?"

He scratched his chin and from the counter picked up one of Arthur's massive science journals. Shuffling noisily through the pages, he said, "Alex's house."

"You're making him drive all the way out here to get you? Can't you just drive there?"

"We've – He wants to rent a movie first."

Then came a honk from the driveway, and he hustled past her into the laundry room. He stomped his shoes onto his feet, and she knew he wouldn't bother to bend and tie the laces. "Home by one," she called.

"Night, Mom." The back door slammed shut.

By now her head had cleared. What had come over her this afternoon? She wondered whether the pressure of Arthur's leaving and the hope she'd felt all morning had brought on a touch of fever. Now Stanley was back under the bed, immobile, and of course she would still take care of him, would do whatever she had to for as long as it might take. She was ready, too, to deal with the house and glad to have it to herself for the evening – though she did think of poor Arthur, alone in his hotel room, either too hot or too cold, tossing on a lumpy bed, gassy from fried food, unable to read.

The house was Hannah's; it wouldn't get the best of her. She dressed in an old pair of jeans and one of Arthur's flannel shirts and pinned up her hair. From the laundry room closet she took a pile of rags, bottles of carpet cleaner and wood polish, a dust pan and hand-held vacuum. She started with the popcorn kernels in the family room. They were every-where: under the couch, in the fringes of the area rug, on the coffee table. Some were wedged inconceivably between the TV and VCR. Next she went for the dining room, the orange stain on the rug she and Arthur had bought at an auction, for what they at first thought was a bargain and later discovered to be a crime. She sprayed blue liquid from a can, allowed it to foam, scrubbed, and sprayed again. Up close the spot seemed to fade, but each time she stepped away it reemerged, just as sharply as before. This agitated her more than she could have imagined, and she found herself growing furious at Arthur, whose chair was nearest the stain. He'd watched pasta sauce or pot roast gravy drip from his plate onto the rug and said nothing, ignored it, hoping Hannah wouldn't notice until it was too late to blame him. This was something Daniel might have done; so maybe the boy did pick up his bad traits from his father.

Just then the doorbell rang. Daniel, she guessed, forgotten something and also forgotten his keys to get back in. She ran for the back door, almost ready to accuse him of staining the dining room rug. But just as she grabbed the knob, the bell rang again, three times in quick succession, from the front of the house, not the back. No one but electricians, plumbers, and sales-men ever came to the front door. And on a Friday night? She was out of breath by the time she opened it. Three boys, Daniel's age or slightly older, stepped back at the sight of her. The one in front had hair to his shoulders, in perfect ringlets, the way, she guessed, Daniel wished his would grow. He smiled brightly and said, "Is this thirteen-thirty-six Crescent View?"

Behind him stood a boy a full head taller than Hannah, with a squared-off buzz cut and a football jacket from a high school whose colors she didn't recognize. His arms were crossed, his head turned toward the street. The third boy was squat with a comically pointed face. His lips seemed to fit uncomfortably over his teeth, which, she gathered, were horribly crooked. She imagined the other two always calling him by a nickname, "Rat" or "Weasel," until they'd forgotten his real name. He stood slightly hunched, his finger still hovering above the doorbell. "This is thirteen-thirty-six," Hannah said.

Still smiling, the boy in front said, "I guess we're looking for three-thirty-six."

"This isn't three-thirty-six."

The doorbell rang again, and the mousy boy looked around guiltily. The long-haired boy backhanded him in the shoulder without taking his eyes from Hannah. The tall boy seemed to hug himself tightly. "Right," the long-haired boy said. "Sorry to bother you. You wouldn't happen to know where three-thirty-six is, would you?"

She pointed left, and again the doorbell rang, three, four, five chimes. This time she saw it: the mousy boy lurching forward into the bell, his whole body following his finger, eyes wide, horrified, it seemed, by a plea-sure he couldn't control. The other two grabbed him by the collar, and then all three were running, straight down the lawn to an enormous black car parked on the curb, the type popular fifteen years ago and now driven only in movies by drug dealers and pimps. In her puzzlement, Hannah forgot to shout for them to use the walkway until they hit the street. The car squealed off in the opposite direction from the way she'd pointed.

She closed the door, shook her head, and returned slowly to the stain on the dining room rug. The afternoon's confusion came back to her. The boys seemed part of the dream she was in, already half forgotten or pushed away. In less than five minutes, the bell rang again. This time she felt an illogical fear — not that the boys had come back to do her any harm, but that the smallest one, fascinated with her doorbell, would camp on the stoop, ringing and ringing, day and night. She flung open the door and said sharply, "Three-thirty-six is down the hill." But instead of three boys, there was a girl in front of her, pretty, with straight brown hair to her shoulders, a soft pink sweater over black slacks, very little make-up, rare among the girls in Hannah's school. She'd never met any of the girls Daniel was friends with; she'd always been afraid to. She'd suspected they would be the type crunchy with hairspray and caked with eyeliner, cigarettes clenched between press-on nails three-quarters of an inch long. This girl was a surprise and a pleasant one. "It's okay if we park in the driveway, yeah?" the girl said in a lazy, cheerful voice.

"Daniel's not here," Hannah said, but the girl was already past her, into the house, halfway down the hall.

"Who?"

"Daniel. My son. He lives here."

Something wasn't right about the girl. Her gait was halting, and as she reached the kitchen she seemed to stagger. Hannah's first thought was that she'd been in an accident – maybe those boys had run her down with their car, and now she was in shock. But then, from the open door came a deep voice, "Carrie. What the hell are you doing?" From the stoop a handsome boy was beckoning. He looked older than the others, far older than Daniel, with a sharp jaw and a shadow on his upper lip. His face was familiar; he might have graduated from Hannah's school, two, maybe three years ago. "Jesus, Carrie. Come on."

The girl looked at Hannah gravely and said, "I guess we'll have to go to Deer Run." She pulled a pack of gum from her back pocket and held out a piece. It wavered in front of Hannah's eyes. Part of her felt she should take it, wrapped as it was in silver, an unexpected gift. But she kept her hands at her sides. After a moment the girl unwrapped it and folded it with difficulty between her teeth. The paper slipped from her fingers and fluttered to the floor. Only now did Hannah realize how drunk the girl was, her eyes glazed, jaw working carelessly. She snapped out of her trance, grabbed the girl by the elbow, and pushed her toward the door. She tried to speak forcefully, but her voice came out as a thin whisper: "Get out of my house."

Still smiling brightly, the girl reached out and gave Hannah's arm a quick squeeze. "See you later," she said, and weaved to the boy, who grabbed her around the waist and hustled her down the steps. They made their way to a fiery red sports car, where another boy had an aluminum barrel halfway out of the trunk. He let it roll back in and darted to the driver's door. The girl went headfirst into the back seat. The car screeched out of the driveway, swerved for no reason, stopped in the middle of the street, and made an awkward five-point turn. Another car approached, this one blaring a music that rattled the dining room windows and shook the stoop where Hannah stood from fifty yards away. A light came on above a neighbor's front porch. The two cars pulled parallel, and the girl leaned out of the red one, shouted something to the driver of the other. Then her pink sweater disappeared behind tinted glass. The red car's tires spun. Something flew out the back window of the new car, and from the sidewalk came the sound of shattered glass. Then both cars were gone. Only a cloud of exhaust hung over the street.

It took her until now to put everything together. This bothered her more than anything. Weeks ago she should have realized Daniel had planned a party. She could only blame her distraction and weariness from a month of worrying about Stanley.

A party. In her house. This was the reason he'd so desperately wanted her to go away – because he'd invited half the kids in north Jersey to drink beer in her living room, to throw up in her flower pots, to roll naked in her bed. The rage that overtook her now made her fingers tremble so violently she could only stop them by gripping handfuls of her jeans. Some evil fluid rose from her stomach to her throat and burned there. The bell rang ten, twelve more times, and she sent kids running with curses and threats and an uncontrollable waving of her fists. Finally she taped a note to the front door, promising to send the police after anyone who so much as looked at her doorbell.

She waited for Daniel in his bedroom, in the dark. A streetlamp cast enough light through the half-drawn blinds for her to make out posters on the walls, of rock stars, baseball players, a blonde model in a skimpy bikini. Most of the carpet was covered by clothes and the CDs he worked so many extra weekend hours to buy. Cracks in their cases caught the light and glinted, not one of them unscarred. She sat on the edge of the mattress, hands in her lap, conserving her energy. But she couldn't calm herself enough even to come up with punishments or lectures – all that would have to wait. As much trouble as she'd had with Jared, he'd never done anything so blatantly deceitful as this. She'd been stricter with Jared. She hadn't let him have his own car; he'd had to ask to borrow hers on weekends. Before he could watch TV, she'd always made him show her his homework. Had it been such a mistake? For years he'd despised her, and she'd feared he always would. But now he respected her, and they got along better than ever. She'd been strict with Alyssa Silver, too, and look what had happened with her: she'd scored a b- on an admittedly savage make-up exam. She'd even sung beautifully for Hannah in front of the entire class. The truth made her dizzy: she'd let Daniel run wild, and now he would have let Stanley die in order to have strangers tear apart her house. Not only would she have come home from Mexico to find the cat dead and buried, but her vases smashed, her antique bowls filled with cigarette butts, all her sheets soiled.

He never missed a curfew and didn't tonight – this was the one thing going for him. At ten minutes to one, a car accelerated up the driveway. A door slammed, then another. There were boys' voices, a loud cackle, not Daniel's. She went to the window and listened for the creak of the back door, but instead came a heavy rustling in the bushes along the walkway. Again, a light came on in the neighbor's house, this time in an upstairs window, and a face pressed against the glass. She was too far away to see if it was the husband's or wife's; she knew neither by name. A car appeared at the end of the driveway, the same black, bulky, 1970s model the three boys had driven off in earlier. Were they friends of Daniel's? She'd had the feeling they'd never set eyes on him before. Finally, the back door opened. Daniel's shoes clunked against the floor as he kicked them off, and then nothing. He stayed in the laundry room five minutes, nearly ten, no movement, not a sound. He knew how much trouble he was in, she guessed. Knew and was genuinely aching with guilt, the way he always was when expecting a phone call from the vice-principal. By now she was devising punishments – no car for the summer, no concerts or baseball games, no weekends at the shore, no overnight fishing trip on the Delaware river –

and already the force of her anger was leaving her. He wasn't a bad kid, this she knew. On a whim, she imagined, he'd told a few people the house would be empty. Told one friend, maybe two. From there it had spread in a matter of days, until it was beyond his control. He'd spent the whole week on the phone trying to call it off. Not bad, just stupid, so stupid. She wanted to blame his difficult birth, the four transfusions. Maybe he'd suffered brain damage after all. Maybe the new blood pumped into his veins had been donated by a moron.

Now the laundry room door banged open and heavy footsteps crossed the kitchen and clomped up the stairs, not careful or discreet as she'd expected. This didn't sound at all like guilt. Did he think he'd gotten away with what he'd done? She was furious all over again. She pictured him in her garden, a faint smile on his lips as he threw aside a shovel and dropped Stanley's dead body into a shallow hole. He'd feel enough guilt when she was through with him, that was for certain. He'd be awake until dawn imagining all the punishments she would save for the morning. His foot-steps now were strange, two quick ones, a pause, then a forceful stomp. She kept back from the doorway, and he didn't seem to see her. His head blocked the hallway lamp, so she was left with only his silhouette: a crown of writhing hair, the pouchy cheeks he'd inherited from Arthur, the large ears from her own father, arms crossed over a surprisingly narrow chest.

She took a step forward, but still he didn't notice her. Nor did he come into his own room, where she'd hoped to confront him, waving her arms at his stereo, his computer, all the things she could take away from him. He went straight into Jared's room without hesitating, without even switch-ing on the light. Then came a loud crash as he stumbled – as she knew he would – over the StairMaster. By the time she followed him into the room and flicked the light switch, he was already on his belly, halfway under the bed. His skinny legs splayed in a way that should have been painful. His socks had holes in their heels and flopped an inch longer than his toes. "What's wrong with you?" he said so loudly he couldn't possibly have cared whether or not he woke his mother, whether or not she knew about the party. This time it didn't take long for her to know he was drunk, at least as drunk as the pretty girl who'd walked so casually into her house and offered a piece of gum. "Don't you want to eat?" Daniel said. "Aren't you hungry?"

That he was drunk should have steeled her anger and made it all the worse for him. But despite herself, she was overcome with a wave of pity. Was it so terrible that he'd wanted to throw a party? It would have turned out badly, without question – she'd been teaching high school long enough to know that. She'd heard plenty of stories about parents coming home to find broken windows and furniture, about alcohol-poisoned kids carted off to hospitals, about families sued for things they hadn't known about and never would have condoned. But the wanting itself? Wanting friends to come see him, wanting girls in his house. He looked so much younger than all the other kids she'd seen tonight, a little boy in comparison. He had to do something to get noticed. And she'd ruined it for him.

"What's a matter with you," he said, and now his voice was quieter, exhausted. "Why you gotta fuck everything up? You always fuck everything up." Then his body heaved forward and let out a wet, guttural groan – with it came what sounded like water spilled slowly from a glass. He heaved again while she was pulling him from beneath the bed, and then once more as she held his head against her shoulder. Brown liquid thickened with hunks of bread and undigested sesame seeds ran down the front of her shirt and into the loose pockets of her jeans. But what she saw now made this easy to ignore. It shocked her, but at the same time seemed so inevitable that shock immediately gave way to the deepest sense of loss. Someone had scrawled over Daniel's entire face with a thick-tipped black marker. On each cheek was a phallus, graphic and grotesque in the way only teenagers knew how to draw – shaded for dimension, hair in the appropriate places, squirting cartoon drops onto Daniel's nose. His chin had been cleft to look like buttocks. A rounded, girlish script on his forehead stated bluntly, "Dickface."

"It's all right, Mom," he said. "Don't cry. Stanley's gonna make it. I only drank three beers. Only three. I love that cat. He's not going to die." He touched her cheek with a finger that came away wet. Was this crying? Her face was soaked with tears, but no sobs accompanied them, no sniffles or blinking or soreness around her eyes. Water was simply emptying out of her. The kids who'd done this to her son were the same he'd invited to drink beer in her house. Not one of them was his friend. When had things gone so wrong? At his bar mitzvah he'd seemed accepted, if not popular. So many kids had shown up to dance, to congratulate him, to give him presents. Hadn't he been happy then, even if he didn't join in the dancing? After he'd thanked her for the party, she'd gone back to chatting with relatives, friends, and colleagues. The next time she thought to look for him, almost all the guests were gone. He was collecting Mets hats, t-shirts, mugs, pennants other kids had left behind. His suit jacket was gone, his shirt untucked, his tie loosened and tossed over a shoulder. He was still smiling. She didn't know if he'd talked to a single person the whole afternoon.

So this was the truth of it: she'd had no idea whether or not he'd been happy. She hadn't known if the kids at his party had been his friends. Seventeen years ago, she'd saved him in the hospital – since then she'd left him to survive all on his own.

For the first time she saw the loneliness at the bottom of him, in everything he did. Loneliness in both his sweetness and his belligerence, loneliness all through his day at school and work, all through dinner as he listened to his parents complain about their jobs. How could she have imagined Alyssa Silver singing to him, when she'd just as soon draw a penis on his face? She'd observed plenty of kids like him at her own school, sitting in the back of class, lurking at the edges of the cafeteria, but not once had she placed her own son among them.

Now she led him to the bathroom, his arm heavy around her shoulders, his legs doing little to keep him from tumbling to the ground. She wiped the vomit from his mouth and neck as he kept muttering, "Only three. Okay. Maybe four. That's all. Because I felt bad. About Stanley."

The ink on his face she scrubbed with soap and a rough sponge, but the marks barely faded. There was no need for any punishment tomorrow. Daniel would see his face in the mirror and wouldn't want to leave the house for his entire spring break. He wouldn't want to come down from his room. She'd let him stay there. She'd bring him his meals, even carry the TV upstairs. Tomorrow he could have whatever he wanted. But even the notion of tomorrow now seemed murky. She had trouble seeing anything beyond this moment: Daniel's skin – where it wasn't marked – sickly pale, his eyes swimming and red, head in her lap; Stanley perpetually dying under the bed; Arthur away in some far-off, unimaginable place. It would all stay this way. This was the moment she would live in for the rest of her life. The stains on Daniel's face, the vomit on her shirt, the mildew just beginning to grow in the corners of the tub, none of it would fade, not ever.

But then Daniel stirred. "Get off me," he mumbled. She swept his hair out of his eyes, and he said it again, slightly louder. Soon he was shouting, "Get off me! Get the fuck off!" She held a cup of water to his lips, but he slapped it away, the cup skittering across the tiles, water beading around the toilet. He lurched to his feet and stumbled out of the bathroom, still yelling, "Don't touch me!" His shoulder knocked hard against the doorframe outside his bedroom, and he stopped for a moment, staring down the stained wood as if he might strike it. Then he pressed both palms to his temples and grimaced. "Who hit me on the head?" he moaned. "God, my head. I think I'm dying." He took two steps into his room and pitched headlong onto his bed.

She knew she should go to him, force him to swallow some aspirin and water, take off his shoes, tuck him under his sheets. But instead she closed his door and left him to the misery that would only grow worse between now and tomorrow. She stripped out of the filthy shirt and pants and carried a roll of paper towels to Jared's room. The soggy plastic and newspaper she tore off and balled up, and then crawled under the bed to clean the rest. Stanley lay curled in the same ragged ball, eyes closed, his nose only an inch from the putrid puddle. *If only he would sniff at it*, she thought. If only his tongue would jab at a chunk of barely chewed bread – then he could decide between the pleasures of this world and the promise of the next. She reached out a finger, stroked his chin, and silently pleaded her case. Even now she believed all this might still have something to do with her.

# With Equals Alone

MY OLDER BROTHER JARED WOULD GRADUATE FROM HIGH school in a month. At the end of the summer he'd head off to college far away. I was fourteen and would begin high school in the fall. These were the facts, though I refused to believe them.

Jared wasn't, the rest of my family knew but never admitted openly, a happy kid. He breathed, dreamed, perspired resentment. At fourteen, he'd been chubby, quiet, and studious. He'd smiled all the time, his cheeks red and always oily. At school boys and girls picked on him relentlessly. Home wasn't much better; though I was four years his junior, I jumped at every opportunity to tease him about his weight or the amount of time he spent with books.

But as soon as he started high school, all this began to change. His smile disappeared. He went on a drastic diet and began working out with a weight set in the basement. Within a year his stomach was flat, his cheeks were pale, and he joined a gym on Route 10, run by a former professional bodybuilder who'd once competed and lost badly in the Mr. Olympia contest. Jared would soon be making his own entrance into the world of competitive bodybuilding; his application had been accepted for an amateur contest in West Orange, set for a week after graduation.

The transformations had been gradual enough for me to ignore from one day to the next. Only during sporadic, unguarded moments would I notice his widening chest, his forearms beginning to bulge, the tendons standing out like cords on his neck when he turned his head to the side. I'd see each new part as separate from the rest of Jared, as if a calf muscle were something he might have bought at a discount in the department store where he worked as a stockboy, no different from a new sweater or hat. Only reluctantly did I begin to piece together the whole. The recognition always troubled me and was sometimes so startling I had to turn away. Could this really be my brother? He didn't seem at all like someone who could be related to my mother or father. I had the growing suspicion that a stranger had taken over Jared's body and begun sleeping in his bed. If it weren't for the face – undoubtedly Jared's, though leaner than ever before –

I would have been certain. I occasionally searched the pillowy lips we had in common, the wide nostrils, the deep-set eyes and long eyelashes he could only have inherited from my mother, searched closely for any sign of the chubby, cheerful fourteen-year-old, but that Jared was gone for good. Now his voice had deepened, and the mild New Jersey accent shared by my whole family – and which I would never even notice in my own speech until I moved to Delaware – broadened in his mouth almost to the point of parody. Cars for him became "cauws," work was "wook." He carefully combed his hair back from his forehead and let it fall in ragged curls at his neck, a strange combination of *Saturday Night Fever* and Rambo. He took to answering his name with "yo."

Most of his time at home he spent locked in his room, staring at his muscles in the mirror. Sometimes, late in the evening, I heard him on the phone behind the closed door to my father's office, speaking in a boisterous, excited tone I'd never heard from him before, and again I had the uncomfortable feeling of living with an impostor everyone recognized but no one acknowledged. He fought with my parents about everything imaginable, usually at the dinner table, and rarely spoke to me at all, though by this time I'd long since stopped trying to tease him and wanted, sometimes desperately, for us to get along. I'd never believed all those times I picked on him had ever meant anything. I'd never expected to be held accountable for my actions as a ten-year-old, and I certainly never thought they would cost me my brother's love. Now I took his side in any argument he had with my parents, but he didn't seem to notice. His gaze lumped me with my mother and father when he said, "You're always attacking me. Can't you all just leave me the hell alone?"

All this anger and aggression dismayed my parents. We'd always had such a nice family, they mourned. Where had things gone so wrong?

As young boys Jared and I had never been spanked. Not once had either of my parents struck us in a moment of annoyance or frustration or fear. Our punishments were always carefully planned and calmly discussed: banned toys or privileges, extra chores on weekends, painfully monotonous lectures. My father especially managed to keep his anger under wraps no matter how badly Jared or I (rarely Jared) misbehaved.

He prided himself on his cool temperament, which he claimed was a long-standing hereditary trait in his family. It was also somehow tied in his mind to his apparent immunity to the most common infectious diseases. During his childhood in the '40s and '50s – a treacherous, disease-ridden time in his descriptions – he'd avoided not only polio and smallpox, but also the mumps, the measles, and even chicken pox. This didn't mean he was a particularly healthy man. At least once a month he came home with some new ailment: a strained back, a pulled groin, a broken pinkie toe. A doctor had first detected a slight murmur in his heart when he was only thirty-five. By the time I turned fourteen, he'd had two hernia operations, three bleeding ulcers, and a chronically spastic colon.

My mother never had so much as a nick on her finger, despite spending half her waking life chopping vegetables in the kitchen, but she was a magnet for every airborne germ imaginable. She'd had measles, mumps, chicken pox, all before her twelfth birthday. Without fail, she came down with a cold the first week of every December and caught strep throat in the spring of all odd-numbered years. Her assault on bacteria in our house was unyielding; she scrubbed toilets and sinks twice a day, soaked silverware in boiling water, sprayed enough Lysol in the kitchen to give everything we ate a slightly antiseptic, lemony flavor. She, of course, was not so even-tempered as my father. Though she never actually came close to violence, I often and easily provoked her into shouting or hissing warnings through clenched teeth. More than once I'd watched her grip the edge of a counter or chair so hard her knuckles blanched and thought, this is it, this is the moment I've taken things too far. Finally I would know what it felt like to be smacked by someone who loved me. I always felt terrible at these times – angry at myself and sorry for my mother, who'd tried so hard for so long. But when the smack didn't come I was always disappointed, bitter at the predictable grounding or the dull speech about respect or honesty, which still left me stewing with guilt and remorse. Not like a blow, which, I imagined, would have freed me from all feelings of responsibility. I thought my mother must have known this, and was intentionally choosing the strictest possible punishment. Did she really love me after all? Already my mind would be working toward the next time I would stand before her apologetically, head lowered, hoping for the bite of her long fingers, followed by her immediate tears and pleas for forgiveness.

Every time my mother was sick, my father bragged about his genes, of which Jared and I seemed to have gotten the better part – we, too, rarely caught colds or the flu, and neither of us had ever had chicken pox. He often said he was glad we seemed, for the most part, to have inherited his temperament. When either of us acted less than mild-mannered, he blamed our youth and warned us about viruses and bacteria. He sang out at every opportunity, "Keep a cool head, stay out of bed." All of this confused me terribly. If my genes said I wouldn't get sick, why did it matter how cool my head was? If they said I was even-tempered, did I have any choice in the matter? I couldn't make sense of it, but my father was a scientist, and it didn't occur to me to question him.

Only when he claimed his genes as the source of my cavity-free teeth did I begin to wonder. With this I wasn't impressed at all – I may not have had any fillings, but my teeth were so crooked the orthodontist who'd recently attached my braces said I would most likely have to wear them for three and a half years. One tooth grew in a quarter-inch from where it belonged, right through my palate, and had to be removed in a painful surgery. The rest were covered in wire and metal hooks that tore at the insides of my cheeks and rubber bands that snapped against my gums. My best friend, Greg Farisi, had perfectly straight teeth; he was spanked more than anybody else I knew. Whenever my father talked about cavities, I cursed the whole idea of genes and wished there was a way I could still get my traits from Greg's father, who couldn't have cared less about keeping a cool head. At these times I decided to turn my back on my heritage, my nature, as my brother seemed to be doing. I would be hot-headed. If I ever had kids, I would smack them whenever they deserved it.

My mother was equally skeptical. "There's something called fluoride," she said. "I'm the one who made them brush after every meal."

"Don't worry," my father assured her. "They inherited your looks. For that I thank my lucky stars."

If my father saw our healthy genes as a source of pride, Jared took them as a sign – as he did everything else at this time – that he deserved better than he was given, that he was constantly treated unfairly. He had nothing but disdain for anyone who could get sick and still claim authority over him. He'd say about a teacher who'd been out of school four straight days with a cold, "I don't care what she gives me on that test. I don't even want it back. It's probably covered in snot." When my mother called after him to dry his hair before leaving the house, he'd shrug and answer, "What for? I don't have a weak constitution, like some people."

My father still insisted Jared was, at heart, sweet and mild-mannered. "All this anger goes against who he really is. That's why it gets him so upset. He doesn't want to be like this."

My mother snorted. "So what happened to his genes? Do they go to sleep during the teenage years? Is there some sort of pill we can give him? I'll start Daniel on it now, just to be ready."

In the fall, Jared was leaving for a small private college in Tennessee. In three short months I would be living alone in the house with my parents. Though to Greg Farisi and my other friends at school I said, "I can't wait. I'll get two rooms," I couldn't help feeling betrayed. How was I supposed to make it through dinner every night by myself? All my parents' attention would be focused on me. Without Jared to distract them, how could I be anything other than what they wanted me to be? Before it even truly dawned on me that Jared would soon be gone, I found myself hanging around him whenever he would let me, offering to run errands for him, complimenting him on his clothes and hairstyle. I was determined to make up for all the years I'd picked on him. If he began to like me before he left, I thought, maybe he'd call often from college. Maybe he'd come home on holidays and occasional weekends. Maybe – even as I thought it I knew the hope was ridiculous and futile – maybe he would change his mind and find a college in New Jersey.

My parents were also bothered by his choice of schools, though for different reasons. They couldn't understand why he would want to go to Tennessee for anything. "What's wrong with Pennsylvania?" my mother said. "Or Massachusetts? There are so many wonderful colleges in Massachusetts."

"You know what they think of Jews down there?" my father said. "And with your accent? We'll get a call about you hanging from a tree."

They also worried constantly about the cost of tuition. Even at fourteen I knew they would, in the end, have no trouble paying for it. But still, my father couldn't keep himself from musing out loud one evening in early spring, soon after Jared received his acceptance letter, "It's crazy how much they're asking." He absently swirled a hunk of roast beef in the pool of butter leaking from his baked potato. "I don't see how ordinary people can afford an education."

My mother answered immediately, "Ordinary people go to public schools."

Jared laughed without the least bit of humor and threw his fork against his plate. "Fine. You want me to go to Rutgers? I'll go. No, forget that. I'll go to County. Or maybe I'll join the goddamn navy. You won't have to pay a dime."

My father glanced from side to side, stunned. He never seemed to understand where trouble came from. Weren't we all just talking calmly, like human beings? Now he made a feeble attempt at appeasement. "Did I say anything about not wanting to pay?" he said. "We'll find a way. We can always sell the cottage." Every year he talked about selling the vacation house in the Poconos, where we spent no more than a week each summer, sometimes only a weekend. The rest of the year, my father tried – unsuccessfully – to rent it out. But every time his real estate agent came close to selling, he hesitated. "It might still be a good source of income," he'd reason. "We just need to advertise better." The more money the house lost, the more attached my father became to it. We all knew he'd never let it go. But now he went on, "I can call the agent tomorrow. Maybe that couple from Poughkeepsie is still interested. We'll find a way. If the market would just stay steady for once, I wouldn't worry. If there was such a thing as job security anymore – "

Before he could begin the speech we'd heard so often before, about corporate loyalty and the inefficient use of employees as disposable resources, my mother cut him off. "Of course we can pay for you," she said to Jared. "That's not going to be a problem. It's when Daniel's time comes, that's what concerns me. We'll just have to wait and see."

Somehow I'd been brought into the middle of this against my will.

What did college have to do with me? Jared was still fuming, and now his eyes were locked on me, his forehead creased, a muscle in his jaw jumping. "So it's my problem where he goes?"

"I don't care," I said. "I don't want to go to Tennessee."

"If you don't start studying, you won't be going anywhere," my father said.

"We're just trying to be fair," my mother said.

Jared wouldn't stop staring at me, though I hunched down in my chair and feigned interest in the broccoli I hadn't touched until now. "I'll join the navy," he said. "I'll join the navy and you can go to Harvard, you little shit."

"Jared!" my mother cried. "Don't you dare talk like that at my table."

"I like Rutgers," I said.

"Rutgers doesn't take just anybody," my father said. "The kid doesn't read a thing. Not even the funny pages. I don't see how he doesn't fail all his subjects."

"You can go to the fucking moon, for all I care," Jared said.

My mother's chair squawked against the linoleum floor. "That's it," she said between her teeth. She half-stood, leaning forward, hands flat on the table, knuckles white. My father held out an arm in front of her. She glanced at it and inhaled through quivering lips. "I don't want to see your face until tomorrow," she said. "Get marching."

Jared was on his feet. He tugged at his sleeves, which clung to his upper arms. I couldn't tell whether he was pushing out his chest or if it had simply grown big enough to stretch the boundaries of his T-shirt. "Gladly," he said. "Good practice for the navy. Since that's what you want."

"I don't want to hear your voice," my mother said, but already Jared was stomping his way across the kitchen, lifting his knees to his waist, swinging his arms stiffly, occasionally saluting the oven and dishwasher. She settled back into her chair and wrapped her hands carefully around her cup of tea, as if to warm the fury from them. "He's not being funny at all."

After Jared was gone from the kitchen and the back door slammed, I said, "I don't need to go to college." And though it pained me, I added, "Jared can go to Tennessee if he wants."

My mother shook her head. "If you want to finish your dinner, I'd better not hear another word."

"You know what kind of jobs you can get with a high school diploma?" my father said. "Indentured servitude. Cannon fodder for the corporate army."

"Stop," my mother said, rubbing a thumb and forefinger above her eyebrows. "All of you. Please just stop."

IN MY PARENTS' IMAGINATIONS, JARED'S GRADUATION WAS to be a great milestone, a turning point for our family. For months they'd spoken of it in hushed tones, with uneasy anticipation. Afterward, they seemed to think, everything would suddenly change. Finishing high school would lift some invisible burden from Jared's shoulders, and life would become easier, for him and for the rest of us. "Make sure you show him how proud you are," my mother reminded me often. "This isn't a small thing. He's worked hard."

I was also graduating – from middle school – but no one, including me, made much of it. In fact, I didn't want to think at all about switching schools in the fall, and whenever anybody mentioned it, I immediately tried to change the subject. The last few years had been a good time for me. I knew it even while it was happening and didn't take a moment for granted. I'd never been an especially popular kid, but my best friend was, and from that I benefited. Greg Farisi lived at the bottom of my street, and we'd run around the neighborhood together since we were four. For ten years we'd seen each other nearly every day, and though I didn't necessarily fit into his crowd of friends, almost no one questioned my being part of it.

Greg was a small kid with olive skin and a tight, impish smile that formed a dimple on his left cheek, one he was able to deepen on command. He always seemed on the verge of winking. His black hair ended in loose curls above his forehead, and at any given moment he was either fluffing them up or patting them down. He was a natural athlete; until he was twelve he played every sport the township offered and excelled in all of them – as a halfback, a shortstop, a point guard, a hockey forward. But these were all just games to him, pure entertainment. Wrestling was his true calling. After placing second in the state at 106 lbs. his first year in middle school, he quit every other sport and devoted himself full-time to the mats. From then on he was always bulking up or slimming down to make his weight; he'd once spent an entire day spitting into a 7-Eleven Big Gulp cup to shed the few extra ounces that would disqualify him from the next day's meet.

When he wasn't wrestling or training, Greg grew easily bored – especially during school – and looked for ways to amuse himself. This usually meant causing some sort of trouble, and I was always more than happy to help him. This, above all, was why we'd stayed friends for so long. I couldn't wrestle and was lousy at most other sports; I'd pitched in Little League, but my control was so erratic and my speed so fleeting I didn't bother trying out for the middle school team. The only game I could compete in with Greg was ping-pong – he never beat me more than three out of five times. But when it came to getting into trouble, I was a star. I spent enough lunch periods in detention hall for the vice-principal to ask, "Mr. Brickman, are you practicing for prison? Or do you just enjoy silent meditation? Maybe you should consider taking up yoga and stop getting thrown out of class."

Nothing we did was criminal – climbing onto the school's roof, swiping chalk erasers from all the classrooms, writing our names in bug spray on the basketball courts and lighting them on fire. Despite what the vice-principal said, I didn't believe these things would have any bearing on my future; I did them because in my mind nothing I did then could possibly matter one way or the other. But still, my parents were horrified every time they got a call from school. "So he doesn't catch colds," my mother cried at my father, who could only scratch his beard with both hands at once. "Big deal. What good are his genes if they make him act like an idiot?" For every lunchtime detention, I was banned three days from watching TV or sentenced to a weekend of raking leaves.

Greg somehow managed to escape the consequences of our pranks, though they were usually his idea to begin with. In two years, he'd only been sent to the office twice and had never sat through detention. He had a way of endearing himself to teachers, parents, other kids – to everyone except his own father, who'd known him long enough to see through his smile and who kept a black leather belt, far too creased and battered ever to wear, always ready in his top dresser drawer. Greg had once shown it to me and described its sting, especially when his father didn't pay attention to his grip and the buckle accidentally caught the back of Greg's thigh. I never believed Mr. Farisi was a cruel man. Most of the time he was affectionate, even with me, ruffling my hair and telling jokes. But I knew his sense of justice was strict and absolute. Instead of hating him for it, Greg respected him far more than those teachers who let him get away with anything. Though he made me nervous, I liked him because he had no qualms about saying "fuck" in my presence.

But after seeing the black belt, I thought it only fair that I bear the brunt of responsibility for our trouble at school. Not that I had much choice. Once, in science class, we'd purposely sat across the room from each other and had planned to set off a pair of firecrackers at the exact same moment. My fuse must have been longer, or else I'd lit it a fraction of a second too late. Greg's firecracker blew first. The teacher whirled, a hand on her chest. She observed Greg's theatrical shrug and let out an equally exaggerated, exasperated sigh. Already she was beginning to smile in forgiveness. But then my firecracker went off, and her smile stopped short. "That's enough, now," she shouted. "Once might have been funny, Mr. Brickman. Go see Mr. Swaney. Tell him you're guilty of overkill."

I never resented Greg for this sort of special treatment. It seemed worth the trouble at the time. Known to everyone as Greg's friend, I was always surrounded by a group of kids who otherwise wouldn't have spoken a word to me. I never sat alone during those lunch periods I wasn't in detention. Because Greg was afraid of injuring his knees or fingers and missing a wrestling match, he kept out of the regular lunchtime football game, sitting instead with other wrestlers and a group of girls on the grassy slope overlooking the baseball diamond and soccer field. And of course I sat there, too. Happily. It wasn't that I didn't enjoy playing sports, but with girls watching from all corners of the playground, these games had nothing to do with fun. Something strange happened when I was conscious of eyes set on me. In Little League, I'd once pitched three scoreless innings with nearly perfect control, but as soon as my father showed up in the bleachers, my fingers became slippery, my arm rubber; my cleats caught in the ground and the catcher's mitt eluded my fastball, my curve, even my lob. Afterward my father said, "Don't worry. You weren't born for this. There's only one Sandy Koufax in a lifetime."

So I was perfectly content to sit on the hill where Greg lounged on his elbows, chewing a piece of grass, squinting at the football game below, and picking out people in the crowd as objects of amusement. "Look at Wilson," he'd say. "Runs like his pants are falling down." Then he'd stand and do an imitation, and all the girls would giggle.

Almost always one of the other wrestlers tried to top him. Marty Jameson wrestled at 112 lbs. and made the team only because there was no one else to compete at his weight. Even six pounds lighter, Greg could pin him nine times out of ten. Marty had fine, nearly white, blond hair that fell in layers over his ears. His top teeth were slightly bucked, pushing his upper lip half an inch in front of the lower. This combination made him look to me like an albino duck – often, when he threw a glance in my direction, I was certain his eyes had a reddish tint. For reasons I could never put my finger on, my presence had always been an offense to him. He put up with me only because of Greg, whom he hated and envied for his sense of humor, his wrestling ability, and most of all for the attention given to him by the girls. As soon as Greg imitated one of the football players, Marty followed with, "This is how Coach Scholl walks." Then he strutted like the evil duck I knew him to be. But Greg would have no part of it. The coach was hard on him and never fell for his charms; Greg respected him almost as much as he did his own father. So Marty wouldn't strut two steps before Greg snapped, "That's not Coach. That's your mother after I fucked her in the ass till she bled."

Whenever Marty made me his target, saying, "I don't see why this kid sits with us. He couldn't wrestle a chicken," Greg jumped to my defense almost as faithfully as he did for the coach. "Watch out for Brickman," he'd say. "He might look like a pussy, but he knows how to build a bomb."

Only Greg was allowed to make people laugh at my expense. My usual goal at lunch was to keep him entertained enough that he wouldn't resort to making me his entertainment. I'd scan the football game for kids I knew he already disliked and say casually, "I heard Plummer talking the other day. He said wrestling's for guys too pussy to play football and too stupid to do anything else."

Greg would nod and crack his knuckles. "I hate that sonofabitch. I'll show him how pussy wrestling is. You ever hear a guy cry out for his mommy? Wait till I get him in a cradle."

But sometimes, when the football game and the wrestlers began to bore him, when he'd tired of begging one of the girls to show him her breasts, he resorted to making me demonstrate the wrestling moves he'd taught me. Though I was five pounds heavier and two inches taller, I didn't stand a chance. He'd let me take him down once, maybe twice, and then he'd grind my skull or spine with his chin, skid my face along the grass, and finally apply a special hold that split my legs painfully and opened my crotch in the direction of the hysterical girls.

This was a sacrifice I was usually willing to make. I would do whatever I could to keep a firm hold on this life, even if it meant throwing away every third Saturday to rot in detention hall. As the end of middle school approached, I was more desperate than ever to fortify my friendship with Greg. There was no reason for him to drop me when we started high school. But then again, nothing seemed certain, and I often felt myself on shaky ground.

Most afternoons when Greg didn't have wrestling practice, we took off somewhere on our bikes, though from our neighborhood there were few places to go: into other residential neighborhoods guarded by Crime Watch signs, along the strip of dirt beside the freeway sound-barriers, across the train tracks to the private lake where we'd twice been arrested for trespassing and lectured to in the back of a police cruiser, or to the gas station mini-mart on Route 10. More often than not, we rode beneath the column of electrical towers that cut a swath through our neighborhood and strung power lines from Newark to the Pennsylvania border. We'd once decided to follow the towers all the way to the Delaware Water Gap, but after less than five miles, already exhausted, I'd stopped at the sight of an electrical cable dangling from a tilted metal cone fifty feet over-head. It was wrapped in rubber, the whole thing thicker than my upper arm; it snaked fifteen yards along the ground and ended in what had once been the face of a deer. But this no longer looked like the face of anything. The eyeballs were gone and most of the hide up to the neck was burned away. At regular intervals, a surge of electricity singed the remains of the deer's jaw, sending up a plume of white smoke to quickly scatter in the breeze. Greg, who'd been riding ahead, noticed that I'd stopped and came back. He dropped his bike in the weeds and followed the line of the cable. To keep from vomiting, I laughed loudly. "That's the worst thing I've ever seen," Greg said. "You're one heartless sonofabitch, Brickman." When I looked up his eyes were watery, their rims red. For the next week at school, he called me "the iceman," and said to the group of girls on the hill during lunch, "You want to meet the coldest man on earth? He laughs at electro-cuted deer. The kid's got no soul."

The same week, two different girls promised to let me kiss them in the parking lot, in order, I knew, to make Greg jealous. Though both times the girl backed out at the last minute, Greg encouraged me selflessly, say-ing, "Go ahead. I don't mind taking your sloppy seconds." For this alone, I'd gladly have taken a few extra trips to the office or submitted to a head-lock. So far Greg had asked for nothing more. But what about next year? What other sacrifices would be required of me then? The coming fall re-mained a mysterious, hazy time, when, I feared, anything might change without reason at all.

The regional high school where my brother now went and where I was soon destined to follow was set far back from the main road on which my bus passed every morning and afternoon; twice a day I glimpsed a bit of brick and glass and rows of parked cars. Student cars – kids actually drove themselves to this school. I'd only seen the building up close twice while riding with my mother to pick up Jared from an afternoon computer club and had never once been inside. Because it gathered kids from three sep-arate townships, the school was massive compared to mine, three stories high and laid out in a square-cornered C. A rigid, imposing wall faced the parking lot. From either end, a stout wing jutted onto a concrete slab scattered with maintenance sheds and pickup trucks, and fifty yards beyond, the entire world dropped away abruptly into the bowl of the football stadium. The sides were solid brick, broken only by steel doors painted the colors of diseased flesh (which our health teacher had described while flashing nauseating slides) – the top two gangrene, the ground floor a smoker's lung just beginning to blacken. Each door led to a rickety fire escape with retractable ladders that seemed to stop short ten feet from the pavement. The building's front was all glass and aluminum frames, but the promise of open light was deceptive: both times I rode past, all the blinds were lowered. Beside the flagpole, on the tiny patch of lawn leading to the front doors, a splintered wooden sign, punctured with numerous BBs and at least one real bullet, announced, "Union Knoll High School: Home of the Mallards."

I would not spend the next four years of my life in this place – it was unthinkable. There was no grassy hill, no lunchtime football game. Where would Greg spend his days? How would I convince him to let me follow? When I imagined getting into trouble and taking my punishments, I could only picture the bullet hole in the Mallard sign; starting next year every step I took would tremble with a significance beyond my comprehension. Even thinking about the building from afar brought on an agitation I couldn't control. The only way I could keep my breath from growing short and my fingers from shaking was to believe truly and absolutely that I would never set foot in the hallways Jared described as narrow, claustrophobic, and perilously overcrowded. I managed to convince myself it was all a mistake, which someone would soon discover and correct. At night as I prepared for bed and again during my morning shower, I was comforted by glancing down at my knobby wrists and knees, my bony chest and hairless arms and legs, all of which could belong to no one but a boy, and not to someone about to become a man – as my mother often referred to me.

Only my father seemed at all concerned about my entering high school, though not in the same way I was. "You think you can just slide by without studying," he said one evening, when I mentioned watching the Mets game after dinner. "That's fine for now. But just wait until next year. They won't let you get away with that on the Knoll."

Anxiety quickly crept into my fingertips, which I drummed against my knees. "It's an important game," I said. "Doc's pitching. Tonight's his big comeback."

"Who wants more rice?" my mother asked.

"Doc's washed up," my father said, and I slowly began to relax the muscles in my stomach and let the air out of my lungs. "No one snorts cocaine up his nose and goes back to being a star. Inside he's messed up for good. All that potential, such a waste."

And then, for no reason I could fathom, Jared piped in: "He doesn't need to study. They'll give any moron a high school diploma."

What was he doing? We were off the subject. I'd been off the hook. My father said, "He'll be one of those metal-shop kids, the ones who can fix my car but can't read a dinner menu."

"I can read fine!" I snapped. The force of my voice surprised and pleased me. I could be hotheaded, after all. My father's genes didn't control me completely. Already my anger was fading, but still feeling its thrill, I went on. "Any moron can graduate high school. Jared's doing it, isn't he?"

Quickly, my mother jumped in. "You can stop right there," she said. "We all know how hard your brother's worked, and we're all proud—"

But Jared was shaking his head. Instead of matching my anger, his expression was one of mild hurt and resignation. "No," he said. "Daniel's right. It's stupid. It doesn't mean anything. I don't see why everyone's making such a big deal."

"It is a big deal," my mother insisted.

"I'm going to watch the game," I said.

Jared stood. "I'll go with you."

I nodded, bewildered, careful not to let my excitement show. Jared hadn't offered to do something with me in years. He didn't even like baseball. I didn't want to question it but still couldn't help glancing quickly into his face for some hint of motive, and to find out what might be asked of me in return.

My father called after us, "You can both be mechanics. They make good money, you know. As long as you get to be your own boss."

"It is a big deal," my mother repeated as we made our way to the family room. "It is," she said once more and dropped pots into the sink with a despondent clang.

SHE CONTINUED TO THINK SO, NO MATTER WHAT JARED SAID. She planned an enormous party for the afternoon following the graduation ceremony, with relatives coming from Connecticut, Long Island, even Florida. She'd started cooking for it in January and had already filled the extra freezer in the basement with hors d'œuvres and desserts. She'd hired neighborhood kids to serve food and snap pictures. But, of course, Jared didn't want a party. He tried to make her cancel it, and when she wouldn't, refused to give her the names of any friends she might invite.

Graduation for Jared was nothing more than a distraction. His sights were set a week later, when he would compete in the bodybuilding contest in West Orange. This was the thing he'd really been working toward these last four years. How could graduating high school compare? It marked the end of something he hated. The contest was the start of something he loved. My parents pretended he was just being modest, that as soon as he donned the green cap and gown, the gold tassels – the official colors of the Mallards – he would feel the flush of accomplishment and the dawning of a bright future. "He's under a lot of pressure," my mother told me when Jared wasn't around. "Everything's changing for him. Try to be nice to him. Try not to bother him too much."

As soon as his registration was accepted for the competition, Jared doubled his training time at the gym. He came home halfway through dinner, his entire shirt stained with sweat and only beginning to dry. He held his arms away from his sides and didn't seem able to lower them. Each step made him wince. My mother had already served a salad and was beginning to dish out hunks of glazed chicken. "I won't hold up everything for one person," she said.

Jared eased into a chair, visibly swallowing a groan. "I never asked you to."

My father said, "It's not healthy to think about your body all day every day."

"Don't sit down with your stink," my mother said. "Go take a shower."

It didn't really matter whether or not Jared was on time for dinner. He only picked at his meal enough to keep my mother from harassing him. He was on a special diet that was supposed to give him bulk and at the same time trim away excess fat to chisel the outlines of his muscles. He lived on protein and carbohydrate shakes made from a powder I silently swore was nothing more than chalk dust – once, when no one was home, I'd opened one of the plastic tubs, stuck my nose far inside and taken a deep breath. In this powder I'd hoped to find the secret of Jared's drive, of his determination to abandon the person he'd once been, but here instead was the source of his misery. My nostrils burned, and I coughed for half an hour. Who could possibly be happy with nothing but chalk in his stomach day in and day out?

After dinner, he locked himself in his room and hurried through his school work. I knew when he'd finished – through my bedroom wall I'd hear the opening bars from the 2001 film score, the music Jared had chosen as the soundtrack for his posing. Hours on end he worked at choreographing his moves: arms in a circle in front of his chest; a right-hand profile, arm twisted to show a tricep, leg slightly bent with the calf flexed; a look at his back, biceps lifted on either side of his head; left-hand profile, the mirror image of the right; and finally a return to the chest, only this time with one arm stretched straight, fingers extended, and the other curled beside his ear. The whole thing went on for two and a half minutes. A month before the contest, he shaved all the hair from his arms, legs, and chest and began covering himself with Liquid Tan, which refused to spread evenly, instead tinting his skin in rust-colored blotches and streaks.

To my parents, all this was either pure madness or some youthful fantasy they could ignore with a shrug or a wave of a hand. In their bafflement they kept mostly silent, though they often made questioning gestures to the ceiling. "When I was his age, I wanted to race hot rods," my father said. "I guess this isn't so different."

This worked to my advantage. When it came to bodybuilding, Jared was willing to take any ally he could get. Since I was the only one in the house who even pretended to support him, he allowed me into his room while he practiced his routine. This was my last chance, I knew – my last chance to make up for the years I'd called him fat, to make him remember me fondly after he was gone. I made a big show of interest, pointing out awkward moments or changes of speed. "You're rushing through the calf shot," I said. "Hold it another second. One more. That's it. Good."

Two weeks before graduation, I even went so far as to say I wanted to start lifting weights myself. To my surprise, Jared quickly offered to teach me with the set in the basement. His enthusiasm worried me, and I knew right away I'd made a mistake. He scribbled out a long list of exercises with numbers of sets and reps. Around my waist he tightened a bulky leather belt that made it nearly impossible to sit. I curled and squatted and worked my triceps, all while Jared watched, barking what in his mind must have been words of encouragement. "Come on, you wimp. One more. Do you want arms like a girl? I said one more. Do you want to look like Dad?"

Our cat Stanley had followed us into the basement and was rubbing against my legs as I struggled with the weights. Already my limbs tingled with approaching numbness and seemed to be taking leave from the rest of my body. I'd had enough, but Jared led me to the bench press and slid me beneath a steel bar with black plates at either end. The bar dropped straight to my chest and wouldn't budge. The whole thing couldn't have weighed more than eighty pounds, but I was sure it would collapse my lungs. The cat's tail flicked mockingly under one elbow and then the other. I grunted, heaved, shouted, "Get it off me!" Jared only shook his head and said in disappointment, "Come on, you pussy. You can do it. Use those girlie arms."

Why was I doing this? I didn't care about muscles, and I certainly never wanted to shave my legs or paint myself orange. Jared's face hovered above me, the firm cheeks and sharp jaw that still seemed so alien, with patches of stubble showing through the fake tan. Something occurred to me then for the first time: what if Jared's face had never changed? What if he was still the same chubby, happy, humiliated kid my parents had always wanted him to be? Would I care whether or not he was leaving? My ribs were beginning to ache, and I gasped, though in truth I wasn't yet having any trouble breathing. I tilted my body to one side until a steel plate slid from the end of the bar. The cat screeched and tore up the stairs. Then the entire bar seesawed, wrenching from my hands and crashing to the floor. The second plate landed edge-first on Jared's foot. He stomped around the basement, cursing and shouting, and I waited for him to grab me, shake me by the shoulders, sock me in the eye. This was what I'd been waiting for all along. I pictured his fist hurling toward my face, the blinding crash, the sudden release of all my guilt and past wrongdoing – now there would be nothing standing between us. Jared would either love me or he wouldn't, and I would know one way or the other. But suddenly he was calm. He bent and rubbed his foot slowly, then straightened and turned to me for the first time. "You're hopeless," he said. "There's nothing I can do for you."

I groaned without meaning to. Nothing else he might have said could have wounded me more. I would try the bench press again, really try this time, and I was sure I'd lift the bar at least once. Even with a hundred pounds on either end I'd lift it, so long as Jared took back what he'd said. But he was already on his way upstairs. I chased after him and set my foot against his bedroom door just as he was shutting it. "I can still help with your routine," I begged. "I'm better at watching than doing."

He hesitated a moment and then reluctantly opened the door. "All right," he said. "Just sit on the bed and don't say a word until I'm through."

He yanked off his shirt and pressed the play button on his tape deck. The routine was no different than it had been for the last month, still awkward and rushed in the same spots. But now I was barely watching. My eyes wandered to Jared's walls, plastered with cutout pages from muscle magazines, men and women in brightly colored bikinis barely covering their shimmering, oiled skin. My heart was racing. I couldn't stop picturing the door closing on my foot. If I'd been a second later, it would have shut all the way. But somehow this was worse – my hope had returned, my suffering prolonged. Along with anxiety came a sullen jealousy of all the faces on the walls. These were the people who would go with Jared to Tennessee, the ones he would think about all the way through college. He didn't, I thought, even own a picture of me. And if I gave him one, what were the chances he'd hang it on his wall or prop it on his desk?

The music stopped. Jared let out a long breath and shook his arms. "So?" he said. "What do you think?"

"Great," I said, surprised at the gurgling sound deep in my throat. I had to sniffle hard to go on. "A hundred times better than before. It's almost perfect."

"Really?" He frowned conspicuously to keep from smiling. "You think so? What about the profile, the right side?"

"You still need another half-second on the calf. But otherwise it's there. The music's excellent."

"I wish I had another month to practice," he said.

"You don't need it," I said. "You know you'll win, hands down."

"I think I'll run through it once more. You don't have to stay if you're bored."

"I'm not," I said. "Not at all."


THE NEXT DAY IN SCHOOL I TOLD MY FRIENDS ABOUT JARED'S routine. But in front of them I told the truth. "His muscles are pretty big," I said. "But his moves suck ass. He looks like he's dancing with a bear."

It was an especially hot day for early June, and the football game was sluggish. Greg had been picking aimlessly at the grass and had only shrugged when I'd pointed to a kid on the football field who'd dropped three passes in a row. Something struck my ear, and beside my hand dropped a balled-up gum wrapper. From behind, Marty Jameson said, "Why don't you go sit with your own kind, Brickshit. They're letting the retards go down to the pond."

Along the service road beside the baseball diamond, the school's five special-ed kids bounded in a ragged line toward the winding green pond that marked the edge of school property. None of us had ever seen these kids up close; their teachers wisely kept them separate. I didn't know what might be wrong with their minds, but even from far away, I could see that they had received the worst fate imaginable: bodies completely out of proportion, balloon heads on stick necks, stumped legs, bloated bellies and buttocks.

"Those kids have more brains in their teeth than in your whole family combined," Greg said, without even glancing at Marty. Then he motioned lazily to the girls. "And anyway, if you get rid of Brickman, you'll lose all these pretty ladies. Why do you think they hang around with us at all?"

The girls snickered, but in a tense, expectant way. Several of them were leaning forward. Everyone seemed to be waiting for something to happen. Greg went on, "Besides, he can wrestle now. Didn't I teach you that half-nelson the other day?" he asked me.

I could already imagine my shoulder slamming against the ground, Greg's chin digging into my back. In a panic, I said, "I tried it out on my brother. Did I tell you he entered a bodybuilding contest?" I spoke rapidly, feeling my cheek burning against the grass, my braces serrating the insides of my lips. Briefly I wished I was with those kids walking toward the pond, wished my head were twice the size of my body so I'd never even have had the chance to sit on this hill or lead an ordinary life. Wouldn't that somehow have been easier? "He's been dieting on chalk dust for the last two months. He has to shave his legs every week."

Of all the kids on the hill, only Greg had ever met Jared and remembered him best from his fat years. Only he found all this funny, but that was enough for me. I was able to relax, and soon got carried away. I stood in front of everybody and ran through a parody of Jared's poses, singing out the 2001 theme. Greg rolled to his side, laughing uncontrollably. I mimicked Jared's accent. I told how he almost took off a nipple while shaving his chest. I described his awful tan, even lying about a bright white patch on his back where he couldn't reach with a brush – in truth, he'd had me cover that spot for him. Greg hooted, howled, wiped away tears. "I bet he even shaves his balls," he cried. All the girls laughed. The wrestlers chuckled. Even Marty Jameson cracked a smile, his duck bill parting slightly, his pink eyes squinting. This was my moment of glory – all sights were on me, and I didn't stumble once. Even as I spoke, I was admiring my composure. I would have given anything to let this go on forever, but already I was imagining the moment lost, swallowed by the swiftly approaching summer and the dark mystery of next fall: in less than three months, no hill, no playground, only a concrete slab littered with cigarette butts and flattened pieces of gum. I tore off my shirt and started running through the routine a second time, my movements now even more exaggerated and ridiculous, but the laughter was dying down. Greg caught his breath and spit. "Jesus Christ, put your shirt back on," he said. "You're blinding everybody."

Marty Jameson, leaping at the chance, said, "He's a walking rack of ribs. I've never seen anybody so skinny in my life."

"That's funny," Greg said. "I thought you saw your mother naked every day. That's what she told me, anyway."

A WEEK LATER, GREG CAME UP THE HILL TO MY HOUSE. THIS was a rare occasion. Though we lived less than a quarter-mile apart, I almost always went down to his place. Not because he wasn't welcome at mine – my parents were as charmed by him as everybody else. Whenever I got into trouble at school, the first thing my mother said was, "Tell me you at least didn't drag Greg into this. It's one thing for you to do something stupid. What's his mother think of us? Turning her nice boy into a hoodlum."

My excuse for never having Greg over was that it was easier to go downhill than up. No one questioned the logic of this. But the truth was, I felt more comfortable in Greg's surroundings than I did with him in mine. There was an unmistakable difference between our two houses. His wasn't dirty by any standard, but it had an atmosphere of relaxation completely foreign and agreeable to me. Three-day-old sports pages often lay spread open on the living room floor though no one was reading them. In the kitchen, Mrs. Farisi, a round woman with massive bosoms and graying hair tied in a long, fraying braid, was always walking the tightrope between control and pure chaos – used pots, bowls, baking trays teetered in stacks, lettuce leaves, raw ground beef, wobbling eggs covered every inch of counter space, flour dusted her cheek. When Mr. Farisi wasn't at work, he sprawled on the couch in a sleeveless undershirt and held lively conversations with characters on TV.

My house was spotless and hushed on any given day. My mother, too, spent all weekend cooking, but there was never so much as a dirty fork in the sink or a drop of splattered sauce on the stovetop; nothing but the exact ingredients she would need in the next five minutes sat out on the counter. My father grumbled if anyone talked loudly while he was trying to read the newspaper. He wouldn't lay the paper down for a minute before my mother snatched it from the floor and tossed it onto the stack in the laundry room. No shoes were allowed past the kitchen – a single sneaker smudge would stand out on the shining hallway tiles like a fresh bruise on pale skin. I was embarrassed to have my friends think I lived in a museum; I didn't want to watch everything they said or did.

But today, Greg insisted on coming up. He'd had an argument with his father over TV channels and had to get out of the house. "I just wanted to watch football," he told me on the phone. "But he was watching some stupid black-and-white movie on Lifetime. He's already pissed off about some client. I called him Mussolini. Fucking Mussolini, actually. He's on his way to get the belt."

Reluctantly, I told him to ride up, but in my mind determined we wouldn't stay here long. The minute he came in the door, I'd suggest heading off somewhere on our bikes – even after seeing the burnt deer, we were both still fascinated by the electrical towers, and I knew Greg wouldn't object to riding there. I waited nervously for him to come up the hill. Today was Sunday, and everybody was home. My father was reading on the back porch. My mother had been in the kitchen since dawn, browning onions for a soup – another dish for Jared's graduation party. I'd woken to the smell, and by now it filled the house and seemed to coat my tongue. I waited for Greg in the family room, where Jared lay on the couch with Stanley in his lap. He was watching a videotape of last year's Mr. Olympia contest and kept rewinding the same segment over and over: a series of poses by a smiling black man with a sensitive gap between his front teeth and otherwise inhuman proportions. His chest, I was sure, must have been inflated with air. When he moved his arms a certain way, black wings seemed to sprout from his back. The man could have swallowed three of me whole without affecting his size. But at the same time, his muscles appeared too delicate to have anything to do with strength. Each ripple, every protruding vein, all of it seemed incredibly fragile, ready to crumble at the slightest touch. I found myself growing anxious for him, afraid the next pose would put him in his grave.

Jared didn't look at all like a bodybuilder today. His hair was matted against the couch cushion, sticking up in back. The collar of his white sweatshirt was stained a rust color where Liquid Tan had rubbed off from his neck, but despite the tan, the skin under his eyes was gray. "Look at that motherfucker," he said, with a mixture of awe and frustration. "It's not just that he's huge. He moves like he's wearing a goddamn leotard. I can't do that."

"He's been doing it a long time," I said. "I don't know why you're watching this. You can't compare yourself to Mr. Olympia."

Greg came in the back door without knocking. He called out something to my father on the porch and said to my mother, "That smells great, Mrs. B. Nice to see you. My mom would love the recipe."

My mother's answer was lost beneath the sizzling of onions. I hopped up from my chair and tried to divert Greg directly to the garage and our bikes. But he was already walking past me into the family room. "What's up, Jared?" he said. He pointed to the black man on the TV screen, who was now flexing his biceps, each the size of Greg's entire head. "Man, you're looking huge. Daniel told me you bulked up, but I had no idea. You're not taking steroids, are you?"

Jared didn't say a word. He stroked the cat gently and kept watching the video. I was suddenly ashamed of the orange stains on his collar, the orange streaks on his face and hands, nearly the same color as Stanley's fur. Even his bulging neck muscles seemed artificial with Greg in the room. Greg was Jared's opposite in every way – I saw it clearly now. No matter how big his muscles were, Greg would always carry himself easily, with confidence. He could never have been fat or lonely; he would never be anything other than what he wanted to be. "I don't see how you could lose any contest," Greg said. "But I think you spent too much time in the tanning booth. Maybe it's just the video, but from here you look kinda like a Negroid. You'll have to go for a Jamaican accent."

Jared's hand paused in the middle of the cat's back, and then continued on its way to the tail. "Aren't you the kid who likes to roll on mats with other guys?" he said.

Greg smiled, but he shuffled his feet, widening his stance. His hands balled into fists. He was digging in. "I've been working out, too," he said. "Take a look."

He circled his arms in front of his chest. Why was he doing this? He knew what kind of trouble it would make for me. I stared at him hard, and he must have sensed my agitation, for he shot me a quick glance before turning back to Jared. *I'm sorry*, his look suggested, *but I can't help it*. It said something else, as well: *Don't tell me you didn't know this was coming*. Immediately I felt an onrush of guilt and troubling satisfaction. Greg flexed his arms and began singing the *2001* theme; when he no longer knew the tune, he switched to the theme from *The Flintstones*. He ran through an excruciating parody of my parody of Jared's routine. But Jared watched him for no more than a few seconds. The orange tint of his cheeks reddened; for a moment he seemed to have a real tan. He wouldn't look at me, but the set of his jaw charged me with the most inexcusable treachery. I was torn with shame and regret, but at the same time tried to feel indignant. Why should I care if he hated me? He was leaving. No matter what I did or said, he was leaving. Still, I shrugged apologetically and said to myself, I didn't want this. This was never what I'd wanted.

Greg wouldn't quit. He pointed one arm straight toward the ceiling, curled the other beside his ear, and let out a sickly groan. He finished with a ferocious sneer. Then, as if nothing had happened, he turned back to the TV and said, "Do you have to shave your balls, or just your chest and legs?"

By now I was trembling with anger, perhaps the first real anger I'd ever felt in my life. "Don't be an idiot," I muttered through my teeth. I was glad to feel the sharp metal of my braces catching on my lips. Jared was staring straight ahead, no longer at the TV, but at a bookshelf filled with my mother's cooking magazines. He took deep, rumbling breaths, his nostrils flaring. Slowly, his fingers sifted through the fur on Stanley's haunches.

"Don't call me an idiot," Greg said. His arms were crossed, and all trace of joking was gone from his voice. He eyed me closely, his jaw jutting slightly forward, the same look he used to intimidate an opponent before the start of a wrestling match.

But I was in no mood to be intimidated now. "Then don't act like one," I said.

"Are we going somewhere or what?" Greg said. "It stinks like onion farts in here."

He left the room and turned the corner to the bathroom. As soon as the door shut behind him, I went to the couch and whispered to Jared, "He's an asshole. Don't listen to him." He lifted the remote control, pressed a button, but said nothing. On the TV, the giant black man zipped backward through his poses. "I think your routine's great," I said. "Really. I never made fun of it. I was just demonstrating –" I took a step forward, and Jared jerked his knee. The cat, startled from sleep, pushed off from Jared's thigh, claws extended. Jared cried out and grabbed his leg with one hand. The other arm – accidentally? on purpose? I would never know – swung behind him, its elbow catching me just below the ribs. I hit the floor in an instant. Snot and spittle exploded onto my lips and chin. Whatever noise escaped me brought everybody running, my mother from the kitchen, Greg from the bathroom, my father all the way from the back porch. Through stinging tears I could see them all standing above me as I gasped and sputtered. Jared, too, was on his feet. "I barely touched him," he said. "He chased the cat off my lap."

"He's your brother," my mother said, astonished. Her voice was uncertain, confused in a way I'd never heard before. "Your own brother." This was the worst thing she could ever have imagined, her greatest fear, I suddenly felt sure, since giving birth to a second son – in her own house was playing out a biblical story of jealousy and vengeance. And worst of all, she had done nothing to prevent it. "How could you?" she choked.

My father, for the first time in my life, raised his fist. It came down slowly, opening on the way. By the time it connected with Jared's shoulder, it hit with no more than a light, backhanded tap. Still, all of us sucked in a unanimous breath of shock and horror – all except Greg, who couldn't have understood what this meant. Jared's face altered instantly. He blinked and swallowed twice. His chin trembled. His mouth opened and closed without speaking a word. Finally, he managed to say, "You hit me?" My father, dazed, glanced over his shoulder to see if Jared was talking to someone else. "I can't believe you hit me," Jared said. "I barely touched him." His face twisted and purpled with all the rage he'd ever held back in his life, all the hurt he'd never avenged. "I wish I'd really punched him," he said quietly.

By now I was able to sit up, though I still held my stomach with both hands. Greg stood a few feet off to the side, smirking. He was, I knew, thinking about the story he would feel compelled to tell tomorrow at school. Why's everyone so upset? he must have been thinking. Where's the black belt? My mother stooped with a tissue to wipe up the spit that had been dribbling from my chin onto the hardwood floor. She was shaking and, I could tell, making an effort not to face my father; I hoped she would make a crack about his genes and warn him about the coming onslaught of germs, but she kept silent. My father slumped on the couch, staring at his hand as if it were no longer part of him. He might have been considering whether or not to lop it off. I was waiting for Jared to storm out, up to his room or out of the house, but instead, he sat in an armchair across from my father. His shoulders were hunched forward, burdened, it seemed; he made no effort to puff out his chest. He and my father gazed at each other, both shaking their heads. Without a word something passed between them, a substantial gesture, like a handshake or a signature, ending an unspoken but long-standing dispute. Neither looked down at me.

BY THE TIME GREG AND I HEADED OFF ON OUR BIKES, MY STO-mach no longer hurt at all; the pain that had seemed so intense was now as distant and hazy as a memory, not of something I'd experienced, but of something I'd watched or been told about. Instead I felt mostly mortified by what Greg had seen and full of self-pity – Jared had hit me, but it hadn't changed anything. He hated me more than ever. I tried to imagine what might have happened if he'd hit me harder, done some life-threatening internal damage, so he'd have no choice but to feel sorry and let me forgive him. At the same time, I couldn't help envying him: for the rest of his life he could tell people, "My old man hit me once. I never let him do it again."

Of course, I didn't say any of this to Greg. As we whizzed through our neighborhood, I shouted curses and threats of revenge. "The sonofabitch," I said. "Couldn't even stand up and fight me. Throws a sucker punch when I didn't even do anything."

Greg rode a yard or so ahead of me. He didn't respond, but seemed to be nodding. We sliced through a neighbor's lawn, kicking up clumps of sod, and dropped into a shallow gully that led to the power lines. Soon, the first tower loomed above us, wide as a garage at its base, narrowing as it rose, until arms heavy with wires branched off near its peak. Greg skidded to a halt in a sweeping half-circle. Dust clouded behind him and drifted forward over his shoulders and head. I stopped my bike, still ranting about Jared: "I can't wait till he's out of the house. I hope he never comes home for holidays."

Greg laid his bike carefully on the ground. "I'm an idiot?" he said.

"What are you talking about?"

He didn't answer. He glanced up the length of the electrical tower and then suddenly charged at me, toppling me from my bike and slamming my cheek in the dirt. My braces knifed into my lower lip, and my tongue was flooded with a salty, metallic taste. Instantly Greg had my arm locked behind my back. "You called me an idiot," he said.

"I didn't mean it."

He wrenched my arm higher and added a knee to my tailbone. A current buzzed through the wires overhead – for a moment I thought the sound was of my joints grinding, my muscles stretching and tearing. My nose was only an inch or two from a tangle of thorny stems, and with each pull on my arm it slid closer. But the pain was only minor compared to the sheer panic that struck me. I saw the life I'd so recklessly tried to preserve suddenly slipping away – tomorrow Marty Jameson would have free reign to banish me from the hill. I imagined myself on the bank of the slimy pond beyond the baseball diamond, staring up toward the slope where the wrestlers sprawled on the grass, where the girls who would never talk to me again held their hands in their laps to keep Greg from looking up their skirts. What would I say to those kids I'd have to sit beside now, with their giant heads on withered bodies?

"You think I'm an idiot," Greg said.

"I don't," I said. "You're not."

"Who's an idiot?"

"I am," I said.

"Who? I can't hear you."

"Me," I shouted. "I'm an idiot."

"Say it again."

"I'm an idiot!"

"You are," he said. "You really are."

He let me up and brushed a clump of dead grass from my shoulder. I massaged my throbbing arm, shook out my wrist, and spit blood at my feet. Greg kicked clods of dirt into the weeds, sheepish now. Nothing was over yet. Tomorrow he might tell everyone how I'd called myself an idiot, but he would still protect me from Marty Jameson. He would still wrestle me to the ground to make the girls laugh. But for how long? In two weeks the hill above the baseball diamond would be a memory. At the end of the summer there would be nothing but an ugly, C-shaped building and a slab of concrete where I could stand only if I learned to smoke. There would be no more Jared, just me alone in the house where my father would lie awake at night wondering how his hand had closed into a fist, where my mother would double her efforts to sterilize everything, where I would fight to keep my mild manners at bay.

"Come on," Greg said. "Let's go."

He picked up his bike and pedaled slowly toward Pennsylvania. I hesitated a moment, glancing in the direction of home, fearing the time had come to face what I couldn't change. Maybe it would be better this way: to give up trying, to let go of everything at once, to take whatever might come. The thought brought with it a momentary exhilaration, a wash of freedom, and was quickly followed by cold terror. Not yet, I pleaded. Not today. I flexed my sore wrist, bony and thin enough to circle with a thumb and forefinger. High above, sagging from the electrical tower's outstretched arms, the power lines buzzed dully. Not far off, Greg was weaving figure-eights in the tall grass, waiting. I hopped on my bike and hurried after him, knowing and at the same time refusing to believe that this ride or the next – any, any at all – might be the last.

# Mr. Mervin

EARLY EVERY SPRING, DANIEL'S MOTHER POINTED OUT filth on windows all over the house. Rain streaks, smudges from finger-prints, grime left by melting frost. Ordinarily she'd make a joke of it. "Don't you love living in a church?" she'd say. "All this stained glass!" But this year she carried a bottle of Windex and a roll of paper towels into the family room, where his father was reading the sports pages. Daniel, ten and a half, sat on the hardwood floor at the edge of the carpet, arranging his model cars and trucks. He'd spent weeks gluing together minuscule pieces and could finally set up an elaborate freeway accident. His mother went to the wide windows that started at Daniel's chin and rose all the way to the ceiling. "What's the point of these," she said. "I can't see the backyard. I can't even see my garden." She pumped the trigger of the spray bottle so fast it snorted, and clutching a paper towel, shoved her hand between the screen and window frame.

"Why kill yourself?" his father said. "You know it's silly to bother now."

"I can't even see Daniel when he plays outside."

On the floor, seven cars were ready to collide when a dump truck slammed into the carpet and turned on its side. But Daniel momentarily forgot the freeway. "You don't need to see me," he said.

His mother kept scrubbing, and his father said, "It's silly. You know Mr. Mervin will call soon enough. Next week at the latest."

"You don't need to see me," Daniel said again, but softer. Mention of Mr. Mervin made bubbles the size of ping-pong balls rise to his throat, and he didn't want to breathe. He remembered only a hunched bulk perched high on a ladder, a slow voice, and heavy footsteps, but still he didn't want the windows cleaned, ever. Once, late at night, he'd woken for no reason, and it was Mr. Mervin's name he'd found himself whispering. Right away, he knew he'd never go back to sleep. He crept down the hall to his parents' bed-room, raised his hand to knock on their door, but then hesitated. There was no sound, no snoring or rustling of sheets. They were gone, he was sure. Something had taken them away or made them want to leave. Back in his bed, alone, he lay with his ear against the wall separating his room from his older brother's. All night there was some noise from Jared, a cough, a sniffle, the squeak of a bed spring, and this was the only thing that kept him from crying. His eyes were still open when the first bars of sunlight appeared on his carpet and, down the hall, pipes hummed from his father's shower.

Now his mother pulled her arm inside and held up the paper towel, already black across the middle. "Mr. Mervin," she said. "That's exactly why I'm cleaning them myself."

"I thought we'd agreed on this," his father said.

"Is it so much to ask to have my windows cleaned properly?"

"It's a mitzvah. Didn't we agree it was?"

"It's not so much to ask," his mother said. "We can give to the UJA. We can buy seat cushions for the Center. This year I'd like to have clean windows."

"He needs our business."

"We can sponsor a starving African baby. I saw that girl – Archie Bunker's daughter. On TV. She was asking for our help."

"Be serious," his father said. "If you're really unhappy, I'll get someone else to come after Mervin."

"You want to throw away your children's money." She squeezed the spray-bottle trigger, and a blue mist bounced from the glass into her face. She winced, slammed the bottle on the end table, coughed. His father went to her, but she waved him off with the paper towel. "Go on," she said. "Go empty Daniel's savings account and flush it down the toilet."

"Mr. Mervin's stupid," Daniel said and immediately felt better.

His father shook his head and dropped his gaze to the sports page. His mother stared at the ceiling and said, "Whose son is this?"

A mistake. He tried to go back to the freeway. Two cars spun, women and children screamed, but it was too late. His mother's hand gripped his arm quickly enough to make him flinch. She led him to the corner of the sofa farthest from the door, where he always had to admit he'd done something wrong. His legs dangled too far above the floor. There was no escape. She bent to one knee and tapped her fingers on his leg. "We don't say things like that about people. We've discussed this, haven't we? I know we have. It's not nice."

"He doesn't know how to wash windows," Daniel said. "You said so."

"He's not as fortunate as you are. You have to learn to be kind. Didn't we talk about what a mitzvah is?"

Daniel kicked his heel against the sofa's cushion until his mother grabbed his ankle. He pictured his father giving away his money to every window washer in the phone book. "I know how to wash windows," he said.

From the other side of the room, his father called, "Some people are just born brilliant."

"I don't want to hear you calling people names," his mother said, and let him up from the sofa. He hurried to his cars, slammed two head-on, hard. Both fenders cracked and a bullet-shaped headlight popped straight up, a foot into the air. His mother carried the Windex and paper towels back to the kitchen. The argument with his father was over. He'd messed up and knew how it would go: two weeks later Mr. Mervin would call, and when Daniel scanned his mother's calendar, he would find penciled into a square at the top of the page marked May, "Mervin – windows (ha!)."

But Mr. Mervin *was* stupid, no matter what his mother might say. His father had told him, on more than one occasion, he should never lie. He preferred the rule about lying to the one about being kind. Even listening from far away as his father gave thanks and handed over a check, he could tell Mr. Mervin was the stupidest man alive. He told this to Greg Farisi and tried to tell it to Jared, who was in the basement, swinging black barbells from his thighs to his shoulders. A year ago, Jared's cheeks had been bloated and red, and his stomach hung an inch over his belt. Now, his belly was nearly flat and slick with sweat. Veins stood out on his thin arms. "Your muscles are getting big," Daniel said, carefully. When Jared had been fat, Daniel had teased him all the time, but now he tried to compliment him whenever possible. Jared had always noticed the teasing, but never seemed to hear the compliments. The basement was cold and damp, but he stayed despite an occasional shiver. He kept his toys here, and his mother wouldn't let Jared lock him out. "Washing windows is easy," he said. "Anybody could do it."

"If you don't shut up," Jared said, nearly out of breath, "I'm going to drop one of these on your head."

Greg had been different. He lived at the bottom of the street and was the toughest boy in the fifth grade. He was almost always mean, and everybody wanted to be his friend. "I hate stupid people," he'd said.

HIS FATHER NEVER CALLED MR. MERVIN. IF MR. MERVIN DIDN'T call, his father would skip the mitzvah and hire a regular window washer. But every year, no matter how much Daniel might wish for all the telephone poles in New Jersey to be swept up in a sudden tornado, the phone rang one evening during the second week of April, just as his mother was setting dinner on the table. "Can't he at least remember when we eat?" she'd said last year, as his father jumped from his seat and reached for the receiver, his paper napkin fluttering to the floor. His greeting had been loud, excited. Whenever Daniel called him at work, his father answered with a stern, solemn, "Brickman speaking." No matter how many times he called, the tone always startled Daniel; this was the way his father would sound if he died in a plane crash in the middle of the ocean and his ghost, late at night, crept out of Daniel's closet or dresser drawers. "Melissa and Nicole talk about you behind your back," the ghost would say. "Mr. Pearl thinks you're too cocky to be a good ball player." But with Mr. Mervin on the line, his father laughed, and nearly shouted, "Yes, yes, I've been expecting your call." Then, after a long pause. "Well, our windows could certainly use your visit. This was an especially dirty winter, wasn't it? Let me put my wife on. She's the planner."

His mother shook the oven mitts from her hands, grabbed the phone, and – glaring at his father – said sharply, "Hello, Mr. Mervin." His father sat and stared at a magazine, but his eyes didn't move across the words. A short pause, and his mother touched her hair. "Thank you, I'm fine." Then a slight smile. "Yes, the boys are fine, too, thank you." She scanned the pages of her calendar, tapping a pen on the narrow wooden bookshelf stuffed full with phone lists and recipes. Somewhere in that mass of paper was the secret formula to Daniel's favorite meal. It had a Yiddish name, but he always called it meat-pie. Once a month, if he'd been good, she made it just for him. In the morning, he smelled the slight burn of onions, and when he came home from school, the kitchen was doughy. In between, during class, he imagined himself at the dinner table, a perfect steaming wedge before him. He would make a pile of the crumbled meat and slowly chew the crust. The crust was the true secret: outside it was yellow and flaky, but underneath it dripped with a heavy, dark-tasting juice. "The twenty-ninth?" his mother said. Daniel tasted the juice on his tongue, though he knew tonight they were having baked chicken. He hated Mr. Mervin for making him think of meat-pie. He hadn't been good this month or last and didn't know if he'd ever eat it again. His mother scratched her pencil on the calendar and said, "Let's make it the third."

This year, after the first ring, Daniel bolted to the phone before his father could rise. In as low a voice as he could manage, he answered, "Brickman speaking." His mother held up one finger and tilted it to the side in warning. He smiled at his father, who seemed confused, as if he had no place in the family now that someone was answering for him. From the phone came a slow, trembling, "Hello." The voice might have belonged to someone reading a flash card held up by a teacher across an enormous auditorium, and Daniel felt a reluctant sympathy for its owner. For some time now he'd wished for a fiery end to all vocabulary flash cards. He knew the definitions, he always knew the definitions, but when a card jumped in front of his face and a teacher called his name, his mouth froze and the answer caught in the back of his throat. Greg said his tongue always stuck out, and he looked like a moron. The teacher, Mrs. Ringle, knew he was smart and tried hard, knew it was only flash cards that turned him stupid, but called on him anyway, at least twice each lesson, flipping the cards relentlessly. Most of the girls in the class laughed, and a few of the boys, until Greg gave them a look or raised his fist. All afternoon, Daniel stared out the classroom window to the filmy green pond at the end of the playground and imagined Mrs. Ringle's car slowly sinking. And then, after school, or the next morning waiting for the bus, he'd have to do something to make everyone forget. He tipped garbage cans into the street, stole boxes of ice cream from the cooler behind the gym, took a *For Sale* sign from one neighbor's lawn and stuck it into another's. Once, during recess, he planned to scatter thumbtacks across the teachers' parking lot. Kids watched from the basketball court, far enough away that no one could see the only thing he dropped from his pocket was lint. For the rest of the day, tacks poked into his thigh, but boys he'd never talked to clapped him on the back, and one girl drew a picture of him standing next to a car with a flat tire.

None of this should have happened. When his parents had time to help him practice, he had no trouble with the flash cards. But last week, when they'd both been out at meetings and Jared had locked himself in his room, he'd tried to practice by himself, holding each card first in front of the bathroom mirror and then the one in his parents' bedroom. What good were mirrors if they made everything backwards? He struggled for several minutes trying to read the word "WOLAGNUB" in its proper order. His voice stuttered, as stupid sounding as the voice now on the phone. But he wasn't stupid, he knew he wasn't, and he hurled the stack of cards at the trash can. Most plunged right at his feet, though others lifted, turned quick loops, and settled on his parents' bed.

"This is Mr. Mervin," the voice said, "of the Pane Relief Window Washing – "

"I know who you are," Daniel said.

"May I speak to Mr. or Mrs. – "

"I know what you want," Daniel said, but by then his father was up from the table, a hand on his shoulder, the other cupped, waiting for the receiver. He handed it over, but before he could return to his seat, his mother took him by the arm. His father disappeared into the laundry room, the phone cord stretching over the dinner table. His mother pulled him from the kitchen. She was trying to lead him to the corner of the sofa, but in the hallway he broke free. She snatched his wrist before he could run upstairs.

"Do we have to talk about your phone manners? Do we have to do this again?" She spoke through clenched teeth. Her words were edged with a gritty, hissing sound. Daniel stared at his socks, long and floppy at the toes. After a moment he shook his head. "I want a real answer," she said. Her fingers pinched the skin of his wrist.

"No," he said.

"No, what?"

Tears were leaking onto his nose. There was nothing he could do. "No, we don't have to talk."

"About?"

"No, we don't have to talk about my stupid phone manners."

"Okay." She ran a thumb under his eyes. "Go up and wash your face. And tell your brother he should come eat with his family for a change."

ON A MORNING THREE WEEKS LATER, DANIEL SAT ON HIS bedroom floor, waiting out the half hour before he had to catch the bus to school. Downstairs, his mother's heels clicked from the kitchen to the living room to the family room, dusting, he guessed, or watering the plants. Last night his father had left for a business trip to Switzerland and would be gone for two weeks. He'd tried to be good all day, had even promised to stay that way forever if his father didn't leave, but none of his pleading had changed anything. "I wouldn't go if I could help it," his father had said. "I'd retire tomorrow. But colleges aren't cheap." Already, Daniel missed him. He didn't want to think about the plane floating high over the ocean; Mrs. Ringle could never explain how jets stayed in the air, though he asked nearly every week. Instead, he thought about the chocolate his father would bring home, and the original Lego sets. A Lego motorcycle with mufflers and wires and real rubber tires, a Lego helicopter with propellers that twirled, maybe even the Lego castle with four towers and a working drawbridge.

Through the wall, his brother's stereo blasted the refrain, "*Urgent, urgent, urgent, urgent emergency. It's urgent.*" In front of him on the floor was a box of baseball cards – the brand new 1983 complete set in mint condition – and a pile of plastic pages, each sectioned by nine rectangular pockets. Careful to keep the set's order, he slipped each card into a pocket, and referenced its number to his *Official Baseball Card Price Guide*. Most cards were worth no more than fifteen cents, but several topped the dollar mark. And somewhere in the middle, a hidden treasure, the Wade Boggs rookie card: twelve dollars and forty-eight cents. The pockets were a tight fit; on occasion he frayed a card's corner on the plastic edge and had to stand, pace, breathe deeply, the way he'd seen his mother do after breaking a favorite flower pot. Sometimes this wasn't enough, and he had to pummel his fists into his pillow to keep from shouting.

He'd just slid number 228 of 792 from the box, when pounding footsteps reached the top of the stairs. At the end of the hall, an ogre, massive body on thin legs, rounded the banister. It carried a bucket and some sort of weapon, a T-shaped stick with a blade at one end. His door was wide open. Where could he hide? He glanced toward the closet, but then imagined waiting in the dark, the door flinging open, the ogre's claws tearing through his clothes. What could be worse than being eaten in his own closet?

But this was no ogre. Even before he reached the doorway, Daniel knew who it was, could see the weapon's blade was made of rubber. Still, a sound squeaked through his nose when Mr. Mervin said, painfully slow, "Hello there." Daniel had never seen him so close. Usually he didn't show up until after Daniel had gone to school, and by the time he came home Mr. Mervin would have finished inside and would be high on a ladder in the front yard. Until he went away for good, Daniel would follow his mother from the laundry room to the kitchen, folding towels, fetching ingredients, setting the dinner table. "You're being very good today," his mother would say. "Did you get in trouble at school?" But now Mr. Mervin stood right above him. The shape of his face was like a skeleton's, worse than a dying person's. No skin sagged under his chin or on his cheeks the way it had on Daniel's grandfather when Daniel had kissed him goodbye in the hospital. His hair was greased back in three strokes, over the top and above each ear, leaving long strips of bluish skin from his eyebrows to the back of his head. Everything on his face was large and simple: drooping oval ears, a squashed triangle nose, perfectly round eyes opened so wide a ghost might have been following him around all day whispering, "Boo!" when he least expected it. Daniel counted only five teeth in Mr. Mervin's mouth, and those were square and brown, belonging to a horse or a family of giant rabbits. "Base – ball – cards," Mr. Mervin said, so slowly he might have been speaking three separate words in three separate sentences. "Mickey Mantle?"

"He's old," Daniel said. He gathered the plastic pages, put the loose number 228 back in the box and shut it. His hands were trembling. He had to be tough, he told himself. If Greg were here, he'd say something cruel and wouldn't be afraid at all. "This is 1983."

Mr. Mervin nodded, smiling. "Mickey Mantle hits home runs." He strode to the nearest window. On the orange carpet, muddy footprints trailed backward to the door and into the hall. Daniel stood to leave, but Mr. Mervin pointed to a poster over the dresser. "Mickey Mantle?"

"That's Tom Seaver," Daniel said. "He's a pitcher. His rookie card's worth ninety-eight dollars." He knew all this and he wasn't even eleven. Even Jared, who hated baseball, knew who Tom Seaver was. It wasn't right for someone so big to be so stupid. It wasn't right for him to come into the house when his father had to go away. To keep from crying, Daniel tried to imagine himself as the boss of a company. Mr. Mervin would work for him, and he would get to fire him. When his father had to fire someone the next day, he didn't sleep for a whole night; at the breakfast table his eyes were red, and he kept shrugging for no reason. Daniel would sleep fine. He'd just point his chin at his office door and say, "Get lost." Now, he waved a hand at the poster and said, "Don't you know what a pitcher looks like?"

Mr. Mervin turned slowly, his smile gone, his mouth a hole. "I know things," he said.

"You don't know who Tom Seaver is," Daniel said.

"I know lots of things."

"You don't know what a pitcher looks like. You don't know how to wash windows."

"I know lots of things!" Mr. Mervin said, his voice rising just short of a wail. The bucket slipped from his fingers, and soapy water sloshed over its rim onto the carpet. He clutched the T-shaped stick to his chest, wringing the handle. "I know – "

Daniel ran. He went to his brother's door and tried the knob, his knees ready to buckle if it didn't turn. This time it opened. Jared jumped from his chair and scattered papers over his desk. "Jesus," he said. "I thought you were Mom. Can't you learn to knock?"

Daniel closed the door behind him and pointed at the wall separating their rooms. "In there," he shouted over the music, and then gasped. "In my room. Mr. Mervin. He's crazy. He wants to kill me. He thinks Mickey Mantle's a pitcher."

"Shut up and come here," Jared said. "You've got to look at this." Daniel went to the desk. Jared cleared the papers to reveal a magazine open to a wrinkled page, its top corner curled. A woman, naked, squatted. Streaks of white and blue paint marked her arms and shoulders and middle. She held a paintbrush, the wrong end forward, too far between her legs. "Can you believe this?" Jared said. "I can get as many of these as I want. Cheap." Between his braces stuck bits of soft, wet bread. His breath smelled like peanut butter. In the black background beside the woman's head, a fingerprint, sharp and clear, a perfect swirl. Jared's? Daniel reached out a finger, but Jared slapped away his hand. "No touching. Only look and admire." The record ended, and the speakers hummed softly. He tried to peek between the woman's legs, but couldn't. Instead, he stared at the fingerprint, listening for his mother's footsteps approaching in the hall. The only sound came from his own room, the stuttering squeak of rubber against glass. He put a hand on Jared's shoulder, and Jared didn't shrug him off.

WHEN HE CAME HOME FROM SCHOOL, MR. MERVIN'S CAR WAS still in the driveway. Not a van or truck with the company's name stenciled on its side, but a station wagon with wood-colored doors, rusty fenders, and three antennas poking from its hood and roof. He saw the car from the street and immediately wanted to get back on the bus, but it was already pulling away from the curb. He wouldn't be able to follow his mother around the kitchen or family room. In the fall she'd gone back to teaching for the first time in fifteen years and didn't come home until late in the afternoon. By now his father's plane would have landed in Switzerland, or else crashed into the ocean or into the slope of a towering, snowy mountain.

Jared wouldn't be home either. Now that he was in high school, the barbells in the basement were no longer enough for him. Every day after school, he rode his bike down Route 10 to Market Street Monsters, a gym where men and women in brightly colored underwear posed before the large front window, their muscles oiled and jumping. On a day too cold for riding a bike, Daniel had gone there with his mother to bring Jared home. Even from the parking lot, with the car door closed, he could hear the terrible grunting, and was sickened by the smell of sweat. Jared slumped into the back seat without speaking, breathing hard, rubbing his shoulders and neck; he didn't seem any happier for the hours he spent here. After dinner, Daniel glanced over the mantle to a picture of the whole family from three years ago. Jared was smiling and had an arm around Daniel's neck. He didn't seem to care at all about the dimpled flesh beneath his chin or about the way his T-shirt bulged around his waist. It was Daniel's fault his brother spent every waking moment worrying about his body. He hadn't once missed an opportunity to call Jared fat and knew it was too late to take anything back. How could he explain now how hard it had been to be the younger brother by four and a half years? How could he explain his reasons, which he barely grasped himself – that Jared would never have paid him any attention had he always been kind and generous?

So it was his fault, too, that he'd now be alone with Mr. Mervin, who might try to kill him or might set his baseball cards on fire. Carefully, peering first around the corners, he circled the house. The front yard was empty. In back, leaning beside Jared's window, a ladder, but no stupid ogre on top. He was still inside. Maybe even in Daniel's room, waiting. He reached into his shirt for the key dangling on brown yarn. Without pulling it over his head, he leaned forward to unlock the back door. Immediately, from upstairs came the heavy thumping of clumsy boots. He crept through the laundry room into the kitchen, gently lifted the phone, and dialed. Greg answered, "Wha'chou want?"

"You've got to come over," Daniel said. "In the fort. Five minutes."

"Is it the magazine?" Greg said. "Did you get it?"

"Just come."

After three steps of flat lawn, the backyard rose steeply toward the strip of woods separating the neighborhood from the freeway. Daniel charged up the hill, weaving between the evergreen bushes his father had planted last year, most already brown and crumbling. Every weekend his father walked from one bush to another, pumping an enormous metal squirt gun that clogged after every three sprays. "Goddamn fungus!" he yelled, even when he knew Daniel was listening. Once, he'd lifted the gun above his head, hurled it behind the rotting woodpile, and disappeared into the garage. After a moment, Daniel followed him. Behind the car, his father sat on a stack of yellowed newspapers, rubbing his fingers on his shirt. "I'll spray for you," Daniel said. "I'll kill the goddamn fungus."

His father shook his head. "I'm going into town," he said. "Bring down your library books. They're due by five."

Now he hurried past the bushes, the first cluster of tall trees, and dropped into a patch of stomped earth cleared of dead leaves and protected by a semicircle of half-buried boulders. Among the rocks were the remains of Matchbox cars he'd once loved to polish and now loved to smash. This summer he and Greg were going to build a real fort. They'd steal wood from one of the fancy new houses being built at the top of the street and nail it high into a tree. Greg insisted they build it on his property, though there were almost no woods behind his house and anybody would be able to see it from the road.

This fort was hidden and had a view. From here he could stare unnoticed into the kitchen and family room. He could see both his own and his brother's windows, though Jared's blinds were lowered. His own were raised as high as they could go, and there, framed in one of the window's sectioned squares, was Mr. Mervin's face, his mouth a brown smear. His lips were moving, talking, maybe, to his rubber stick as it passed over the glass, followed by a gray cloth. Daniel couldn't wait for him to be out of the house and on top of the ladder, where he could imagine for him a long and terrible fall. But this, he was sure, would be the last year Mr. Mervin came to wash the windows. After the phone call, he'd wandered through the house, pressing his thumb into the corners of every window he could reach. This afternoon, his mother would find smudges everywhere. "Mitzvah or no mitzvah," she'd say the moment his father came home. "I've had enough."

Soon, Greg leapt over the boulders into the fort. "What is it? I was watching *What's Happening*. Did you get the magazine?"

At lunch, Daniel had told Greg about Mr. Mervin and about the woman with the paintbrush, told him that without seeing it, he could never understand. For the rest of the afternoon, Greg had asked only about the magazine and wouldn't believe that Jared always kept his room locked. "That crazy retard," Daniel said. "I told you about him. He's in the house." He pointed to his window, but now it was empty.

"Check this out," Greg said. "I can walk like Rerun." He held his arms away from his body, thrust his head forward, and strutted two steps forward, two back.

"That's a chicken walk," Daniel said.

"You're a chicken. You're afraid of the window guy." Greg was smaller than Daniel, by an inch or two, and just as skinny, but he was dark and quick. He was Italian. "Italians are tougher than Jews," he'd said, more than once. "That's just the way it is." Daniel never argued with this. He'd seen Greg throw his eraser at Mrs. Ringle when she accused him of cheating. He'd seen him get punched in the eye by a sixth grader and stand up without a single tear. He knew Mr. Farisi kept a worn leather belt beside his bed and used it whenever he got the chance. Daniel only objected when Greg insisted Italian mothers were also better cooks than Jewish ones: "You've never had meat-pie." When Greg stayed for dinner and tried it, he said, "Well, Italians are still tougher."

Jared's window blinds rose. Mr. Mervin lifted the frame and unhooked the screen. "He's ugly," Greg said. "He's the ugliest person ever."

"His teeth are brown," Daniel said.

Greg picked up a rock. "I bet I can hit him from here." Nothing could stop Greg from breaking windows. He'd smashed his neighbor's with a baseball, the school's with the same eraser he'd thrown at Mrs. Ringle. Despite his father's belt, he'd twice shot holes in his own bedroom window with a BB gun. Daniel stood and grabbed Greg by the wrist. On his own wrist he could feel his mother's fingers, pinching, pinching, if she came home to find shards of glass on Jared's floor. Greg pulled his arm away and threw the rock on the ground. "Don't touch me," he said.

"If you hit him, he'd know we're here," Daniel said. "Let's spy on him."

"Don't ever touch me."

"I bet he'll steal something."

Greg dropped to the dirt and watched. The rubber stick and the gray cloth passed over each of the window's sections. Mr. Mervin's lips moved slowly, the enormous teeth sliding into and out of view. "He's talking to his squeegee," Greg said.

"His what?" Mr. Mervin's face drifted away from the window into the room's darkness.

"He's crazy," Greg said. "We've got to go see what he stole. Your brother's records, probably. And your cards. You didn't leave the Seavers sitting around, did you?"

Of course not. This was a dumb question. He always kept them – every Tom Seaver card since the year after his rookie season – in a cigar box sealed with a lock he'd taken off one of his father's suitcases. The box was buried under piles of clothes in the back of his closet. He took it out only late at night with his shades drawn. Greg always asked where he hid them, but he would never tell. Still, he couldn't help picturing Mr. Mervin rummaging through the rest of the cards, bending the plastic pages to look for Mickey Mantle. "We've got to stop him."

Greg left the fort without a word. He ran skidding down the hill, leaving long streaks in the red mulch. He stomped in the center of a bush, and most of its branches snapped and hung to one side. Daniel stood, then hesitated. This wasn't what he'd wanted. He didn't want to go anywhere near the house or Mr. Mervin and wished, for once, that Greg would be scared. From the bottom of the hill, Greg waved him on, and he followed carefully. He went for the back door, but Greg darted to the ladder. "This way." Daniel didn't move. "Come on," Greg said. "He left your brother's screen off."

"I have a key," Daniel said, and reached into his shirt.

"We've got to get that magazine," Greg said. He bounced his hands against his sides. "Now's our chance."

"What about the retard? He's got my Seavers."

"You know where he keeps it? Under his pillow?"

"In his desk drawer."

"Go get it," Greg said. "I'll keep a lookout." Daniel glanced up the length of the ladder to the high window. Waist down, his skin tingled. He started for the back door. "Where you going?"

"Jared's room must be unlocked. Mr. Mervin was just in there."

"You want the retard to see you? And tell your mom? Go up this way."

"He won't see me," Daniel said. "He's too stupid."

"You're such a chickenshit. I always tell everyone you're not, but I guess it's true."

"You go."

"I bet you're even too chickenshit to be lookout," Greg said. "If someone comes, you'll run away and leave me up there." He put a hand on the ladder. Daniel pictured him snooping through his brother's room and then his own, digging in the closet until he found the box of Seavers, easy enough to break open without the key. "I always tell people you're the second toughest kid in the class. I always tell them you're not stupid when you can't do the flash cards," Greg said. "I always stick up for you."

Daniel knew he should punch Greg for this, but didn't dare. Not because Greg would beat him up, but because there would be nothing to stop the laughter during the next vocabulary lesson. What would he have to do then to make people forget? Put poison in Mrs. Ringle's food or build a bomb to blow up her car? "I'll go," he said.

Greg backed away from the ladder. He turned his face when Daniel tried to look at him. "If anyone comes I'll whistle," he said.

The first step was the hardest. He had to stretch his leg to reach the rung, and something in his knee popped. The railing was cold against his hands. But with each new rung it became easier, more regular than climbing a tree, which never scared him until he was too high to jump down without breaking all his bones. He concentrated on each ridge of beige fiberglass siding, and soon he was at the top edge of the living room window, level with the roof of the porch. Wet leaves and pine needles clumped in the seam of the porch and the house. He glanced down, though he knew he shouldn't. But it didn't seem so terribly high, and he had no sensation of falling. Greg crouched beside a shrub and gave a thumbs-up sign, then shrugged.

By the time he reached Jared's window, the insides of his legs were sore, and his breath came fast. He reached out a hand to slide the glass open, but then stopped. There was movement in the room. Mr. Mervin, snooping or stealing. But not Mr. Mervin. Jared was home. He must have come back while Daniel and Greg were in the fort. Or else been there the whole time. He stood before the mirror, wearing sweatpants but no shirt. Against the wall leaned a magazine, propped open. Not a naked woman, but an enormous black man in bright blue underwear. He held up his arms on either side of his head, his muscles giant lumps, each larger around than Daniel's waist. His white smile gleamed. In the mirror, Jared imitated the man's pose, though instead of smiling, his lips were clamped, hiding his braces. His muscles – only bumps, but large enough, Daniel thought – gathered and fell quickly. His mouth moved. Daniel couldn't hear through the window but could read the words clearly: "You're shit."

Jared took a step backward, shook out his arms. Then, a different pose, his arms in a circle, wrists crossing at his belly. His shoulders quivered, his face grew red, but nothing happened on his chest. He let out his breath and spoke again. "You're goddamn shit." He stomped in a circle, then sprang into another position. One arm curled behind his head, the other extended, fingers pointing to the joint of the wall and ceiling. He looked more like a rock 'n' roll star than a bodybuilder. The black man in the magazine seemed to be laughing, and Daniel wanted to join him. But then Jared threw his fists against his thighs and shouted loud enough for Daniel to hear through the glass, "You're fucking shit!" He went to the door and punched it with the heel of his hand, then kicked the desk, the chair, the dresser. Finally, he flung himself on the bed, and lay on his back, staring at the ceiling.

The ladder rattled against the house. Daniel was laughing now, trying not to make a sound. Nothing was funny, but he couldn't stop. His body shook, and an occasional snort escaped his nose. The ladder was shaking harder, and he knew he should be still. He wanted the black man to stop smiling. He wanted Jared to get up from the bed and pose again in front of the mirror. No. He wanted Jared to be fat again and happy. He was crying now and wished he was on the ground, in the fort or safe in his room with his cards spread around him.

From below came a long, wavering wail. "No! No – no!" To his right, far, far to the ground, Greg, a bug, burst from the shrub and scuttled around the side of the house. From the opposite direction ran Mr. Mervin with his bucket and T-shaped stick, half-hobbling or dancing, waving his arms above his head. The stick chopped up and down like an ax, and dark water spilled from the bucket onto Mr. Mervin's shoulder and back. His hair had come unslicked and writhed in three wild clusters like fat worms cut in half. He shouted, "No, no, no, no!" and hopped from one side of the ladder to the other.

Daniel felt his legs going numb. He forced himself to climb one more rung so most of his body was even with the window. Now, on the other side of the glass stood Jared, staring at him. Jared glanced over his shoulder, at the mirror, the magazine, and shook his head. "Your muscles are big," Daniel said, and reached a hand toward the window. Jared peered over the sill at the ground and laughed. Nothing was funny, nothing. "You're strong," Daniel said. "I'm sorry." Jared reached a hand toward his. But instead of lifting the window, he grabbed a string and yanked. The blind zipped to the ledge, replacing Jared with slats of light blue plastic.

He climbed another rung. The roof was only a few feet above the end of the ladder, but far out of reach. Beyond stretched the same blue color as the blinds, everywhere, forever. The blue where his father's plane could hang for hours, though nobody could tell him why. He wrapped both arms around a rung and watched the ground. A blur through his tears, Mr. Mervin dropped his bucket and stick, stomped and wailed, no longer forming words. Here was his parents' mitzvah. They'd started something terrible and then left it to him alone. If only he could make it off the ladder. If only, he pleaded. If he made it off the ladder, never, never in his life, he swore, would he do a good thing for anybody. Mr. Mervin, mouth open, horse's teeth gnashing, put both hands on the ladder's rails and took the first step toward him.

# Kosher

AT THE END OF THE SUMMER I TURNED TWENTY-FOUR I FOUND myself back in New Jersey. I had almost no money and owed two months' interest on my credit card. My parents took me in under the condition that I find a job by the end of the first week. Reluctantly, I accepted. They'd let me stay in my old room for free, but I had to pay for my food. While I'd been gone, they'd turned kosher, and the cost of their groceries was outrageous. On the way home from the airport, my mother complained incessantly about having to drive all the way to West Orange to find a kosher butcher, and when she did, the meat was lean and dried out and had no smell. I was happy enough to buy my own food.

More than a year earlier, I'd left New Jersey on what was supposed to be a two-week quickie-tour through Europe before starting a job with a marketing operation in Morristown. But once I'd crossed the ocean, the idea of traveling through sixteen countries in fourteen days no longer seemed right to me, and by the time the two weeks were up, I hadn't yet left Paris. I called the head of human resources at Immediate Marketing, Inc., and after explaining several times who I was, told him I was sorry to leave him hanging without notice. After a short, expensive stint in the Alps, I headed east, where my money would go further. In another month I had a job making beds and cleaning bathrooms in a Budapest hotel in exchange for free room and board. On the side I helped a Hungarian businessman write letters and e-mail to his customers in England. My pay was absurd, but I learned to live on almost nothing; I ate canned meat and hunks of cheese, and snuck beer back to my room rather than spend three times as much to sit in an overcrowded bar. In six months I'd managed to save up enough to travel for another three. This, I decided, was the perfect way to live. All I needed was what I could stuff into my backpack. Who would want any more? On a morning when my stomach was rumbling and I had nothing to eat but a stale heel of brown bread, I'd written in my journal, "My most precious possessions will be my experiences, my sensations, my memories." Afterward, every time I was hungry I reread this sentence and underlined it, until my pen tore clear through the page.

My parents were appalled. They'd worked their whole lives to acquire piles of things that needed to be dusted once a week. My older brother had recently begun to do the same, and I was certain he was miserable, despite his new car, his oak dining table, his silver candlesticks. When I showed my mother some of my photographs and talked about the things I'd learned, she shook her head and said, "Waste of a mind." It was dignified of her to talk about my mind, when I knew she was really thinking about the cost of my education. My father, on the other hand, didn't mince words; he just called me "the money hole."

I tried to take their disappointment lightly. What did they know about living? My father worked at a pharmaceutical company, managing a group of lab technicians whose jobs he didn't understand. He shuffled papers for fifty hours a week, wishing he was still just a simple bench chemist in the days before computer modeling and bioengineering. My mother now taught at a private Jewish high school and spent much of her time and energy arguing with her students' parents about the grades she'd given their kids. She also exhausted herself trying to prove to the other teachers at her school that her recently found faith was genuine, despite her secular background. When I was a kid and my mother taught at public school, "kosher" was a word she used only to describe what should have been happening in the government. We'd always eaten bacon with our Saturday morning pancakes. Now, she wouldn't even light the oven on Saturday. She and my father didn't miss a single Friday night service and had their names entered on a gold plaque at the synagogue in recognition of their large yearly contribution. Though they tried, the other teachers could find no flaw in her observance and were forced to flash her broad, false smiles at kiddushes and bar mitzvahs. But now I'd ruined all that for her. How could she tell the teachers what her son was doing with his life? A smart Jewish boy who'd given up great opportunities to become a bum.

"An international bum, at least," my father said with a short laugh, but my mother only crossed her arms.

Kosher or not, I was convinced what my parents practiced had nothing at all to do with being Jewish. Just a month before, I'd walked three miles along the train tracks from Auschwitz to Birkenau and stood for an hour on the platform where screaming children and sobbing grand-parents had been unloaded from cattle cars. I'd dipped my hand into the slimy pond overgrown with weeds where the ashes of fifty thousand Jews had been dumped. I tried to tell my parents about it, but they didn't or couldn't understand why I'd go to Poland rather than the Swiss Alps or the Italian Riviera. "I wanted to share the suffering of my ancestors," I told them, though if someone had suggested that's what I'd wanted while I stood on the platform picturing all sorts of horrors, I would have protested with my entire being. What I wanted now, for once in my life, was to have my parents congratulate me for doing something admirable and honest, for making them proud.

"Your ancestors were all in Minsk," my father said. "What Stalin did to them makes Auschwitz look like nothing." I turned away. He had no idea what it meant to suffer, I told myself. For my parents, the most difficult hardship was forgetting to buy salami and having to make an extra trip to the butcher in West Orange. For six months, I'd slept every night on a cardboard-thin cushion with no sheets, no pillow, and only a sleeping bag to cover me. If they couldn't see the value in this, why should I care whether they were proud of me or not?

I stopped trying to explain what I'd seen. In humility I would lower my head, taking their comments and insults silently, and work steadily for six months. My Chevy Nova, which had sat in the driveway since I'd left for Europe – untouched except for the scratches in the paint my father had made while shoveling snow from the hood and trunk – needed new brakes and back tires, and once I could afford them, I'd head off again. This time I'd go to Canada and take three months to make my way from Quebec to Vancouver. Then I'd work again, six months out west, until I'd have enough money to cross the Pacific and spend the next few years in Asia. And not once would I look back.

But first I had to score a job here in New Jersey, a place I swore I'd never come back to, except for the briefest visits. It was a miserable state, freez-ing in winter and brutally humid now in summer, with so many cars crowd-ing the freeways it was impossible not to curse while driving. The spring before, when I'd left Budapest, I'd traveled briefly with a guy named Jeff from Gary, Indiana. I told him how much I hated New Jersey, and he said he'd been there, and it wasn't nearly as bad as Gary. He claimed to be from the worst city on earth, nothing but smokestacks and traffic, and a view across the lake to Chicago, whose skyscrapers glittered like towers in the Promised Land. But one day we stopped at a pension in a little town in southern Bohemia famous for its brewery. The owner, an old woman who never stopped giggling and flashing her rows of silver molars, showed us to our room and took our passports. First she read Jeff's and sighed deeply, shutting her eyes. "In-di-ana!" she exclaimed, drawing out the last two syllables so the word sounded like the name of some beautiful Czech princess who'd died for the sake of forbidden love. It didn't matter that Gary was cold and ugly and full of crime. When the woman read my passport she tried to sigh the same way, but I could see the effort it cost her. She glanced at me to see if I believed her and read slowly, "New Cher-sey." Jeff had to bite his lip to keep from laughing, and for the rest of the week we traveled together, he called me Chersey. Every time he said it, that "ch" sound made me flinch. He might just as well have flicked my earlobe with his finger. By the time we parted in the Prague train station, I'd decided the only way I could keep from killing him was to promise myself never to come home.

And here I was. On my second day back, I found an old business card from Immediate Marketing, but the number had been disconnected. That afternoon when my mother came home from school, I insisted that I'd made all the right decisions. "Look," I said. "They went out of business. I would have worked a year and then been back on the street."

My mother shook her head. "They probably made it big and moved to California."

"People move to California, Mom, not businesses."

"Oh? And what does a bum know about businesses?" I wanted to argue but could think of nothing to say. The one real business course I'd signed up for in college I'd dropped after the first week. So instead I offered to take out the trash. "There's a job for you," my mother said. "My son, the garbage collector."

For the next few days, I spent most of my time in my old room, lying on the bed, flipping through the classified pages, or through my pictures from Europe, and staring at the walls. None of the jobs advertised in the paper suited me; I was overqualified for all the crappy ones and under-qualified for everything else. I answered one ad for a cabinetmaker's app-rentice – a useful skill, I figured, one that might be in demand anywhere in the world. But when I showed up for the interview, a burly guy covered in sawdust asked to see my skill with a table saw. I didn't know how to turn it on. "Isn't that what an apprenticeship is for?" I said. He laughed mysteriously and handed back my application.

The walls of my old room were more interesting than the classifieds. I hadn't changed the posters since high school, and each wall marked a stage in my life. Over the desk were the Mets and the Knicks, Daryl Strawberry and Patrick Ewing. Between the windows stood a model in a blue string bikini with a poofy shell of blonde hair and earrings dangling to her shoul-ders. And above my bed, it was all Led Zeppelin, the four ugliest men I've ever seen, grimacing and sweating beneath hazy stage lights. Sports, women, and rock and roll. Who had I been kidding? I'd only taken one guitar lesson in seventh grade and spent most of Little League sitting on the bench. Girls wouldn't come near me in high school. The closest I'd come to a rock con-cert before college was sitting behind the cafeteria during my lunch hour, listening to headphones, closing my eyes, and pumping my fist in the air. Once, after I'd finished singing along with the final verse of "The Rain Song," I opened my eyes and saw a half-circle of boys with long hair and heavy metal T-shirts, girls in short skirts and fringed black boots, sur-rounding me, smoking cigarettes and laughing hysterically. I pulled off my headphones and stood to leave. One of the girls said, "Come on, we want an encore." A few of them waved lighters in the air, and two of the boys held me against the wall until I sang the opening verse of "Black Dog." Afterward, they made me smoke six cigarettes at the same time and I threw up on my Walkman. And now, staring at the poster of Jimmy Page embrac-ing his ridiculous double-necked guitar, I wished for nothing else but to hop on a train to a town whose name I couldn't pronounce, where the only things that interested people were whether I could pay for my room in dollars and whether I had ever seen David Hasselhoff in person.

By the end of the week I still didn't have the slightest prospect for a job. My parents wouldn't throw me out, of course, but I wouldn't have put it past them to wear mourning clothes, beat their chests, plead with God that they had done nothing wrong, that they didn't deserve such a scourge for a son, and otherwise make my life so miserable that I would have to take a job at Burger King just to get out of the house. I scanned the classifieds one last time, resigned to something worthless, assuring myself I could handle anything for six months. But the only ad that didn't immediately turn my stomach was one that read, "Telemarketer for charity org. Wage + comm." That plus sign kept my attention. All I'd have to do was call people and make them feel guilty for having more money than they needed. The better I got the more money I'd make, but even if I was lousy, I'd get paid something. I called the number, and the woman who answered cut me off mid-sentence and told me abruptly to come for an interview that afternoon. I was hesitant at first, picturing the burly cabinetmaker with his table saw, but worse, I imagined my mother rending her sleeve and saying, "What kind of boy goes to college for five years and then sits around all day with no job? Next, he'll start selling drugs." I hurried to my father's closet and searched for a pressed shirt and a tie.

The address the woman gave me was only the next town over, but when I got there I thought I must have taken down the wrong street number. I'd expected an office building, or at least a strip mall. But this was just a drab apartment complex. Not a slum, but one of those functional, bee-hive places with thousands of units and little kids running around the parking lots. I drove around for nearly ten minutes, rolling slowly over speed bumps, avoiding strollers, until I found number 1412 on the first floor of a building toward the rear, almost all the way back to the freeway. Beside the door was a wide window blocked by heavy white curtains. I knocked and stood with my hands together behind my back. After a moment, the door opened and I looked into a dim living room with almost no furniture, only a velvety orange recliner in front of a TV on an overturned milk crate. It smelled like my grandmother's apartment in Queens, a mixture of Lysol and something burning in the oven, though here there was another smell on top of those, either a dog or a couple of cats.

"You're Daniel," a voice said, beneath me.

I jumped back. A woman in a wheelchair was holding the door open. She was ancient, crouched over, her legs hanging useless in baggy blue sweatpants. She stared up at me from an angle that seemed painful. Her lips, almost white and cracked, moved steadily, working up and down over her teeth, though she wasn't speaking. Occasionally, her short, bluish tongue slipped out and ducked quickly away. She might have been sucking out bits of meat caught between her teeth. I tried to say something, but the only word I could manage was "Phone."

"Yes, we spoke," she said. "I'm Helen." Her voice was normal, even pleasant. I would have expected it to be garbled by the movement of her lips, or else throaty like most old women's voices, but it was clear and strong, the voice of a woman younger than my mother. It seemed unconnected to her body and made me uncomfortable. "Come on in," she said, turning her chair and leading me inside. I wanted to make sense of this, but couldn't bring myself to ask her any of the questions running through my mind: Was this supposed to be an office? Did she work here, or was she one of the organization's charity cases? I kept looking for dogs or cats as we went past the living room into a narrow kitchen, but didn't see any. Most of the space in the kitchen was taken up by a folding chair and a bridge table stacked with papers. In the middle of the table sat a simple black phone. My hands began to sweat. "Here's the script," Helen said. "Let's see what you've got."

"Don't you want to interview me first?" I asked.

"This is the interview."

I looked over the script, but couldn't concentrate on the words. My mouth went dry. Here was the table saw all over again, but this was even worse. What was I doing here? I'd always hated telemarketers. When I was in college, I'd never had any money, but whenever I got a call asking for donations, I couldn't help but feel I was being judged, that someone was keeping account of my good deeds. No matter what the charity – whether for the homeless or for the police troopers' dog fund – I pledged ten bucks I knew I would never send. But as soon as I hung up the phone, I felt as if someone had picked my pocket during a moment of confusion. I asked Helen, "Could I get a glass of water before I start?"

"If you're wasting my time," she said, "you might as well leave now." Again, her voice startled me. It wasn't a truly beautiful voice, the type you hear from soap opera stars or late-night deejays, but it was full of confidence. I didn't see why she wasn't doing the telemarketing herself. If I'd gotten a call from her during college, I wouldn't have hesitated before making my ten-dollar pledge. But I'd always been susceptible to attractive voices. Not long before I'd heard one so beautiful it made me tremble. It was announcing arrivals and departures in the train station in Poprad, Slovakia. I couldn't understand a word the woman said and missed my train, which left from a different platform than the others heading north. But I didn't mind the extra hour listening to her voice echoing in the busy waiting area. I even considered searching for the room where she was making the announcements, but then thought how ridiculous I would look, unshaven, carrying a battered backpack, smiling at someone I'd never be able to talk to, who would dismiss me after a first glance. And who knows what she looked like? She might also have been hunched in a wheelchair, her body mangled, paralyzed even, except for her mouth.

"Just follow the script," Helen said. "You'll do fine." She handed me a list of phone numbers. The skin on her forearms was smooth and tight, her hands thin and muscled. I leaned far back in my chair, away from her, queasy. She wasn't an old woman at all, despite the patches of white hair over her ears and the wrinkles on her slack cheeks. I suddenly wanted to call everyone I knew and ask for donations to help her. My parents could afford to give plenty, but if the charity wasn't Jewish they'd never even consider it. "How can I give to this person if I know somewhere there's a Jewish child without enough to eat?" my mother would say. Not once did she invite one of these hungry children to our Shabbos meal. I took the list of numbers, picked up the phone, and dialed.

After the first ring, a woman's voice answered, nearly out of breath, "Mike?"

"No, uh, I'm Daniel."

"Daniel?"

"I'm calling for the, let's see, the Robowski Fund for the Disabled."

"This isn't a good time," the woman said.

I was botching it. Helen's lips slowed, and she shook her head. I put aside the script. "I'll only take a second of your time, ma'am." I closed my eyes and pictured the woman on the other end of the line. She was in her late thirties, I guessed, with light brown hair pinned to the top of her head. She stood smoking a cigarette in her kitchen, wearing shorts and an oversized white T-shirt that read, "I'd Rather Be Gardening." Her purse lay open on the counter. On the Budapest subway, I'd watched teenage gypsies pickpocket tourists and businessmen and had always sympathized when the police chased them through tiled stations into the dark tunnels. Now, I imagined myself in their ranks. I crept toward the woman's purse and said, "We've just begun our annual fundraising campaign to benefit people with physical and mental disabilities. Basically, we need lots of money to help people who can't take care of themselves." Helen coughed, and I cursed myself. Not only was I ruining the call, I was offending the person who would hire me. But when I opened my eyes and glanced at her she didn't seem angry. She even smiled, I think, though with her lips moving again it was difficult to tell.

The woman on the line said, "Well, I couldn't do much."

I stood beside her purse now, and while her back was turned, plunged my hand inside. "You know, that's OK," I said. "Because every little bit counts. You can't imagine how much a small donation of fifty dollars would help."

"Fifty, oh, that's too much, I think. I'll send twenty-five."

The woman gave me her address and slung her purse over her shoulder. Only later would she realize what I'd done. I thanked her and hung up. My heart was racing. This was the first time I'd ever stolen anything, and now I was handing it over to people who needed it. I'd be the Robin Hood of the phone lines. I beamed at Helen. "Good," she said. "You took the pity approach."

"What?"

"She felt sorry for you."

My face went hot. "Hey, didn't I just get twenty-five bucks? How's this commission work?"

She gave me a choice. Five bucks an hour plus ten percent commission, or forty percent, no wage. Forty percent! Who needed wages? She shook my hand firmly, and I sat down to make more calls. She wheeled herself out of the kitchen, head thrust forward, arms pumping too fast for the speed she moved, and after a minute I heard voices from the TV in the living room. I spent the next two hours making calls, but got only one more donor. It was a man who cut me off mid-script and said, "How much did I give last year?" This was too easy for a gypsy: he held his pocket open so that I might cleanly slip out his wallet. I told him fifty bucks, and, he said, "Afraid I can't do more than that this year. Put me down for another fifty."

In two hours I raised seventy-five dollars – forty percent of that meant thirty bucks for me, fifteen an hour. That was more than I would have made as a marketing assistant. Maybe I'd be able to leave here in less than six months, maybe even three if I worked full-time, six days a week. When I left the kitchen, Helen sat slumped in the orange recliner in front of the TV. I thought nothing of it then, though on my way home I couldn't stop wondering how she'd gotten out of the wheelchair. I kept picturing her using those strong arms to swing like a gymnast on parallel bars from one chair to the other. But in the living room, I could only think about the money I'd made. Helen gave me the first day's pay in cash, in case, she said, I decided not to come back. After that, she'd give me a check at the end of every two weeks. I told her not to worry, I'd be back every day for six months. She shrugged and said, "It's better not to promise anything," and I hurried out to my car, whispering to the brakes and tires to hold out just a few more months. I rubbed the three worn ten-dollar bills between my fingers and drove to the nearest Burger King drive-through.

When I got back to the house, my parents were already sitting down to dinner. My mother looked up from her plate and said, "You got a job?" I reached into my pocket and pulled out a crumpled ten. For a moment, I considered throwing it onto the table, the way a rebellious and misunderstood son would do in the movies, but then thought better of it and stuck the ten back in my pocket.

"Who gets paid in cash?" my father said. "Drug dealers and beggars."

"And waiters," my mother said. "You're a waiter, right?" She waved at the bag in my hand. "Not at Burger King, I hope."

"There's no such thing as waiters at Burger King," my father said.

"I wouldn't go into one of those places if it was the last restaurant on earth," my mother said.

"I'm not a waiter," I said. "I'm working for a charity organization. I'm doing a mitzvah and getting paid for it."

"It's not a mitzvah if you get paid," my father said. "It's just a job."

"I'm helping people in wheelchairs," I said.

My mother pointed at the bag again. "You can't eat that garbage in here."

My heart sank, though I knew I shouldn't have been surprised. They don't get it, I told myself. They'll never understand. Their lives have been too easy. I went out to the back porch. It was still uncomfortably hot, even with the sun going down. In Budapest, I would walk along the river at this time of night, usually with a bottle of beer, when the air would start to cool no matter how hot the day had been. I'd find a bench and sit beside the Danube until each swallow of beer made me shiver. By the time I'd get back to the hotel, I'd be shaking and would have to wrap myself in my sleeping bag and blow into my hands. The cold wouldn't let me forget that I was alone in a country whose language I could never hope to learn, whose words I could barely pronounce. But it also shocked me into remembering that this was the way I had wanted it. I had no one to blame but myself.

And now as I ate my Whopper and fries, still sweating at dusk, I stared through the glass door at my parents sitting at the kitchen table and understood there had been something right, something necessary, in that cold summer wind. My father grimaced every time he took a bite of chicken. My mother waved her fork in the air as she talked, shrugging and shaking her head. I'd been trying not to think about Helen since I'd gotten home, but now I could picture her sitting between my parents, her head barely topping the table, her lips working uncontrollably as she aimed a forkful of chicken toward her mouth. She glanced from my mother to my father and said, "What are your problems? You walk every day of your lives." I finished my food and swore I would never be like them, promised myself I would never be lulled by comfort into forgetting what was most important. I would never spend even a moment fretting over what other people thought of my life.

The sun finally set. Though I couldn't see it, I knew that beneath the orange glow on the horizon sat the freeway with its four lanes heading west, and I quickly pictured myself speeding along the miles and miles of pavement. And then, more clearly, I imagined Helen, years after I'd left, sitting in an electric wheelchair in a comfortable, well-furnished room, nodding and saying to my parents, "Daniel? Yes, I knew him. He did good for people. He changed my life." Then, my mother dictating with tears in her eyes, my father, unable to stop clearing his throat, writing the letter apologizing for all the times they'd judged me unfairly. And my letter, after months, maybe years of consideration, forgiving everything.

DON'T GET ME WRONG. I WASN'T NAÏVE. I KNEW HELEN WAS running a scam. The invoices we sent to people who pledged money were printed with a black-and-white picture of Helen in the corner, above the words, "There are thousands of people like me who need your help." But the Robowski Fund for the Disabled benefited only two people, Helen Robowski and me. And why shouldn't she do it? She hadn't walked a step in her life. She lived in an empty apartment and couldn't get a job if she wanted one. The government gave her enough money to keep alive, but what kind of life was that? Anyone would have done the same thing, no question.

Over the next two weeks, I worked at Helen's apartment every day, even Saturday, though my parents groaned when I stood up after breakfast and headed for the car. "Cripples are still crippled on Shabbos," I told them. By the third day, Helen was leaving a key under the mat for me so I didn't have to knock. She would still be asleep in the bedroom with the door closed when I started making calls. The smell of dog or cat was strong in the morning, though I discovered quickly that she didn't have any pets. I had no choice but to assume the smell came from Helen herself. For the first two or three calls of each day my stomach would stay jittery, my mouth dry. But once the nervousness wore off, the job was pure boredom, duller even than making hotel beds and scrubbing bathrooms. I spent the entire day in the tiny kitchen whose walls, after a few hours, seemed to lean closer together, pressing into the bridge table and folding chair.

When you're in a room that small for hours at a stretch, with nothing to look at but phone lists and your fingernails, you can't help but notice things. The first thing that struck me as I rooted around the kitchen was that the cabinets above the counters and sink were all empty. This shouldn't have been a surprise – of course Helen couldn't have reached them – but still, it startled me. I'd never once considered how useless things like high cabinets would be to a cripple.

But something I noticed on my third or fourth day in that kitchen troubled me until my last: there was no dust in there, not a speck. Everything gleamed as if on display in Sears. Not only the counters and stove, which Helen might have reached with a stretch, but also the hood above the stove, the top of the refrigerator, the insides of the high cabinets. Nobody could have dusted those places from a sitting position. At first I thought she must have hired a cleaning service, though after glimpsing her government check on the counter, I didn't see how she could afford it, even with the money I was bringing in. But in two weeks, not a single person had come into the apartment during the day. And if a cleaning service came less frequently than every two weeks, then surely there would have been at least a trace of dust in the interval.

The point is, in two weeks, I hardly got to know this person, despite spending all day with her in a lonely apartment. After the first day, I'd imagined that the job would have two components, telemarketer and daytime companion. But Helen didn't seem terribly interested in either my companionship or in the donations I solicited. Every morning, she would roll out of the bedroom into the kitchen between ten-thirty and eleven and wheel past my chair to the refrigerator. She always wore the same rumpled blue sweatsuit, which it appeared she also slept in. If I was on the phone she'd nod to me, or if I was between calls she'd say, "Morning, Daniel. Did you have a good night?" My nights were always the same: I'd sit on the floor of my bedroom, flipping through my pictures from Europe, while voices from two TVs – my mother's downstairs playing a nighttime soap, my father's at the far end of the hall tuned to a baseball game – competed outside my door. Occasionally, I'd leave the room to ask my father if the score of the game had changed or to grab a handful of my mother's microwave popcorn, which she shared willingly but which had no butter or salt and was usually burnt. But I didn't want to tell Helen about this. Why should she know I didn't have a single friend within twenty miles of my hometown, or that when I left her apartment for the night I spoke no more than five sentences to anyone until I came back the next morning? So instead, I'd say, "Some old woman in Parsippany just pledged a hundred bucks." She'd answer as if she hadn't heard what I'd said, with a mumbled, "That's nice," or "Oh, really?" and continue taking things out of the refrigerator and cupboard – orange juice, milk, coffee, cereal. She always ate at the counter, though I offered to clear part of the table for her. I would continue calling numbers on my list, trying to ignore the slurp of coffee and the crunch of cereal behind me, self-conscious as the line connected and I began my pitch. One morning, I asked Helen if she'd make an extra cup of coffee for me, and every morning after that, a steaming mug would appear on the table beside me as I worked.

After she finished breakfast, Helen would wheel herself into the living room, and the TV would come on. If I got up to go to the bathroom a minute later, I'd see the wheelchair empty and Helen slumped in the orange recliner. I never saw how she moved from one chair to another, never even heard grunts or squeaking springs. She always timed her move to the living room when I was in the middle of a long or difficult call. And once the TV came on, she wouldn't move for the rest of the day, except occasionally to pick up the mail or some groceries at the corner store. Around twelve-thirty or one, I would take a break for lunch and walk down the road to a cluster of fast-food places. They were always crowded, so I'd carry my to-go bag back to the apartment and drag the folding chair out of the kitchen into the living room where I could see the TV. Before leaving I'd always ask Helen if I could get her something, but each time she said, "I'm fine, thanks." On the day she first made me coffee, though, I decided to get an extra cheeseburger for her anyway. When I held it out to her, she took it without looking at me. She thanked me, but then let it sit in her lap until a commercial came on. When she finally unwrapped it, I could see that her lips had grown slick. Every day as I ate, her mouth must have been watering. After that, I brought her something each time I went out, and no matter what it was, fried chicken, pizza, burritos, she'd hold it in her lap until a commercial break and then eat it slowly, chewing each bite for so long before finally swallowing I thought she'd begun to gnaw the inside of her cheek.

Helen wasn't like the daytime TV watchers I knew. My grandmother would turn on the same programs day after day, comforted by the familiarity of soap opera characters and game show hosts. But every time I sat down to lunch with Helen, she'd be watching something different from the day before – black-and-white war movies, nature documentaries, cooking shows. She watched each with the same concentration, slumped forward slightly in the recliner, her lips moving slower and slower, until, just before the cut to commercial, they would seem on the verge of stopping altogether. When the commercial came on she'd snap out of her trance, lean back, and pick up whatever food I'd brought her, her lips working madly. During commercials I would try to engage her in conversation, though she focused mostly on unwrapping her food and chewing. Once, I asked her what she would do with all the money we were making. She shrugged and said, "I haven't thought much about it yet."

"What made you start this in the first place, then?"

"I could use a new TV," she said.

I glanced at the TV, which looked fine to me – it had a reasonably wide screen and a clear picture. Her wheelchair, on the other hand, was a wreck. Its treads were completely smooth, its seat cracked in places, exposing the dirty yellow foam inside. "A TV," I said. "Sure. And the rest you'll donate to charity."

She was silent for a moment, and then said, "OK. Ten percent of mine, ten percent of yours."

I didn't say anything, and she started laughing. I told her what I planned to do with the money, and she said, "That's nice. I never got to travel. My mother always talked about bringing me to Poland to show me where she was born. But we never got a chance. Who'd want to go to Poland anyway? Canada sounds nicer."

Poland! I'd been there for more than three weeks just before I came home. I told her all about the old town square in Krakow, about the night clubs in Warsaw, about the vast salt mines and the High Tatras mountains in the south, about the beaches and wild dunes along the Baltic Sea. Then, in a lower voice, I told her about the walk along the train tracks from Auschwitz to Birkenau, about the tiny pond full of ashes. I told her things my parents never gave me a chance to explain: that what disturbed me most about Auschwitz were the tourists with video cameras recording rooms full of shoes and human hair; that you could still see prisoners' drawings on the barracks walls in Birkenau, and often they were scenes of heavenly bliss; that even on the sunniest day the place was suffocating and gloomy and smelled evil. I even told her about a piece of ceramic tile I'd picked up beside one of the gas chambers and smeared with a bit of algae from the pond. I meant to carry it in my pocket wherever I went, as a reminder of what I'd seen, but when I reached for it on the train ride back to Prague, it was gone. I tore apart my backpack, spread my clothes all over the seat, nearly burst out crying, but no ceramic tile. "I think I left it in a youth hostel in Gdansk," I told Helen, almost out of breath. "Someone probably threw it away without ever knowing what it was."

"That's why I wouldn't want to go back there," she said. "My mother left before all that happened. But she hated Germans and Jews. She talked about them like they were the same people."

Nothing I'd said had touched her. The TV commercial ended, and Helen returned her attention to an episode of *I Love Lucy*, leaning forward, absently crumpling the fast-food wrapper in her hand. I wondered if she knew any Polish, which wasn't very different from Slovakian. I'd ask her to recite train schedules. She didn't care any more about me than had the woman announcing arrivals and departures in the Poprad train station. She wouldn't think twice about me when I left. The next day she'd put another ad in the paper, and someone new would start making calls. I'd be halfway across Canada, and she'd be watching a new giant-screen TV. By the time I reached California, she might even have a satellite dish.

Only my parents would miss me. No matter how much grief I caused them while I was home, I knew my absence would pain them more than my presence. When my older brother had moved in with his Catholic girlfriend after college, my mother slumped for weeks as if she had a fifty-pound sack of flour draped over her shoulders. My father suddenly developed bad knees. Even after they broke up and my brother married a Jewish girl, my parents didn't fully recover their former postures. That night, I watched them through the porch window, wondering what my abandonment might do to their bodies, fearing that one of them would discover a tumor or rare blood disease the moment my car pulled out of the driveway. And just as that thought crossed my mind, my father began coughing and pounding his chest with his fist. My mother stood and went to him, hammering her open palm against his back. His face reddened, veins stood out on his neck. My mother leaned close to his ear. I hurried into the kitchen, but when I reached the table, he stopped coughing and spit something into his fingers.

THINGS AT HOME AND AT HELEN'S MIGHT HAVE STAYED THE same way for a few months if I hadn't struck gold on the second Sunday I worked. I was running through my pitch without much excitement to a man with a deep voice who kept saying, "Yes, I see," at the end of each of my sentences. In my mind, he was older than my father, but lean and fit, the relaxed, well-groomed type who could wear his bathrobe around the house all day and still not look like a slob. When I finished, he said, "This sounds like a very worthy cause. Unfortunately, this is a slow month for me." I imagined myself rummaging through his sock drawers searching for loose change, and told him any little bit would go a long way toward buying new wheelchairs and walkers and whatnot. He replied, "Yes, I see. Well then, how's six thousand?"

I nearly dropped the phone. In the sock drawer sat a roll of bills I'd have to grab with both hands. I was almost afraid to touch it. It might be a trap – the man might have a cop hiding in his closet. "Did you say six thousand, sir? Six thousand dollars?" I was already doing the math in my head. Forty percent of six thousand meant twenty-four hundred for me. With that much, I'd be able to fix my car and leave New Jersey the next day. After the man hung up, I spent a few moments slowly tracing three round zeros onto the pledge card and stared at the black-and-white photo of Helen in its corner. In the picture she was even more hunched than usual, and her hands were hidden in her lap. She looked like the neediest person in the world. I was already picturing myself telling her about the six thousand. She would take both of my hands in hers, squeeze them and say, "Daniel, you're wonderful. You saved my life." I would close my eyes and listen to the clear voice that could have belonged to a woman who walked on healthy legs and smiled with ordinary, steady lips.

Then, as I finished filling out the man's address, I read the words beneath Helen's picture, "There are thousands of people like me who need your help," and heard my father's words, "It's not a mitzvah, it's just a job." I imagined six thousand people in wheelchairs lined up before me, waiting for their cut of the man's donation. I'd hand each a dollar and none would be any better off than before. It made sense then that Helen should get three and a half thousand dollars that might actually make a difference in her life. It made sense that the man's money should really help one cripple rather than tease six thousand. But as I carried the pledge card into the living room, I couldn't stop hearing my mother's voice, "Next he'll start dealing drugs!"

Helen was leaning far forward in the recliner, watching a panel of political analysts bickering about foreign policy. I stood to the side until the show broke to commercial. "Helen, you're not going to believe this," I said, and held out the pledge card. She turned slowly. Her eyes were half-closed, her face puffy. She didn't seem to know who I was or what I could possibly want from her. "Sorry," I said. "Did I wake you?"

She took the card from me, glanced at it, and handed it back. "Wow," she said.

I didn't really expect a shout of joy but had hoped at least for some sign of relief or gratitude. The line of six thousand cripples stretched out before me, each clamoring for a dollar. "You can get that new TV," I said. "As soon as the check comes in."

"That's true," she said.

"What'll you do with the rest?"

"I'm not sure."

I had to breathe deeply to calm my anger. She didn't seem to care about the money one way or another. She couldn't care less how hard I worked or how successful I was. "Remember the other day, when I said something about charity?" I asked. "You said ten percent of yours, ten percent of mine.

Why don't we really do it with this one? Six thousand's a lot of money."

She turned back to the TV. On the screen, a man in a tuxedo was gliding across a bright lawn on a riding mower the size of a small car. Beneath him, a caption in white letters read, "Why settle for less than luxury?" Helen held up the remote control, and the image blinked off. She turned back to me and said, "Is that really what you want to do?"

"I told you what I'm going to do with the money," I said. "What do you need four thousand dollars for?"

She shook her head. Her lips were moving in their ordinary way, mechanically up and out, but now there seemed to be a heavier quivering at their corners. "What do you think a cripple does with her money?" she said. I shrugged. "Jesus, Daniel. Do you have any idea what my medical bills are like?"

"I hadn't thought of that," I said. But I had. I'd seen all her bills in the pile of mail on the kitchen counter. Phone bill, electric bill, cable bill. Not a single medical bill. In two weeks, I hadn't once seen her go to the doctor. Whenever she did leave the apartment, she always came back within half an hour with the mail and a carton of milk or a package of hot dogs. "They're pretty expensive, huh?"

She put a hand over her eyes. It was trembling. "For someone who's traveled all over," she said, "you don't notice much what's happening in front of you. Can't you see how sick I am? I'll be lucky to make it through the year."

It took an enormous effort for me not to say out loud, Bullshit! I'd noticed plenty. I'd noticed there was never any dust on top of the refrigerator. I'd noticed she'd never left the apartment long enough even to get a checkup. But I said, "I'm sorry. I didn't know. Maybe you should keep the whole six thousand."

She took her hand away from her face, which seemed calm again. "Don't be ridiculous. You did all the work. I just sit on my ass all day." She lifted the remote again, and the TV screen flashed on. The three analysts had continued bickering, now about U.S. policy in the Middle East. I went out of the living room. Helen called after me, "Thanks, Daniel."

In the kitchen, I doubted myself for a brief moment and shuffled through her mail again, but still no medical bills. She couldn't really have been dying. Not with such strong, healthy-looking arms and hands. If her arms showed even a hint of withering like her legs, I might have believed her. But now, glancing at the top of the refrigerator, spotless and shining, I couldn't believe anything. Maybe her legs weren't withered at all, just hidden in the loose sweatpants. After I left the apartment every afternoon, she might have pushed aside the wheelchair and danced through the kitchen, dusting and laughing and counting her money. Maybe she was just an ugly, greedy woman, and the only thing wrong with her was a pair of cracked lips that she couldn't keep from moving.

For the rest of the afternoon I was distracted and couldn't concentrate on my calls. I brought in only one new pledge for fifteen bucks. The sound of the dial tone was beginning to make me dizzy. I got up to leave an hour earlier than usual. In the living room Helen was asleep in the recliner. I tried to walk past quietly, but she woke with a start before I could reach the front door. She turned to me, blinking. "I'm off," I said. "Have a good night."

She looked confused, and I paused by the door. After a moment, she grabbed her right arm with her left hand and squeezed. "My arm's asleep," she said. "I hate that."

"Rub it down like this." I showed her until the skin on my forearm grew hot. "It'll go away in a minute."

"My bladder's about to explode," she said. "Can you give me a hand into the wheelchair?" She stretched her arm and flexed her fingers. Even asleep her arm was stronger than mine would ever be. I went to the recliner and stood over her, not really sure what to do. "Hurry," she said. "Unless you want me to wet myself."

She lifted her arms, and I grabbed her around the middle. My nose was in her hair. I expected to be overwhelmed by the odor of dogs and cats, but instead the scent was fresh and lightly floral, no different from the hair of the few women I'd dated in college. No different at all. I lifted her cleanly over the arm of the recliner, but knocked her right leg against the side of the wheelchair. She settled back against the seat and said, "You don't carry women around often, do you?" I took a step back, and she said in a hurry, "Wait. I'm just kidding, Daniel. Thanks."

I wheeled her down the hall to the bathroom and set her beside the toilet. The mirror was fogged, and the dampness made the smell of her hair grow stronger. "I'd ask you to pull down my pants, but I can tell you're squeamish," she said. "Go on home."

I went back into the hall and closed the door behind me. The smell of dogs and cats hit me again and I clenched my fists in a sudden rage. Helen wasn't dying at all. She was a healthy woman stealing money from hard-working people. Like my parents, she thought I was just some loser who couldn't get a decent job. She'd use me for a while and quickly forget about me. I turned to leave but then stopped at the closed door to Helen's bed-room. It hadn't once been open since I'd worked here. What was she hid-ing? I was suddenly convinced that she had a tall, hairy man stowed away in her bed, that the two of them lay in the sheets laughing at me the moment I left the apartment every afternoon. My hand shook as I turned the knob. With my shoulder, I pushed the door inward as quietly as possible.

The room might have been in an entirely different apartment from the living room or kitchen. A floral bedspread lay crumpled at the end of a narrow mattress, and clothes were scattered across the floor. The night table was stacked high with magazines. Above the bed hung a painting of a dark city street glistening in spots with rain puddles. Guilt pinched my stomach. Not for doubting what Helen had told me – I still didn't believe she was sick or dying. But there was no question that she spent every night in this apartment all alone. No one waited down the hall for her to ask about the baseball scores or to share a bowl of burnt popcorn. The last thing she needed was my resentment. I eased the door closed and called toward the bathroom, "See you tomorrow. Have a good night."

"Tomorrow's payday," she called back. Payday. The word made me forget the lonely night that stretched before both of us. By the time I got home I could think about nothing but the four westbound lanes of the freeway, the fields that would slide past my windows as I drove across the Canadian plains, the flashing neon signs of gas stations and motels, the phone booths from which I would occasionally call my parents to let them know I was still alive. Just inside the back door, my mother startled me. In a hurried voice, she offered to defrost an extra chicken breast for me for next Shabbos. "You don't have plans, do you?" she said.

I hesitated, scratched my chin. "Probably," I stammered. "I think I do, actually. Thanks, though." She blinked several times and quickly turned away.

THE NEXT DAY, I DIDN'T GET A SINGLE PLEDGE. HELEN STAYED in bed until almost noon and then wheeled directly into the living room without stopping off in the kitchen for breakfast. For lunch, I went to Kentucky Fried Chicken and ate in a greasy booth looking out toward the freeway overpass. For most of the afternoon, I ignored the phone list, instead dialing over and over the numbers for the time and the weather. Just before I got up to leave, Helen wheeled into the kitchen, holding out a check. When I took it, her arm didn't drop immediately. It hung in the air and floated slowly to her lap. The check was made out for almost four thousand dollars, forty percent of every pledge I'd brought in for two weeks. Most of those pledges hadn't even been paid yet. The check felt heavy in my hand, the number in the box too large. I no longer imagined myself slipping discreet bills from an innocent woman's purse. Instead, I was beating her over the head with a crowbar and taking her entire wallet, credit cards, driver's license, and family photos included. I asked Helen whether she wanted me to wait before cashing the check, but she said, "Don't worry. It won't bounce. Happy traveling."

She knew before I did that I wouldn't be coming back. With this much money, there was no reason for me to stay. My parents were beginning to get used to my being in the house. That morning at breakfast, my father had begun reading to me from the sports pages. He would have told me the score of every game in every sport in the whole world if I hadn't said I was going to be late and excused myself. I had to leave soon, or I'd never get away. But still, I said to Helen, putting a hand on her shoulder, "See you tomorrow."

She shrugged and said, "If you say so." I hurried out before she could ask me to lift her into the recliner or wheel her to the bathroom.

In the morning, I didn't call to let Helen know I wouldn't be coming in. I went to the bank and cashed her check, and then had my brakes fixed, bought new back tires, and got an oil change. Helen had the number at my parents' house, but she didn't call either. For a few days I sat around my room, packing for the trip, flipping through my pictures from Europe, which now no longer satisfied me. Most of them were shots of architecture – steeples, columns, gargoyles, flying buttresses. I wished I'd taken more of people. Each morning I woke up and told myself I should drive to Helen's and apologize for not coming back. I wanted to thank her for helping me on my way and tell her a proper goodbye. But as soon as I made up my mind to see her, my heart picked up speed and blood rushed to my face. I was afraid she'd lift her arms above her head, saying in that voice that belonged in a more beautiful body, "Can you help me into the wheelchair?" If I smelled her hair, I knew I'd go back to the kitchen and start making calls. Maybe after she hired somebody new I'd be able to see her and leave. Every day I checked the classifieds to see if she'd put in another ad, but after three days there was nothing. Most likely, I told myself, the new ads wouldn't come out until the following Monday.

Finally, at the end of the week, I was ready to go. In the driveway, my mother kept wiping her eyes with her sleeve. I kissed her forehead and, for a moment, worried that her skin felt feverish. "Promise me you'll get a job in California," she said. "A real job."

My father couldn't look me in the eyes. He patted the hood of the car and said, "Don't drive too fast. They have speed traps in Canada."

He put his arm around my mother's waist, and they watched as I loaded the trunk. They looked older than they should have, and small. I wanted to say, "Take care of each other," but all I could manage was, "I'll call every other day." I didn't turn around as I backed out and took off down the street. I knew they would stand waving until I was out of sight. If I'd glanced once in the rearview mirror, maybe I would have stopped the car, stood on the street, and shouted for the whole neighborhood to hear, "Why can't you wish me well? Why can't you accept who I am?" Instead, I kept my eyes straight ahead, trying not to look at any of the things I wouldn't see again for a long, long time, the familiar houses and yards, the strip of woods where I'd first pretended to be an adventurer, climbing trees, sloshing through a creek, spying on neighbors in their gardens, chucking rocks at bird feeders. I managed to keep from shaking until I passed my old high school. From the road, I couldn't see the building, just the tennis courts, a corner of the football stadium, the parking lot where I'd spent so much time listening to Led Zeppelin on my headphones. The names and faces of a few kids I'd known forced their way into my mind, but I couldn't attach them to any specific memories. The only thing I could remember clearly was the clotted perfume and cigarette smell of the girls who would pass me in the halls without even a glance of disgust. Before I entirely realized what I was doing, I'd turned the car toward Helen's apartment.

I wasn't thinking about saying goodbye or thank you, or making one last call for a donation. What I needed to see was that she'd bought herself an enormous new TV. Or even an electric wheelchair. I needed to see that the money we'd made had nothing to do with medical bills.

The apartment complex was wild with children running across the parking lot, dodging my car. I'd only spend five minutes here, I promised myself, not a second more. I'd still make it to Montreal by early evening. From a distance, I could see that the curtains of number 1412 were open. Not once had Helen opened them while I'd worked there. At first I thought this was lucky for me, because I could look in the window and see the new TV without having to talk to her. Or even better, I could knock on the door and watch how she would swing from the recliner into the wheelchair. Part of me even hoped I'd catch her walking around on healthy legs when she thought no one could see.

But when I reached the window, my knees almost buckled. There was no new giant-screen TV. There was no TV at all, and no recliner. Dropcloths stained with white paint covered the carpets, and beneath the window sat a bucket and roller. I couldn't see any painters, but they might have been on their lunch break, or else painting in the bedroom. I could barely glimpse the kitchen but saw enough to know that the table, the phone lists, and the pledge cards were gone as well.

My first and only thought then was that the police had taken her away. No one could run a scam like that for very long and not get caught, no matter how crippled she might look. I pictured two red-eyed, unshaven detectives carrying her from the apartment, wheelchair and all, and tossing her into a squad car in front of all her neighbors and their children. I backed away slowly, glancing in every direction, half-convinced somebody was hiding behind a car or hedge, watching me through binoculars. If Helen had been caught, maybe the police knew about me as well. The vast map of Canada appeared before me; I wouldn't simply be a traveler there, but a renegade. Women would flock to me, to my scent of danger. I hurried to my car and tore out of the complex, my backpack rattling in the trunk as the new tires jumped over the speed bumps.

Not until I'd driven a long stretch down the freeway, curving toward the Delaware Water Gap, on the verge of leaving New Jersey forever, did it occur to me that Helen might not have been arrested. And then, without warning, I was overtaken by a flood of possibilities: maybe she'd found a new apartment to keep the scam running and evade the cops, maybe she'd moved in with a relative, maybe her new telemarketer had scored a hundred-thousand-dollar pledge and taken her to Florida to live in luxury, maybe she'd been rushed to the hospital, maybe she'd dropped dead all alone in front of the TV.

I nearly drove off the road. Not because I really believed she was dead, but because I could never know one way or the other.

Only when I crossed into Pennsylvania and stopped for lunch was I able to convince myself that Helen was fine. Right now she'd be leaning forward in front of a TV somewhere, entranced by a how-to show on building your own deck and patio. I pictured her arms and recalled the smell of her hair, and my breathing began to slow. Then, as I ate my fries, I forced myself to concentrate on the details of the trip, deciding how many miles I would drive each day, where I would stop for gas, how much I would pay for a motel room. For the first few hundred miles I couldn't stop glancing in the rearview mirror. But slowly, the expanse of road heading north and west stirred a thrill in my blood, and by the second day nothing could distract me from the flashing white lines.

I never made it to the west coast, or even to the Rockies. Canada was so much more expensive than eastern Europe that no matter how cheaply I tried to live, money poured out of my pockets. And after two weeks in my parents' house, I was no longer comfortable with the ascetic lifestyle I'd led in Budapest. I'd never realized how much I appreciated a firm mattress and soft pillow. My car broke down twice in Ontario, and by mid-October, I found myself in Detroit with almost no money. It took another year to make my way around Lake Michigan, past the smokestack skyline of Gary, Indiana, to Chicago, where I gratefully accepted a respectable entry-level position in the public relations department of a large advertising firm. My father didn't think much of this. "Advertisers are the worst kind of criminals," he'd say, his voice far off, older than I remembered. "I'd rather be robbed at gunpoint." I told him I tried to be as honest as possible. My mother just asked when I thought I might get promoted.

In the evenings I walked along the lakeshore, where, even in summer, the wind blew cold against my face, colder than the wind off the Danube when I stood facing east. I tried to remember the three-mile walk from Auschwitz to Birkenau, where I'd stopped halfway to snap a picture of the train tracks. That day I'd shot three rolls, savoring the electric buzz of my new camera, thinking not of the cattle cars packed with children rolling toward flaming ovens, but of my parents' expressions when I would show them the photos. They would cup their hands around their eyes, I thought, nod, and say, "We always knew you'd do well. You're a good Jew. You're a good boy." I never showed those pictures to them or anyone else. They sat in a box under my bed in New Jersey, in Detroit, and somehow disappeared when I moved to Chicago. By the lakeshore, I tried desperately to recall the bright, clear sky above the terrible tracks, but suddenly I would be back in Helen's kitchen, nearly gagging on the smell of dogs and cats, the phone pinched between my shoulder and ear, a long list of numbers before me. Behind my chair I heard the smacking of Helen's lips, and though I couldn't see them, I knew my mother and father flanked her on either side, all three in rusted, worn-out wheelchairs. They watched carefully as I dialed, cataloguing my deeds, good and not so good. After comparing notes, my mother's tears sputtered softly, and my father offered Helen the chicken breast I'd refused.

# Anything You Need

THEIR PARTING WAS MUTUAL, FRIENDLY, AGREED UPON A month before Jared was to move out. They'd always respected each other, admired each other, enjoyed each other's company. Their two years together had been scattered with moments of tenderness. But to spend their entire lives this way? A mistake. In neither of their minds, they both told all their friends, lingered even a shred of doubt. The night they'd come to this decision had been tearful, but in the morning, over breakfast, they'd been able to examine it calmly, from a distance. "People just grow apart," Robin had said with a smile that no longer seemed strained, despite her sad eyes, still swollen and discolored. She reached for the sugar bowl and dropped one, two, three, four cubes into her mug. "Any tea with your sugar?" Jared had joked too often, but wouldn't today. She dropped each cube from a height of several inches, and light brown splashes spread from the cup in rays. The glass table would be sticky by this afternoon, but he knew neither of them would bother cleaning anything now, not this morning, not this evening, probably not tomorrow. "Somehow, we –" she began and then paused. "Our values. We want – We're just too different. It isn't anybody's fault. It just happens. There's nothing we could have done about it."

Jared nodded. For a moment he could think of nothing to add. Then, groping for a phrase he'd read in a magazine or heard on a talk show, he said, "No magic. We lacked passion."

For a month they continued to share the same bed, large enough for them to sleep comfortably without touching. Though late at night, groggy, darkness and sleep making them feel drunk or blind or forgetful, their bodies met in the tangle of sheets, and that, too, was friendly. They didn't discuss it ahead of time, but when it happened – neither remembering whose leg had first hooked the other's, whose lips had first sought the neck, the chin, the mouth buried in the opposite pillow – what could they do but accept it as inevitable, even somehow necessary? Their friends had warned them to make a clean and utter break. But what was wrong with a little comfort and nostalgia? Who was it hurting?

"I've got the best of both worlds," Jared told Andy, a buddy from Rutgers, over a quick lunchtime beer. Andy had looked better. Since the last time Jared had seen him, his cheeks had sunken deep into his mouth, nearly separating his jaw from the rest of his face. In college, Andy had gone by the name "Shock," because his eyeballs had always been sizzling with mescaline or mushrooms. He'd graduated, barely, with a political science degree, and was now waiting tables in Chelsea. Jared was paying for their beer. "I still get laid," he said. "But none of the bullshit. No talking, no cuddling. Just bang and back to sleep. What could be better?"

Andy shook his head. "Danger, bro. Danger."

Jared shrugged. "It's all under control," he said, and flashed his Visa Gold at the waitress.

What he and Robin shared at night was harmless, he knew. There was no need for them even to talk about it. At breakfast, after the first time, she'd said simply, "I feel good about things. Don't you?" And from the refrigerator, where he'd rattled bottles and cartons, shuffled mysterious leftovers wrapped in foil, he'd answered, "Can I make you some toast?"

Mornings were different. Only then did Andy's warning seem to echo from the bedroom walls. Touching in daylight wasn't allowed. This, too, they'd never discussed, but he should have guessed. One morning he reached across the empty stretch of sheet between them, stroking two fingers along the warm underside of her knee. He found a vein and traced it, matching the faint pulse to the red numbers on the clock – ten minutes before the alarm would shout for him to face the world, nine minutes, eight. Seven minutes left, and his fingers followed the vein to the top of her thigh, around the curve of her hip, but then she rolled to the far end of the bed and feigned a heavy, hissing breath.

If there was a time he most needed their bodies to meet, it was in the morning. At night, in darkness, it was easy – no, not easy: effortless – to believe in endings. He could say to himself, *We're finished, this is over*, and nothing in his mind rebelled. He could watch the sun disappear over the hills toward Pennsylvania and understand another day was gone. He could close his eyes and convince himself his present life was coming to its conclusion, that tomorrow he would awake a new man. And even if, in the middle of the night, he felt Robin's weight pressing onto him, her fingers groping parts of him without acknowledging who he was, it didn't matter – this wasn't a return to the life he'd given up when he'd fallen asleep. It was a shadowy, timeless state, in between yesterday's life and tomorrow's, somewhat like not being alive at all.

But in the morning, even crowded by their bedroom's tiny window and filtered by navy linen shades, the early April sunlight brightened their closet, the sliding door pushed to one side, their suits, dresses, shirts, slacks, hers and his mixed together on the same rack. Through the narrow space where the shades didn't quite meet, a beam fell across the carpet, across the end of the mattress, lighting up her pale feet poking from the blanket, yellowed with calluses at the heels. Always before the alarm his eyes opened painfully in the bluish light, and yesterday's life came rushing back to him. In the morning, with an entire day to face, there were no such things as endings. In another ten minutes they would rise and shower, eat breakfast side by side at the table barely wide enough for two plates, ride a bus together into Manhattan. No matter how late he had to work, sometimes not coming home until close to midnight, she would wait to eat dinner beside him on the soft, sunken cushions of the inviting couch, and together they would crawl back into this same bed.

In the morning, when he tried to say to himself, *We're finished,* sharp cries rose to his throat and threatened to shake the room. He'd felt this way before, but not since he was a young boy in his parents' house, only ten miles from where he and Robin now lived. He'd never intended to settle in New Jersey, but after a single lonely and confused semester at a private college in Tennessee, he'd transferred, shaken, to Rutgers, where he'd been comfortable from the first moment – and now he blamed the nearness to his childhood home for his regression. In boyhood, the feeling had usually come at night, his parents asleep at the far end of the hallway. He'd wake for no reason and, finding himself alone in the dark, break into an immediate sweat. Through the wall just beside his head came the wispy breathing of his younger brother. But this was no comfort. Even at three years old, Daniel, like his parents, seemed to live in a secret, private world in which Jared played no role. No one was thinking about him, not Daniel, not his parents, and a terrible fear gripped him and wouldn't let him close his eyes. The fear wasn't of monsters hiding in the closet or under the bed, or of thieves circling the house, slipping from shadow to shadow, unlatching windows or picking locks; these thoughts would reach him later. His terror now came in the form of questions, raging louder as the night wore on: How could his parents close him in a dark room? How could he be expected to stay there quietly, for so many hours, night after night? How could the world go dark for half of every day?

He lay with these questions clamped tightly between his teeth, biting his lip to keep from crying out. But once, after an hour, or maybe two, he could hold out no longer, and his mouth opened. The strength of his scream startled even him. Immediately, footsteps pounded along the hall, his door flung open, and his mother rushed to his bed. Tufts of her hair stuck straight up, but her eyes were awake, her hands clenched into fists, ready to protect her son. She seemed to expect some kind of threat, and this terrified Jared even more. It was only then that he began to fear monsters and thieves and soon, when he learned about it in school, nuclear war. But now his mother's arms went around his neck, and his father appeared in the doorway, lingering there. "What is it, baby?" his mother said. "Did you have a nightmare?"

He knew he couldn't tell her about the questions boiling inside him. She wouldn't understand; they might even make her angry. "A nightmare," he repeated, sensing that this was something for which he couldn't be responsible. "Big red crabs. They were crawling all over me. One had its claw on my ear."

"They're all gone now," his mother said, prying him from his blanket. "You'll sleep with us the rest of the night."

"No crabs in our bed, I hope," his father said, and winked. His mother laughed and smacked his father's shoulder. Daniel, blinking and barefoot, tottered out of his room. He held up to Jared a battered blue dog, with floppy ears hanging by threads and cotton stuffing spilling from its belly. Jared kept his arms around his mother and clamped his teeth shut. He tried to forget his questions, though none had been answered.

Eventually, he did forget them. By the time he entered high school, he believed he knew the answers to everything and no longer held back his feelings; he spent four years shouting at his mother, his father, and his brother, and brutalizing himself with weights. In college he stopped caring so much about his own body and focused instead on those bodies he wanted to sleep with. He learned to be open and share with women whatever he thought they wanted him to say. But now, even on the worst mornings, he was again at a loss for words. He clenched his jaw and couldn't cry out. He couldn't let himself reach for Robin. He avoided looking at their closet, at her feet, at the strands of hair fluttering over her mouth. He lay on his back, staring at the ceiling, swallowing hard. He counted the rectangular ceiling panels, made of so many fibers pressed together until they stuck, counted them like the days remaining on this month's calendar, and thought how easy they would be to shatter with a single swift blow. He waited for the alarm, waited for his turn to shower, waited to face her over steaming cups of coffee and tea, her eyes cheerful, her words polite and spoken from miles away.

FROM THE BEGINNING, LATE IN THEIR SENIOR YEAR AT RUTGERS, soon after they'd been brought together in a mutual circle of friends, he'd felt Robin watching him carefully. At the time, they'd both been involved with other people: he at the end of a brief series of casual flings that always ended bitterly, she in a nine-month relationship turning sour. They were introduced at a party, chatted on line at a coffee shop, waved when passing in the middle of campus, and, celebrating their last set of mid-terms with a large group at a crowded New Brunswick bar, found themselves side by side in a dark corner, a pitcher of beer between them. Her boyfriend had stayed home to study, and his lover had gone out with other friends.

Robin was different from the other girls he'd dated. Not necessarily in the way she looked: she had a slim body and the round, full-lipped, expressive face he was often drawn to, either cheerful or angry or confused, never passive, always easy to read. Her shoulder-length hair, soft brown, would lighten in summer, and, he suspected, the faint freckles beneath her eyes would show even through a dark tan. In her nose was a delicate gold ring she would probably take out after graduation, but the sight of it now, occasionally glinting green with the light of a flashing beer sign, made him feel weak. What was different about her, rather, was the way she questioned him – about his studies, his future plans, his current romance – leaning back in her chair, fingers crossed over her stomach, thumbs tapping her ribs. She listened intently to what he said, but with obvious amusement, unsympathetic, expecting him to lie. "So what's wrong with her?" she asked about the girl who later tonight would leave an angry message on his answering machine – she expected him to stop by on his way home, probably spend the night, but he had already decided against it.

"Nothing's wrong with her," he said, though in his mind the list went on page after page. "She's a sweet girl. We're just really different."

"That's okay," Robin said, shrugging. "You don't have to tell me."

Later, the conversation shifted to her boyfriend, and emboldened by the beer, Jared said, "You're not in love with him. I can tell." He refilled her cup. The pitcher was nearly empty. "Who would want to marry a social worker, anyway? You think he complains a lot now. Wait till he hangs around with battered wives all day."

"You might be right," she said, and then added angrily, "But who the hell are you? You don't even like the girls you sleep with." He jerked back in surprise. She burst out laughing and kicked his shin under the table.

Halfway through the second pitcher they both admitted to being miserable with their partners and agreed to make a change. And why not? Everything would soon be changing. In two months he'd graduate. At the beginning of July, he'd start working as a systems programmer for a financial firm in the city, grinding out code ten to twelve hours a day in an office eighteen stories high. He'd move into an apartment the next town over from his parents and start making car payments, payments on his student loans. He'd have to give up flannel shirts and ripped jeans for suits and quiet ties, steel-toed boots for polished loafers. He'd have to shave every day and keep his hair trimmed. He took a long gulp from his beer and fought off a rising panic. In two months, there would be no more wild parties, no more bars full of college girls who would believe anything he said so long as he made them laugh. Four years gone, and he'd spent not a moment looking for someone he might fall in love with. And now he'd enter the world alone. "Let's make a pact," he said, and held out his hand.

Before he could say another word, Robin tried to shake it. "Wait," he said. "I'm serious. You've got to listen. Starting right now. From this moment forward, you understand? No more fucking around. That means for both of us. If it's not the real thing, we won't waste a minute of our time. Not a second."

She gave an exaggerated nod and set her face with a solemn, mocking expression. "You're completely full of shit," she said, and grabbed his hand. He held on tightly, and half an hour later they stumbled into his room.

It took less than two months for her to learn his habits, to begin laughing at the pattern of quirks he wasn't even aware of, to intimate his moods. By the time they graduated and moved in together, he had the feeling she'd been watching him since he was a small boy. No matter how stoically he might try to carry his frustration or anxiety, the moment he came home from work she could guess from his expression when he'd had a run-in with a difficult coworker or harsh words from his boss. Four nights out of five, she could predict the very thing he would most want to eat for dinner. Just short of reading his mind, she knew exactly what he was feeling without his ever saying a word. He might have been living with a more sensitive version of himself.

Once, early in their first summer together, they'd taken a drive into the Catskills for the weekend, and strangely – had it been the clear sky? the fresh air? – words flew out of his mouth, about the scenery, about his ideal career path, about the type of house he would like to buy, not at all like his parents' house if he could help it. He couldn't stop talking or touching her bare arm as he drove. Suddenly, she turned to him and said, as if she'd never before thought of it, "You really do love me, don't you?" The surprise and confusion on his own face must have been obvious, though he only nodded. Of course he loved her. Didn't he say it at least twice every day? But now, she slid closer to him, rested her head on his shoulder, pulled lightly at the hairs on his thigh. In less than a mile she spotted a motel and pointed with her chin. It was only then that he realized this was what he'd been wanting all day – not to be driving, admiring the hills and fields, but to shed their clothes across a matted carpet, to tumble on a starchy, anonymous bed. As they strolled hand in hand to the motel office, gravel crunching hungrily under their feet, he nearly thanked her out loud.

But no matter how well Robin seemed to know him, Jared couldn't feel the same about her. Despite her open face, her broad gestures, he could never put his finger on what she wanted from one day to the next. Every emotion showed clearly in her features, but what good did it do if he couldn't guess which emotion would follow the present one, and which after that? He wanted badly to express how much she meant to him, to tell her about the effect she had on his life. When he said, "Sometimes I feel sick when I don't see you all day," she kissed him, but her smile was sarcastic, and the next day as he left for work she handed him a bottle of Tums. For a time he said whatever came to mind, prepared for Robin to laugh, startled when tears formed in her eyes and her voice quivered, "Oh, Jared. You're way too sweet for me." But with each passing month, his uncertainty grew. He was afraid of repeating himself, of boring her, of driving her away. The closer he felt to her the more intense his expectation of impending loss. He stopped saying the words that popped into his head, instead waiting for Robin to ask for the words she needed. When she heaped affection on him without warning, he nearly panicked, fearing he was being given a gift he didn't deserve. When she rolled away from his touch at night, he shuddered with both relief and toppling sorrow.

The change, though he'd expected it, dawned on him only gradually. Had it begun last December? January? Without any specific incident to trigger it, the nature of Robin's observation altered. She no longer watched him with amusement. He'd open the bathroom door, and there she'd be, waiting. Without a word, she'd slip past him and a minute later appear in the bedroom doorway as he dressed, her arms crossed, not simply annoyance on her face, but bitterness. What had he done? Left the shower dripping? Spit a gob of toothpaste into the sink and not washed it down? Dropped a pubic hair on the toilet seat? She followed him into the kitchen, hovering, peering suspiciously over his shoulder as he rooted through the refrigerator. She refused to forgive him for eating an entire tub of strawberries before she'd had a chance to taste them. Once, when he drank Coke straight from the bottle, she slumped to the floor and wept.

It was then that he began to sense – and soon to feel with certainty – he was no longer loved. But he wasn't yet ready to give up. If he was careful, he still believed, there was a chance to win her back. He walked through the apartment quietly, cleaning up after himself, leaving things as if they'd never been touched. He gave her as much space as she seemed to need. After dinner, he watched the news with the volume turned so low he had to hunch forward to hear it. But even then, she stood at the edge of the room, eyeing him. Finally, she spoke. This day he remembered. It was mid-March, two weeks before they called it quits. "Rwanda," she said from just behind his chair. "Fucking mess. What do you think we should do?"

"I don't know," he said to the TV, holding himself as still as possible. Cameras panned across tangled heaps of black bodies, and then slowly widened to a cluster of huts, an entire village, the sprawling jungle.

"I'm just asking what you think."

"It's complicated," he said.

"You're not the Secretary of State." Her voice was rising, but still he wouldn't turn to face her. "It doesn't matter what you say. I only want your opinion."

On the screen an American official was being interviewed. Jared strained to hear what he was saying, hoping for a quick answer, something he could use. But behind him, Robin was breathing heavily, fidgeting with something on her shirt, and the official's voice was no more than a vibrating hum. "I'm still undecided," he said. "That's what I'm trying to tell you."

Now she was in front of the TV, the news flickering on either side of her waist. "What's to decide? I'll explain it to you. You've got these guys over here," she said, drawing a box with her fingers. Then another box a few inches away. "And you've got some other guys here. These first guys are black, and these other ones are even blacker. The blacker guys are getting their heads chopped off. Should we help them? Yes or no?"

He gripped the arms of the chair and tried to laugh, but the sound from his mouth was sickly. "You know it's not that simple."

"It *is* simple," she said, and now she was hysterical, her face soaked with tears. "It couldn't be simpler. You have no opinion. You don't give a shit about anything. They're all black, they can all die. What do you think of my hair? What color was it yesterday?"

He stood and reached for her, but she ran behind the couch and down the hall. After a moment, the bedroom door slammed. On the TV, Rwanda was replaced by basketball highlights. Reggie Miller threw a nasty elbow, spun, shot, and scored. For the first time, Jared considered what his life might be like without anybody to judge his every action. Pissing on the toilet seat, letting the shower drip for days. But what else? He sank into the chair and held his head in both hands. His own thoughts he heard in Andy's voice, stoned and sluggish, but stubbornly wise: "She doesn't love you, man. You can't share a bed with someone who doesn't love you."

And now she didn't watch him at all. Already, she was working to put him completely out of her mind. In the mirror, the pain in his face was glaring. How could she not recognize it? Right in front of her he tipped the Coke bottle to his lips, but she said nothing. He listened to the news at a volume that nearly deafened him and made a neighbor pound on the wall. But Robin only smiled and handed him a plate of spaghetti, the last thing in the world he wanted to eat.

EVEN THE SLOWEST MONTH EVENTUALLY PASSES. "I'M TELLING you, I can't wait," Jared insisted to Andy over another lunch in the same Wall Street bar. Andy nodded, but his eyes were roaming. He was being evicted from his apartment and would soon be moving back to his parents' house in Toms River. Jared felt sorry for him, but it wasn't his fault if the guy wanted to waste his life. "I wish I'd been out of there three weeks ago," he said. "Time already."

Andy glanced at the clock over the bar. "Time," he agreed.

Jared rented an apartment fifteen miles east, a straight shot down Route 46, two towns away. He had a week to move in and took his time. Friends offered their help, but no, he had his truck, he'd manage. Together, he and Robin could lift the heavier things. One day they carried out his desk and file cabinet. The next he took only a box of sweaters. He ordered a special mattress guaranteed to prevent back strain, ordered it because it took several extra days to deliver. But then the week was over. His bed arrived. He'd taken away almost all his clothes, and now he stuffed the rest into a box with a few kitchen utensils that would keep him from eating with his fingers. Only the last and hardest thing was left to do: on

Sunday afternoon, he and Robin emptied the bookshelves and CD racks onto the floor and began making two piles. There weren't many books. A handful of paperbacks, a few they'd both read, most others given by her mother, never opened. College texts neither would ever look at again, but which both had agreed to keep. His on finance, management, programming, statistics. Hers marketing, advertising, more statistics. "Good reference," she'd said when they'd first moved in together and combined the clutter of their separate lives. "You never know," he'd agreed, though even the thought of reopening *Business and Administrative Communication*, the first three pages feverishly highlighted, the rest untouched and unread, had immediately made him tired.

From the shelves, there was mostly junk they'd bought each other over the past two years, surprise gifts, rarely for any occasion: spiny cactuses in plastic pots, a miniature chess board, picture frames, a glass bowl half-filled with potpourri, a pair of yellow Buddhas, one fat and laughing, the other ascetic and deep in meditation, a deck of playing cards with Van Goghs printed on their backs, an empty brass vase, a crudely carved wooden frog. He wanted her to keep it all. "I got these for you in Chinatown," she said, holding out a pair of clay candlesticks that hadn't once held candles. Glazed red dragons spiraled from their wide bases and breathed fire at their necks. He ran a finger over the etched characters he would never understand – love for all time? death to your enemies? a curse on your children? they might have said anything – and he had to put them down. "You've got to keep them," she said. "Promise me you'll put them on your new shelf."

The CDs were easier, their tastes in music different enough so they didn't have to remember who had bought what. Her stack rose with folk and indie and a smattering of early '80s punk and New Wave. His was nearly all Seattle grunge from four noisy college years. He read the titles fondly and determined to listen to each of them, even those gathering dust, as soon as he hooked up the stereo in his new apartment. But already he expected to feel the pain of genuine loss – never again would he hear these albums through enormous speakers half the size of a tiny dorm room clouded with dope.

With only one disc did they hesitate: The Screaming Trees. He'd bought it soon after they'd met and played it for her that first night they'd staggered home from the bar. She'd lain on his futon, her legs hooked over its raised back, her hair spread on the worn cushion. He sat on the floor beside her, wedged between the futon and the coffee table upon which he'd lit a candle and a cone of incense. Their faces were only inches apart. The music vibrated the floor. "I like these guys," she said, and closed her eyes.

"I saw them last year," he said. "Drove all the way to Buffalo."

He leaned forward and kissed her cheek. She smiled, but kept her eyes closed. He kissed her again, on the jaw, and then on the underside of her chin. He went for her lips, but she turned her head to the side. She was still smiling. She expected him to prove something, but what he had no idea. That he was strong? That he was honest? Carefree? Sensitive? He could be any of these things, but only if she told him what it was she wanted. All night she'd been testing him, making fun of him, but now he'd had enough. He had nothing to prove. He straightened and was about to stand. "Here," she said, pointing to her earlobe. "Kiss me here."

When the CD ended, he spread the futon, then crawled to the stereo and hit Repeat. It was still playing when they woke the next afternoon. For a month they listened to it every day, and then, for another month, at least once a week. It took almost a year to find its way to the bottom of the rack, but now neither of them had heard it since long before Thanksgiving. "*Uncle Anesthesia*," she said, opening the case and sliding out the liner notes. "I still have a weakness for it."

She slid it into the player and sat on the floor staring at her fingernails. He had to walk into the kitchen. He could predict every thick chord and mouth every lyric; he might have written them himself. "It's yours," he said.

"No, I can't – "

He waved a hand. "I'm not taking it. Either keep it or chuck it."

She skipped ahead to the next song, her brows bunching in concentration. She was trying to decide, he could tell, whether she actually liked the music, whether this was something she could listen to for its own sake. She skipped forward again. No. She would keep it in the rack, take it out once a year, listen to the first song and half the second, and quickly shelve it away. "Thanks," she said. "It means a lot to me."

Finally, he'd boxed everything he could bear to take. Robin stood over him as he bit silver tape from a roll. When he glanced up, the rims of her eyes reddened, and he expected her to hurry into the bedroom and shut the door until he was gone. But she only stooped and picked flakes of cardboard from the carpet. He had to step around her to get to the front door. He carried each box out of the apartment, down three flights of stairs, across the crowded parking lot, and shoved it into the bed of his truck. After he'd loaded the fourth and last box, Robin burst from their door – her door. Her hair, almost always down, was pulled loosely over her ears, twisted and pinned in a frayed bun, the way she wore it to scrub the bathtub. Even from far away her eyes looked dark and pouchy. "Jared," she called. "Wait."

A surge of hope took the strength from his legs. He put a hand on the truck to keep from falling. She bounded down the stairs and ran to him, her bare feet dodging broken glass, her sweatpants bunching at the ankles. His arms tensed, ready to reach up and embrace her. But she stopped a few feet from him and said, out of breath, "My teapot."

"What?"

"My teapot. I think you might have packed it."

"I'll bring it to you," he said. "Soon as I find it."

The sun was still high above the office buildings to the west, but a breeze caused plastic candy wrappers and bits of newspaper to skitter across the parking lot. Robin hugged herself and rubbed her bare arms. "It's my mother's. I'd feel strange not having it here."

"I'll bring it tomorrow," he said.

She shook her head. "You won't come back here tomorrow."

He climbed onto the truck bed and tore open the first box he came to. He dug through dishtowels and coffee mugs, but no teapot. On the third-floor walkway, a neighbor appeared, an old woman who never left the building and knew everything about the people who lived here. She spent all day washing clothes, though he'd never seen her wear anything but the filthy bathrobe she had on now, her skinny, bluish legs exposed almost to the knees. Once, in the laundry room, she'd turned to him without warning and said, "When you gonna marry that girl?" He'd been too startled to snap, as he should have, "None of your fucking business." Instead, he'd answered, "As soon as she lets me," though he and Robin had never even discussed it. Now, the woman called out, "You folks moving?"

"Just one of us," Robin said.

Jared tore open the second box and the third, scattered CDs and books across the damp truck bed. The woman called, "That's too bad, honey. You two looked cute together."

"It's for the best," Robin said.

"You wanna talk," the woman said. "Just give a knock on 318."

At the bottom of the third box, underneath a pillowcase, he found the teapot. White ceramic painted with gaudy blue flowers, chipped on the handle. He couldn't remember if the chip had always been there, or if this was something he'd just done. He had no idea why he would have packed it. With its spout between his fingers, it fit comfortably in his palm, and he drew his arm back, testing its weight. He could picture its arc, could imagine the sound it would make against the pavement, a disappointed pop, a brief release of air. He already saw shards skidding beneath car tires and around Robin's bare feet and knew this was what he was supposed to do, knew this would be an answer to something. But then he imagined the old woman, shaking her head as she told another neighbor who couldn't care less, "She said it was mutual, but I didn't believe her. Those things never are."

He dropped from the truck bed and handed Robin the teapot. She clutched it to her stomach with both hands. "Thanks, Jared," she said. The corner of her lip was swollen where she'd been biting it. "If you forgot anything, just call. I'll bring it right over. Call if you need anything."

He nodded and slammed closed the truck's gate, not bothering to retape the open boxes. She set the teapot on the ground and threw her arms around his neck. He touched her waist gently. "I'll miss you," she said, her breath warm on his neck, the rest of him frozen in the chill breeze. "Really. I will."

The third-floor walkway was empty, but he knew the old woman would be watching from her window. "When I'm set up," he said. "When I get everything unpacked, you'll come over. I'll make you dinner."

She stood close to him a moment, her head slightly tilted, expectant. Then she stepped away, wiping her eyes. "I can't wait," she said.

The teapot was back in her hands as she stood watching him roll out of the parking lot – watching still as he idled at the light, waiting to pull onto the highway. Only when he merged into the eastbound lane did she disappear behind the stucco wall of a gas station mini-mart. He wouldn't invite her to dinner. He wouldn't see her anytime soon, he swore. The next time their eyes met, his new life would be settled and thriving. She would barely recognize him.

By the time he reached the second stoplight, there came the empty feeling he'd expected, but with it was a lightheadedness, and he floated from one intersection to the next, past clusters of fast-food joints, car dealerships, Franco's Pizza Parlor struggling to stay in business, a row of furniture outlets. Ahead, yellow lights flashed atop construction vehicles, and the highway narrowed to a single lane. Orange-and-white barrels ticked past on his right, close enough for him to read the black letters stenciled on their sides: United Barricade. His foot seemed to press the brake pedal apart from him, his mind registering his actions only as his eyes took them in – I'm slowing, I'm stopping, I've stopped. The shout he'd been swallowing every morning for the past month came out softly with his breath, in harmless grunts. This was terrible, yes, but somehow not so terrible as yesterday or the day before. Why hadn't he left a month ago?

To his surprise, he found himself pulling off the highway, parking in front of Shop-Rite. Inside, with lights blaring from white walls and waxed floors, he strolled almost casually, nodding to the other men and women shopping alone. He filled a basket with things that wouldn't rot, the things he'd lived on in college: cans of chili and soup, a box of rice, six packages of ramen noodles for a buck twenty-five.

Then the enormous new apartment complex, hundreds of units in more than fifty identical buildings, his tucked away beside the stone sound barrier blocking the noise of the freeway. He forgot to slow down for speed bumps, and the cans of soup and chili knocked together, rustling the plastic bag. He inched his way into the tight parking space with his assigned number, and this is where he expected the lightness to leave him, his energy gone, head sinking against the steering wheel, only to rise hours later, stiff and cold, with the rising sun. But again, his body surprised him. His fingers searched out the door handle and snatched the bag of groceries. His feet carried him out of the truck, up the stairs, and then back down for the boxes in the bed.

The dim apartment was cluttered with the clothes he'd already brought, with second-hand furniture jumbled together in the center of the living room, nothing arranged. Soon, he'd have to decide where to place the velvety orange couch, the scuffed bridge table, the three yellow kitchen chairs whose plastic upholstery was permanently flattened with the imprint of an enormous backside, the sleek black lamp with no shade and no bulb. From the carpet – recently shampooed, according to the apartment manager – came the hairy smell of dog. He carried the groceries into the kitchen, took out a can of chili, and only when he began studying the instructions – *Empty contents into saucepan. Heat, stirring occasionally, until hot* – did he realize he had no can opener. A saucepan, yes, somewhere, in one of the boxes that would still smell of Robin's soap or airfreshener or sweat. A few dishes, two forks, a spoon and knife.

So he wouldn't eat chili tonight. Tomorrow, maybe. He could order a pizza, invite a friend to share it. But no, he hadn't yet bought a phone, or even called to have his service connected. He could skip dinner tonight. He wasn't so hungry. He sat on the orange couch, facing the bare wall and the unshaded window. Tomorrow he would eat plenty. Tomorrow he would buy a can opener, a phone, he would arrange his furniture. Outside, in the parking lot, a black Monte Carlo rumbled, its hood propped open. A teenager in baggy jeans, headphones around his neck, bent over the twisted steel and scratched the side of his head with a thumb. High above, a jet plunged into a ridge of pink clouds, which quickly turned purple. The apartment grew dark. Tomorrow he would buy light bulbs.

# Young Radicals

BY THIS TIME, SHORTLY BEFORE MY TWENTY-THIRD BIRTHDAY, my grandfather lived almost exclusively in the immediate present and the distant past. The last two months, two days, forget it. None of that existed for him. Not long before, my mother had spent a week in his condo. The moment she'd arrived at home, she called to let him know her flight had landed safely. "It was wonderful being in Florida," she said. "We're supposed to get snow here tomorrow." There was a moment of silence on the line, and then my grandfather's deep, rattling breath as he gathered air to shout. "You come to Florida and don't visit me! What kind of daughter are you?"

His second wife, Rose, spent most of her time trying to convince him of the things that had just happened to him. "Your grandson," she'd yell into his hearing aid. "Daniel. He just called. Don't you remember? He wished you a happy birthday." He'd shake his head vehemently. "No. My grandchildren never call me." She still let him drive, though he never had any idea where he was going. They'd be halfway to their favorite restaurant, an all-you-can-eat fish and ribs joint only three miles down a straight road, and without warning he'd screech onto the freeway entrance ramp. "Murray!" Rose would cry, grabbing the dash. "Where are you going?" He'd shift gears, weaving from lane to lane, gunning the car to eighty. "What's a matter with you?" he'd say. "We'll be late for our plane."

Whenever I called, it was safest not to ask any questions about how he was feeling or what he'd been doing since the last time we'd talked. Instead, I'd say something like, "What was the name of the village you were born in?" and then sit back and listen. In the span of fifteen minutes, he'd cover sixty years. Often, he ended up back at his first memory, the spring of 1917, a five-year-old on a steamer docking at Ellis Island. After three weeks in the choking dark of the steerage hold, he first glimpsed the land where his father and brother had already settled two years earlier to prepare a life for the family. But even at five years old, he knew he wouldn't be joining them now. Halfway across the ocean, his sister, a year older, had come down with a sudden sickness. Spots all over her face and arms, shivering no matter how many shawls his mother threw over her. When the ship turned around, back toward Russia, my grandfather stood at the rail watching the Statue of Liberty wave them away. He stayed with his sister the whole trip home, wiping the sweat from her eyes, holding a cup of water to her lips, but as soon as his mother's back was turned, he pulled the sick girl's hair and pinched her arm. By the time they docked in Bremen, his own case of chicken pox was just beginning to sprout across his chest and neck. The first ten days back in Europe he spent in quarantine, a blinding white hall filled with screaming children. "It was punishment," he told me once. "For hating my sister. Poor Dora. I always tell Hannah and Carol, 'Be good to each other. You're sisters. Nothing is worse than hating your own sister.' Yes. Punishment from God. I believed this, then." He laughed quickly, almost giggled. "It's before I was told that God is dead."

THE STORIES ABOUT HIM HAD BEGUN THE DAY I WAS OLD enough to listen. They'd come from my mother, mostly, and occasionally from my aunt and uncle. I was always enthralled by what they told me, torn by feelings of boldness and fear. My mother seemed to enjoy speaking of my grandfather's deep disappointment on returning to Russia, where the first of two revolutions had already taken place in his absence. His family made its way around trench lines to St. Petersburg, and then to the Belarus *shtetel* not far from the Polish border where, three months earlier, his mother had sold their house and furniture to buy their passage to America. They had no home, and my grandfather was sent away to the country, to live on the farm of a wealthy cousin. The cousin was cruel, my mother said, and though he had four extra bedrooms in his house, made my grandfather sleep in the barn with the cows he was to milk every morning. My grandfather worked in silence, speaking not a word to anyone all through the summer and the start of autumn. The cousin and his obese wife, the farmhands and peasants, everyone called him "the mute mouse," because he was small even for a six-year-old and wore a tattered brown coat that fell far past his knees. "Dumb as an onion," the cousin told anyone who so much as glanced in the boy's direction. But then came October, and with it another revolution followed shortly by armies marching from east and west. The farm was ravaged, the cruel cousin gutted in his own house, on the polished banquet table my grandfather had never seen. The hay on which he'd slept shot up in flames, coughing black smoke through the barn windows until the roof, with a wrenching cry, collapsed onto the sizzling cows. He watched all this, my mother said, from the steep bank of a half-frozen river, where he hugged a tree root to keep from tumbling into the current. He held back his tears and stifled his sniffling as an infantry regiment – White or Red he never knew – hurled bodies over his head to bob alongside the floating chunks of ice.

At least part of this can't be true. A member of my family a farmer, milking cows, tilling the soil? Not since the destruction of the Second Temple. I don't even know if Jews could have owned land in Russia at the start of 1917. At my brother's wedding, I took aside Aunt Carol, my mother's younger sister, and recited for her the story my mother had been telling for years. She'd had enough wine by then to let out a loud burst of laughter, and my mother peered at us from across the dance floor. "Hannah's full of it," Aunt Carol said. "Feinstein a farmer? He wasn't cruel. He was a banker. Not in the country, either. He took Pop to Minsk and gave him a nice comfortable bed. Until the pogrom. It's true, they did kill poor Feinstein and his wife. That's when Pop ended up in the river."

Uncle Virgil, the oldest of my grandfather's children, refused to believe the boy had been sent away at all. "The family stuck together," he told me at the same wedding. "They were poor, sure. But he was happy enough. Your mother and aunt, they're just being romantic." He'd never heard anything at all about a river.

Is it any wonder that my grandfather became a kind of role model for me, or at least the object of my imagination? After all, who else was there? My father's father was a pharmacist, born on the Lower East Side. He'd struggled plenty in his time, but I only knew him as a quiet, unassuming man who'd smoked cigars as long as my foot and then died when I was nine. My father himself was a chemist. He did cross the ocean once by boat: he and my mother in a luxurious cabin, sweating and nauseous, clinging to the soaked sheets of their berth. He never saw a war. At the start of Vietnam he was in graduate school, and during the height of the protests at home he was completing his postdoctoral work in Switzerland. Twenty-five years later he was only vaguely aware that strange things had happened while he was away.

It was only natural that as a boy I would imagine myself in the clothes of a Russian peasant, hugging a tree root for hours, the wet clay of a riverbank crumbling away beneath my feet until they dangled directly above swift, icy water. With my eyes closed, I could picture the black smoke drifting above the trees and fields in the distance, so thick that even though the soldiers had arrived at dawn I believed night was falling. Black ash coated the floating bodies, the ice, the shoulders of my woolen coat. I was frightened by the sight of my own hands, the skin blotchy and gray even as I rubbed them against the tree bark. Strange shapes passed close beneath my hanging legs, humped and dark, though luminous in spots, and I was prepared for one of the bodies to rise out of the water, grab my ankle, and pull me under. I prayed, not for the soldiers to go away, not to be home safe with my family, but only for the black dust to stop falling from the sky. For hours I dreamed myself in my grandfather's childhood, growing so desperate and exhausted I even began to cough and shiver with a slight fever. But no matter how much I might have wanted to, I couldn't bring myself to open my eyes and return to my own uneventful life.

At ten years old, I jumped at the chance to visit my grandfather over a school holiday. My father was attending a conference in Europe and offered to take my mother along. My brother decided to stay with a friend. It was the first time I would fly by myself, but even more important, it was the first time I would see my grandfather without the rest of my family to distract either of us. I sat near the front of the plane, and a stewardess checked on me every fifteen minutes, bringing as many Cokes as I could guzzle. She was pretty, though after her bright red lipstick smeared on her teeth, she no longer seemed as kind or caring. When we landed in Florida she led me into the terminal, and I ran to my grandfather and hugged him, wincing at the sharpness of his stubble against my cheek. The stewardess wasn't ready to let me go so easily. She demanded identification before officially turning me over. "Just look at him," my grandfather said, reluctantly handing her his driver's license. "How could he belong to anyone else? He has my ears."

My grandmother was still alive then, though completely blind in one eye. To a doctor she complained of faint shadows beginning to creep into the other. The diabetes had already taken the toes from both her feet, and with difficulty she hobbled around the condo on two canes. I saw her only at meals, and my memory of her is hazy. She had large eyes, slightly bulging, and a gap between her front teeth, but these things I may know from photographs. If nothing else, I clearly recall the smell of gauze and the way she rubbed gently at the dirt she thought she saw on my neck and behind my ears.

My grandfather tried to keep me out of her way as much as possible. We spent a lot of time in his car, in hardware stores, on the shuffleboard courts. There was a fierceness about his moods, whether playful or brooding or irritable, that kept me on edge the entire week. Now it's easy to see why. He was seventy, watching his wife of forty-eight years – she was just nineteen when they married – taken away in pieces by a disease he refused to understand no matter how many times a doctor tried to explain it. And she, who'd never wanted to move to Florida, blaming him for letting her die so far from her family. At the time, though, I was certain of being the center of all his impatience. He was disappointed in me. As a grandson, I didn't stack up. Consequently, I fought for his approval, boasting nervously about whatever came to mind. I'd recently finished my second season of Little League, and as we strolled through a supermarket – my grandfather dropping into his basket anything that caught his eye: pickled onions, coffee ice cream, a baby eggplant, semi-sweet chocolate chips – I told him my coach said I was improving every day, that in two years I would try out for the middle school team. I was a pitcher, but any speed my fastball had wore off after two innings, and my control was fitful. I had little chance of ever making the middle school team, and when the time actually came I didn't even bother showing up for tryouts. Even as I was talking, I only half-believed my own words. But when my grandfather wrapped his thumb and forefinger around my bicep and said, "Who can throw with arms like these?" I put on an expression of genuine hurt and went so far as to let my eyes water. "Don't worry," he said. "A little meat. That's all you need."

I hung my head. "Maybe I should just give up."

Only after a moment did I raise my eyes. His smile was gone, his brows arched. He whispered something in Yiddish that sounded like "go fall." Slowly his voice began to rise. Up and down the aisle heads turned to watch. "Give up? No grandson of mine. You keep trying and trying." He grabbed my elbow and dragged me past jars of pasta sauce and cans of pork and beans, past the fish counter and the bakery. In the produce aisle he rushed to a display of oranges and sifted madly through one crate after another. "Is this size of a baseball?" he said. "Tell me."

"A little bigger," I said. "But Grandpa –"

"This one?"

I nodded.

"Good," he said, and handed it to me. "Now, show me your throw."

"In the store? I can't – "

"Show!" he said, pointing down a long row of coolers to a pair of heavy canvas doors. A stockboy stood off to the side watching us – in disbelief, I guess, because he didn't say a word. The doors were swaying gently in a breeze blowing in from the loading bays. Sprinklers hissed above the lettuce and zucchini, and a cool spray tickled my cheek. I held the orange in three fingers and shrugged. Why shouldn't I throw it if my grandfather told me to? If I had his ears? If I could have, had I been born seventy years earlier, watched dead bodies floating in a half-frozen river? Why shouldn't I do whatever I pleased? I left aside my ordinary, conservative wind-up. Instead, feeling inspired, I thought of baseball games I'd watched on TV and went for a combination of Steve Carlton and Tom Seaver, arms snapping over my head, a leg-kick up to my chest, my back knee sweeping no more than an inch from the shiny, waxed floor. My flat-soled sneaker slid along the tiles, a pain wrenched through my groin, and then I was in a sitting position, my head resting against a rack of stringbeans. The orange, it seemed, had slipped from my fingers sometime before I fell and shot straight up, cracking a fiberglass ceiling panel and thumping in a ring of its own juice not far from my feet. By now the stockboy was running at us, calling, "Are you people out of your minds?" But already my grandfather had me beneath the arms and was lifting me to my feet. In my ear he whispered, "Time to go now, tatala." Out loud he said, "You call that a ripe orange? A crime at these prices." In the parking lot he ruffled my hair and said, "You keep trying and trying. A little practice, a little meat, that's all you need."

AT THE END OF THE SAME WEEK, A DAY BEFORE I WAS TO FLY back to New Jersey, he took me fishing from a concrete pier, the best spot in Florida, he claimed. The water was opaque and sickly green except where swirling oil spots shimmered on the slack waves. What could I possibly catch here? From the start I was skeptical. My grandfather cut strips of squid and stuck them on my hook, and while I watched my bobber, at first with a measure of excitement and then with growing boredom, he chased seagulls away from our bait. After an hour I hadn't felt a single nibble and started to complain. My grandfather only shook his head and crossed his arms. "Mackerel, snapper, sea bass," he said. "Every one I caught from this very spot. Don't tell me good, not good. It's the fisherman catches or don't catch the fish."

I didn't see how it could be my fault. He was the one putting bait on my hook. All I did was stare at the water and wait. But instead of arguing, I threw out my line again, and this time, finally, a tug. The drag made a whizzing sound, and I worked the reel as fast as my hand would turn. "Watch him jump," my grandfather said, but nothing jumped. I yanked the rod, and an enormous blue crab flew out of the water and fell onto the concrete with an angry clack. It turned a full circle and then scuttled straight toward me. I dropped the rod and backed to the ledge, ready, if necessary, to dive into the filmy water. But my grandfather was beside me in an instant, stepping on the crab's shell, sawing off its pincers with the knife he'd been using to slice the squid. He held it in the air, its legs scrambling for something solid, eyes straining on alien stalks, and tapped its underside with the knife's plastic handle. "Not a fish," he said. "But not bad. Crab salad for dinner."

The pincers lay open at my feet, ready to snap. Where they'd once been attached to the crab, white, fleshy fibers trailed an inch along the concrete. I felt queasy and didn't want to think at all about eating, especially not something that didn't die when you pulled out its arms. But at the same time, my heart was racing. I was going to catch something else, a crab, a fish, a stingray, I didn't care what. For my next cast, I bent my knees, swung the rod with two hands over my shoulder, and jerked with all my strength. But the line didn't follow. Behind I heard a swallowed groan and turned slowly to see the hook snagged in the base of my grandfather's thumb. Blood streamed into his palm, and the slimy strip of squid dangled to his wrist. For ten minutes he worked the barb through skin and muscle, grinding his teeth. Not once did he look at me, though I hovered close, ready to cry the moment he did. Seagulls swarmed over our bait, flapping boldly past our ears. When the hook was free, he packed the tackle box and picked up the bucket in which the crab was scratching and clicking in a frenzy. Finally, he turned to me. I waited for the explosion of anger, the words he would later apologize for – "Can't you ever be careful?" or "You're clumsy just like your father!" – and my lips trembled. But he only rubbed his chin, the callused fingers against his stubble as loud as sandpaper on knotted wood, and said, "You've got a lot to learn, boychik. A lot to learn."

Learn about what? Fishing? Hooking someone's finger? This was the worst thing he could have said to me. I was only ten years old. Of course I had a lot to learn. But even then, I knew I could never learn the things he wanted me to. How could I? I didn't grow up in Russia. I would never cross the ocean in a steerage hold. I'd never cling to the bank of a frozen river or watch a dead body float past. Tears welled in my eyes, and as I wiped them away I swore I would never again pick up a fishing pole. And later, back in the condo, while my grandfather dropped the crab, still alive and struggling, into a pot of boiling water, and my grandmother hobbled into the kitchen on two canes and two stumps wrapped in bandages, I swore even more fervently never, never to come to Florida again.

FOR YEARS I KEPT MY VOW. BUT EVEN THOUGH I DIDN'T VISIT, I still saw him at least twice a year, at bar mitzvahs and weddings and at Aunt Carol's midsummer barbecue. And he was often in my thoughts as I graduated from high school and began to think about what a person should do with his life. My grandfather had painted houses for a living, inside and out. Houses all over New Haven and up and down the Long

Island Sound. From seven in the morning to seven at night he painted, and in the evenings and on Sundays he built custom, natural-wood picture frames. He retired at sixty with more money than, as a young boy, he'd dreamed existed in the entire world. But even after his retirement he didn't sit still for a minute. At his condo he poured concrete for the shuffleboard courts and put up an equipment shed in a single day. At seventy he built the porch at my parents' house and painted our trim. Long past eighty he acted as head maintenance man in his building, repairing air conditioners, oiling squeaking cabinets, recaulking bathroom tiles, all for no pay. At eighty-six he stood for a whole day in the hot sun supervising a crew tarring the building's roof. "You don't keep an eye on them, they cut thirty corners on a six-sided brick," he told Rose that evening, exhausted, unable to lift his head from the sofa cushion.

The summer between my sophomore and junior years of college, I took a job with a student painting crew. At the interview, when asked if I had any experience, I told the crew boss about my grandfather, how he'd taught me the trade from an early age, though in truth I'd never once asked to learn, and he'd never offered to teach. The night before I was to start, I called him. "I'm following in your footsteps," I said, and waited for some quiet sign of pride.

"Painting?" he said. "Oh, tatala, it's hard work. I wouldn't wish on my enemies a hot day with those fumes. Make sure you wear a hat."

At the end of the first week, after we'd prepped and puttied and were ready to prime, the crew boss patted me on the back and said, "Okay, Daniel. You've got some experience. Why don't you take the trim on the north side. We'll let the new guys keep their feet on the ground for now." It was a two-story house, and on the north side the ground dipped a good ten feet lower than in front or back. I struggled to raise a thirty-foot ladder, but even fully extended it came five or six feet short of the trim. I hadn't once thought about ladders. I'd pictured myself in my grandfather's white overalls splotched with colors, steaming with the smell of sweat and turpentine, but not once had my imagination taken me through an actual day's work. I'd had no idea how sore my shoulders and back would be after forty-five minutes of sanding and scraping. And now I had no idea how it would feel to climb two and a half stories above the ground and then let go of the rails in order to paint the trim. Halfway up the ladder, a bucket of primer dangling from one side of my belt, a roller and brush clipped to the other, I gagged and had to take the next few steps with my eyes closed. At the top, I hugged a rung and rested my head against the wooden siding. Wood! What century were we living in? Hadn't these people heard of aluminum? What kind of barbaric, primitive system was this, to heave someone thirty feet in the air and expect him to paint your eaves?

To my left, hanging beneath the gutter, a papery nest crawled with angry-looking, black-and-yellow wasps. Directly above my head, a tangle of buzzing wires sagged from the house to a nearby telephone pole. The ladder's rubber caps bounced softly against the siding, and I was sure I hadn't wedged its feet firmly enough in the ground. I'll go down, I thought, I'll go down just to check the footing, but then the crew boss, cheery and blond and already tan though the summer had just begun, rounded the corner and started to prime the first floor window trim. He had experience! Why wasn't he on a ladder?

Even with an extension pole, my roller didn't reach the peak of the eaves. I wasn't about to stand on the highest, or even second-highest rung, so I just closed my eyes, raised the roller above my head, and let the paint go where it would. The smell of my sweat surprised me: it was ripe and feral, almost exactly the same as my grandfather's. This smell belonged to him, I'd always believed, belonged to hard work and a long life. But on me, it was the smell of terror. A few drops of cool liquid fell on my forehead and neck – the primer, I assumed, splashing wildly. But even when I paused my rolling, there was another drop and another, and I opened my eyes onto dark clouds and a mounting drizzle. The blotchy patch of primer I'd rolled was already streaking down the siding like milky tears. From below, the crew boss called, "That's it, Daniel. Can't paint in this. We'll get it tomorrow."

In the morning I called him to say I had a family emergency and was leaving town for the rest of the summer. That afternoon I applied for a job as a picture-framer in a crafts shop. "My grandfather taught me how to frame as a kid," I said during the interview, but then added quickly, "It's been a while. You might have to refresh my memory."

FOR MY FIRST THREE AND A HALF YEARS OF COLLEGE, I MAJORED in marketing. I wrote sample ad copy for Adidas and designed a model five-year plan for Fuji Film. Using a stack of overhead transparencies, I made a presentation on Saab's failed market strategy in the U.S. to a panel of auto-industry representatives. At the end of my junior year, I won a $250 scholarship from a high-profile Manhattan agency, the same agency who, when I applied for an internship the following semester, took three months to send back a form-letter rejection with four typos in two lines of text.

I was sharing a house with two friends, both of whom had serious girlfriends they were planning to marry within six months of graduation. Already, their conversations centered around golf and 401K plans. Late at night, when both couples had disappeared into their bedrooms, I carried the remains of a six-pack to the living room couch and flipped through seventy-six cable channels, searching for commercials. At first, I did it with a pad and pen in my lap, taking notes and trying to predict which ads would hit big and which would get cut after a week's run. But soon I did nothing but guzzle beer and stare at the flashing faces, numbed by the aggressive strings of senseless phrases. Most of the spots used music that had nothing to do with the products they were selling, not even in mood or tone, and some had no product at all: the slope of a mountain, a close up of fallen pine cones, the screeching soar of an eagle, a silver car logo on a black background. I turned from the TV to my marketing textbooks and heard my grandfather's voice: "This is supposed to mean something?"

A week into spring semester of what should have been my senior year, without consulting anybody, I dropped my course in Advanced Business Management and registered for Survey of World Revolutions. Two months later, when I officially switched my major to history – with a concentration on Russia from the freedom of the serfs to the rise of Stalin – I did so against the protests of my professors, my friends, my family. It would take me an extra year and two summers to graduate, and in their eyes this was worse than wasted time. My advisor pulled out all the forms he'd filed for me over the past three years. He kept blinking and rubbing his forehead and, shuffling the papers, reminded me how many hours he'd spent on them. He looked genuinely insulted, as if he'd done all this work as a personal favor and none of it was part of his job. My roommates accused me of not wanting to pitch in for the graduation party we'd planned for May, and though I insisted I'd still be glad to help, they spent the rest of the semester wondering out loud how the two of them would ever pay for all the kegs we'd ordered.

My mother was a different story altogether. She tried to forbid my decision outright, threatening to stop paying my tuition. In return, I threatened to take out a loan and live the rest of my life in squalor. Quickly, she conjured a picture of what I would look like in ten years, poring over the brittle pages of esoteric texts or hand-printing subversive newsletters in a barren loft above a gun shop: she saw me with Lenin's bald head, Trotsky's glasses, a long beard – she couldn't decide between Che Guevara's and Ho Chi Minh's – and Chairman Mao's stony, joyless expression. She was convinced the FBI had started a file on me the moment I'd signed up for a class about socialism. It didn't matter that the Berlin Wall had come down nearly five years earlier. "What kind of jobs are there for history majors?" she asked constantly. I told her I wanted to teach, but though she'd spent the majority of her life as a high-school French teacher, this didn't persuade her of anything. "Did you ever notice all your professors wear patches on their elbows?" she asked. "That's not fashion. New suits cost a lot of money." Once, her voice trembled with hope as she ventured, "Anita Feldman's daughter was a history major. She's in law school now. Have you ever considered law?"

After several explosive phone conversations, we both relented. She sent a check for my summer classes, and I promised to keep marketing as my minor. The following spring, she spoke to the friend of a friend whose husband had recently started an ad agency in Morristown, only a fifteen-minute drive from my parents' house. After a single interview he offered me a job, and, vowing to work there only a year while I applied to graduate school, I accepted. At the end of the summer I'd move back to New Jersey and return to writing copy that hawked running shoes, sport utility vehicles, adult diapers. My mother was thrilled and, as congratulations, offered to send me to Europe for two weeks before I was to start working. Only then did I hear my grandfather's voice again, whispering, "You call this meaning?" Only then did I have the feeling I'd somehow been tricked.

In the meantime, I began to call my grandfather more frequently, twice a month rather than my ordinary five times a year. I listened intently to his stories, holding in my lap the same pad and pen I'd once used to make notes about TV commercials. He spoke of the years leading up to his second boat trip to America, and I scribbled madly. My mother had never gone into detail about this period of his life. At sixteen, she'd told me, he ended up in St. Petersburg, then called Leningrad, as an art student. But that was it. The rest I had to wait twenty-two years to hear from his own mouth: this was the mid-1920s, the Revolution's heyday, and like most other young men and women at the time, my grandfather was caught up in the fever of progress, of community, of ecstatic hope, of the unprecedented freedoms for Jews like himself with an allegiance to the cause of the worker. He joined a Youth Brigade and proudly wore a Communist Party pin on his lapel. In the afternoons, following his classes, he volunteered to help paint factories. He never learned a word of Marx or Lenin but could, nearly seventy years later, sing Bolshevik work songs by heart, his Russian deep and clear, his voice youthful and somewhat ominous.

And along with politics, I imagined, there was a girl. He never told me this – and, of course, neither did my mother – but I sensed it in his tone, painfully nostalgic as he described his subsidized room above a butcher's shop, the sincere greetings from comrades he met in the street, the small gatherings in a teacher's apartment, full of intensity and energy and vodka. A girl lingered at the edges of everything he recalled. She was Russian, I guessed, or Ukranian. Certainly not Jewish. At large brigade meetings he pulled his chair close to hers, letting his knuckles brush against her bare arm. He stared at the shapeless leg of her drab work pants, picturing the curve of her calf, the sticky crease behind her knee, the soft down on her thigh, ignoring the words of the speaker on stage, the enthusiastic roar of the crowd. And afterward, she'd accompany him to his room and praise his paintings, which, she said, evoked the spirit of the new era. In the dim winter light, barely brightened by a single desk lamp resting on the floor for lack of a desk, they'd discuss the ways in which the Revolution had shattered traditional, bourgeois views of morality, and the girl would arrange the sheets on my grandfather's narrow mattress.

So when, just after his seventeenth birthday, his father unexpectedly summoned him, a curt note explaining that he'd finally saved enough money to once again bring the entire family to America, my grandfather wept openly in the telegraph office and howled in despair on the street. He didn't want to leave the Youth Brigade, the room above the butcher, drafty as it might be. He especially didn't want to leave the girl who, I imagined, waited in his bed. He was terrified by stories he'd read in all the pamphlets and newspapers about corruption in the heart of capitalism. But more than anything, he didn't want suddenly to become a Jew again, ready on a moment's notice to flee his home or else burn alive. "But what could I do?" he asked me over the phone, his voice more somber, more resigned than I'd ever heard it. "This was my family. Could I refuse? I didn't believe so, not then. I had no choice. Family calls, you go to your family."

I pictured him explaining this to the girl, on his knees, tugging at her shirt as she tried to turn away. "*We* are your family," she said. "The workers. The Party. Me." When he begged her to come with him, she cursed him and called him a traitor. He told her he would never love another woman, that after the Revolution made its way across the ocean and brought the world together in a harmony of peace, prosperity, and equality, he would return to her. He would come back, yes, if only she promised to wait. She laughed bitterly and wiped away her tears. "The old morality is dead," she said. "I won't wait a day."

For an upper division political history course, I wrote a paper entitled "Jews and the New Economic Policy: A Taste of Freedom," weaving bits of narrative from my grandfather's life with theories and analyses I'd stolen from a variety of reliable sources. My professor was impressed enough to read sections out loud to the class. And on my way out of the lecture hall, I was stopped by a girl with loosely clumped dreadlocks drooping over a shirt that might have been an old quilt torn in half. Her face was round and clean and didn't seem to belong at all with her clothes or hair. "I'd like to read the rest of that," she said, touching my elbow. I felt a quick thrill at the sight of the stud in her tongue and tried to catch another glimpse as she went on about tearing down the walls of misconception. "You really captured the spirit of the time, I think," she said, and I didn't care that neither of us could possibly have known what the spirit of the time was really like. I handed her my paper covered in the professor's scribbles of praise. She gave me a flyer and invited me to join the campus Young Radicals. "We're meeting tomorrow night," she said. "Hope I see you there."

This was why I'd switched majors! There was no doubt in my mind I'd made the right decision. Could I have gotten this kind of attention in marketing? For witty ad copy or innovative public relations strategy? Not a chance. That night I called my grandfather and begged him to tell me more about Leningrad, the Youth Brigade, about painting factories. "Bernard?" he said, speaking to a cousin buried on Long Island four years earlier. "Is that you?"

"It's Daniel," I said. "Your grandson."

"You think about it, Bernard. This woman, I don't know about her."

"Your Brigade meetings," I said, hoping to redirect the flow of his memory. "They were held in an old church, weren't they?"

"Marriage," he said. "It's no joke. Sometimes you don't marry the first woman you shtup."

I thanked him for his advice and laid the receiver down.

MY MOTHER NEVER THOUGHT HIGHLY OF WHAT I WROTE ABOUT her father, no matter what my professor might have said. I didn't tell her about my invitation to join the Young Radicals. I went to only one meeting and struggled to stay awake through two long speeches about our commitments in the upcoming local elections and a heated argument over where to hold the spring picnic. The girl with the dreadlocks didn't show up. She didn't come back to class, either, and I never again saw my paper with the professor's comments. But I did send a fresh copy to my mother, who called me the instant she finished it. "Tell me you didn't let anybody read this," she said.

"Of course I did."

"Wonderful. My son wants the whole world to know his grandfather was a Communist."

I laughed. "Come on, Mom. The Cold War's over. Communism's back in fashion. And anyway, nobody cares what happened in 1927."

"It's none of anybody's business," she said.

"People should know the truth."

"This isn't the truth." Across the phone line I could hear my paper being crumpled. In the background, my father called out, "I thought it was very good, Daniel." But my mother kept on, "This has nothing to do with who your grandfather really is."

I tried not to be bothered by what she said. I struggled to remember the words my professor had scratched in red beneath my bibliography: his "insightful" against my mother's "exploiting," his "honest" against her "disrespectful," his "supple prose" against her "shallow and naïve."

What kind of truth did she want? I could have written about her first dance – this I'd heard from Aunt Carol – when she was supposed to have met my grandfather in front of the school promptly at ten o'clock. At 10:03 she was still dancing, and my grandfather stormed into the gym, shouting above the music, "Hannah! Hankele! Who took my daughter?" When he caught a glimpse of her, swaying slowly, her chin resting on a boy's shoulder, his face went first pale with relief and then red with anger, and he nearly broke the boy's wrist, yanking his arm from around her waist. Was this what she wanted people to know?

Above all else, I made myself believe my grandfather would appreciate what I was doing. This was the best thing anybody could do for him, to make people remember his life as it had actually happened. I considered sending him a copy of the paper, or at least explaining it to him over the phone, but then decided against it. He was too far gone, I reasoned. I didn't want to confuse him further. Instead, I'd trust my instincts. But still, for my next assignment, I wrote a bland essay full of theories and analyses, without any narrative, and received an unenthusiastic B+.

All my mother's objections dropped away, however, the minute I suggested I'd like to visit my grandfather over Memorial Day weekend, between my second senior year and my final summer classes. "Oh, honey," she said. "It'll make him so happy. And who knows how many more chances …?" She'd be glad, she said, to buy me a ticket with her frequent flier miles. That day I bought a miniature tape recorder and three packs of cassettes. I'd record enough material to chronicle his entire life, I told myself, and maybe even write an honors thesis that would pave my way into a highly rated graduate program.

The night before my flight I barely slept, rolling in my tangled sheets until gray light began to seep around the army blanket I tacked over my window for a shade. I was groggy walking down the gangway into the Ft. Lauderdale airport. This, I'm sure, added to my shock at the sight of my grandfather, so much shorter than I remembered, bent over a cane, the sparse hair beneath a bright blue fishing hat now completely white. I'd seen him only a year ago, at my brother's wedding. But in the interval he might have aged five years, or maybe more. Beside him, Rose, always cheerful and jittery, seemed especially nervous, fingers jumping from her enormous pink-tinted glasses to her slacks to her glasses again, already anticipating the terrifying drive home, I suspected. I hugged them both quickly. My grandfather's cane bumped awkwardly against the back of my leg. He kissed me on both cheeks, the same rough stubble that had scared me as a boy scraping my skin, though now my own stubble scraped back just as sharply. He pointed to the book in my hand. "White like a fish and always reading," he said. "Just like his father. Someday you'll grow gills."

No matter how many times I offered, he insisted on driving. Rose chattered the whole way, interrupting herself only to navigate: "That's the golf course where Jackie Gleason used to play," she said. "Left here, Murray. I saw him five times, at least. I waved once, and I think he saw me. The next exit, Murray. No, the next exit. We're going home, remember? Our neighbor, she knows Neil Simon and Arthur Miller. No fooling. She grew up with them on Long Island, her husband was a carpet salesman. He sold carpets to the Millers, you know, when Arthur was married to Marilyn Monroe. Once, Marilyn spilled red wine on the carpet and called Irma crying, 'He'll kill me. I know he will. You've got to get me a new rug.' And Irma, she said, 'Marilyn, now listen –' Straight! We're going home. Home, Murray."

"I know where I'm going," my grandfather said, softly, somewhat hoarse. "What's a matter with you? You think I'm crazy, I don't know?"

By the time we made it to the condo, my hand was sore from clenching the door handle, and my jaw ached. I was exhausted and wanted nothing more than to lie down for half an hour. But my grandfather insisted on showing me off to all the neighbors who hadn't seen me in such a long time and wouldn't believe how tall I'd grown, even if I was still too skinny. As soon as I dropped my suitcase, he led me down the hall and knocked on doors. I stood with an awkward smile as one old woman after another clutched her bathrobe and stepped back in fear at the sight of a rumpled young man with bloodshot eyes lurking in the corridor. I wished, at least, he would have given me time to brush my hair, which must have been oily and matted on the side. "My grandson," he said to each neighbor. "Come to visit me. He started his own business." And lowering his voice, he added, "Computers."

"That's my brother," I explained.

"He's a good boy," my grandfather said. "Tell him he should move to Florida. The girls, they'd go wild."

When there were no more doors to knock on, we sat by the pool for a game of gin. He shuffled the cards with difficulty, his brown, hairy fingers slipping over their corners or sticking to their glossy backs. "My hands," he said. "Daniel, my hands. They used to do so much. Now. Why should a man live if he can't use his hands?"

Rose, sitting nearby, heard what he said. She lifted her glasses and pretended to blow her nose, holding the tissue in front of her eyes. My grandfather leaned forward, chest against the table, to look me in the face. He extended an arm, then hesitated a moment, and let it fall. I fingered the tape recorder in my pocket and said in a rush, "In Leningrad, what kind of factories did you paint?"

He slumped back in his seat and held his hands in front of him, shaking his head. "He wants to know about painting. I'll tell you painting. Fifteen years I worked for my brother. Nineteen twenty-nine to nineteen forty-four. You know what he paid me? Might as well be nothing."

"I meant in Leningrad," I said.

"My brother didn't live in Leningrad."

"I didn't ask about your brother."

"A lazy man, my brother," he said. "Let anybody at all put up the scaffolding. I watched a painter fall and die. My brother cried the whole night, but that was enough for me. In the morning I said so long." Now he was off, and there was no stopping him. Soon, he told me, he'd started his own business with a partner, a man who stank. This was just after my mother had been born, when Uncle Virgil was a toddler. The man's name was Harvey, and he drank whiskey from a flask from morning until night. Never would you see him without a cigarette dangling from his lips. His breath was a sour cloud that followed him from room to room, and his sweat, always gleaming on his balding head and darkening a stripe down the back of his shirt, fumed with a tinge of vomit. My grandfather had recently bought his first car, and every morning drove Harvey to the job site. He, too, smoked then, ten to twenty hand-rolled cigarettes a day, but neither his own strong tobacco nor the cold wind blowing through the lowered windows could cover the stench filling his new Oldsmobile. He'd been planning to drive the whole family to Florida in February, but how could he take them anywhere when the seats, the dashboard, the steering wheel, everything smelled like Harvey?

This wasn't the story I'd been hoping for, and I listened impatiently, waiting for some link to his revolutionary past. But though I didn't hide my fidgeting, he went on without pausing: one morning, the smell was making him woozy, and the road before him began to blur. "Listen, Harvey," he said. "One or the other. The drinking or the smoking. Like this a man can't live. One of them, it's got to go."

"What about you?" Harvey said, leaning so close my grandfather had to hold his breath. "You smoke them things all day long. You think you're better than me? You'll live forever?"

My grandfather stared for a moment at the glowing end of his cigarette and, with a shrug, flicked it out the window. "I'm finished," he said. Next went his half-full tobacco pouch and a packet of rolling papers. "And you?"

Their gazes locked, just for as long as my grandfather could keep from glancing at the road. Only a few seconds, but something important passed between them. In Harvey's deep-set, reddish eyes, my grandfather saw fear and understanding. For the briefest of moments, he didn't notice the man's smell. Then, Harvey reached into his pocket for the flask.

"He poured it out the window," I interrupted, suddenly so bored and disappointed I could no longer hold back. The surge of anger surprised me, but I was glad to have it. Why such sentimentality after all the raw and exciting details of a dying Russia and a young Soviet Union? Why now, when I'd flown so far to visit him? "He threw away his cigarettes, too," I said, with a wave of my hand. "He stopped smelling."

"No, no!" my grandfather said. He was out of his chair immediately, standing without his cane. His fist came down on the table, hard enough to topple the stacked deck of cards. My breath caught in my chest. "What's this crazy you're talking? He stank. He always stank. He never gave up anything. I made him buy his own car. And then he stole from me, I ran him out of town. The whiskey killed him one day, that's my guess." Now, he lowered his voice and dropped slowly back to his chair, his knees quivering visibly with the strain. "A terrible human being," he said. "But he saved my life. He knew he did, I think so. For that, I'm grateful forever. You know how it would be with a black hole in my lung? I'll tell you, tatala, never pick up those cigarettes. Learn one thing from an old man. This I'm telling you."

ALL DAY I DID NOTHING BUT EAT. PISTACHIO NUTS AND POTATO chips, a turkey sandwich and yogurt, two and a half mangoes. When it came to food, my grandfather was the most generous person I'd ever known. The moment anyone entered his home he'd begin with, "You're hungry? Please, eat. Just a bite. Don't say a word until you've eaten. You won't offend me. Only skinniness offends me." He'd always stayed too active to get heavy, but he'd ruined his teeth on the hard candies he kept overflowing from bowls on every end table in the condo. Every Hanukkah, he sent me a crate of grapefruits and oranges – with a note that read "not for throwing" – that lasted me well into February. His favorite restaurants were all-you-can-eat because, he'd explain as a waiter offered more shrimp or ribs or salad or bread, "this is what a person deserves."

At four-fifteen in the afternoon, he announced that we were going to dinner. He dressed in his white linen suit and brown satin shirt with butterfly collar and embroidered gold stitching. For six months in the early eighties, after my grandmother had died and a year of mourning had passed, he'd been a real man on the town. He'd gone to nightclubs at retirement communities from Boca Raton to Miami Beach. He organized a dance in the clubhouse of his own condo. He even called my mother twice to find out recipes for hors-d'œuvres and asked what kind of drinks nice ladies would enjoy. But then, in the food court at the local mall, he ran into Rose, the close friend of a woman he'd known in New Haven. She'd recently lost her husband and was renting a condo for the winter. She hadn't yet decided whether or not she liked Florida. "What's not to like?" my grandfather said, gesturing at the food court's pastel walkway and neon signs, at the bright patch of blue through the skylights overhead. He smoothed his remaining hair, still a dark gray, and smiled. "What else could you want?" Within a year they were married, and my grandfather stopped buying new clothes.

And now, when I came out of the guest room, he looked me up and down. "What's a matter? You got no money to go shopping?" I was wearing a pair of khaki shorts and a blue knit shirt with a collar. It was four-thirty in the afternoon, ninety-seven degrees outside, and we were going to The Olive Garden. I already felt overdressed. "Come with me," he said. "I'll find you something nice."

I followed him into the bedroom, protesting. Rose was standing in front of the closet mirror straightening the neck of a silvery dress. Her hair was coifed and shiny, slightly purplish when she tilted into the sunlight beating through the drawn blinds. "All right, boychikul," my grandfather said. "I'll show you how we dress to go out to dinner." From the closet he took a checkered red and white jacket with shoulder pads. It would have made an ugly cover for a picnic table. There was no way I was putting it anywhere near my body. He held it out and laughed. "Remember, Rose? The cruise to Freeport. We danced all night on the ship."

"That wasn't me, Murray," Rose said.

"It got cold. You wore this jacket over your shoulders."

"That was Clara," Rose said.

"Really, Grandpa," I said. "I don't need a jacket."

"Don't need a jacket? What's a matter with you?"

"Kids dress different today," Rose said. "He'll look like an old-timer in your jacket."

"You want my grandson to look like a bum?"

"He's not a bum," Rose said.

"Not a bum?" He was shouting now. He might have forgotten I was in the room. It only occurred to me a few hours later that this was how he must have reacted every time I got off the phone with him. "Does he have a job? Has he ever worked a whole week? Twenty-three years in school! That I call a bum." As he spoke, he waved his arms wildly, and the jacket slipped from the hanger onto the bed. I picked it up and quietly put it on. Immediately, I began sweating. Soon, my grandfather ran out of breath and gasped deeply, a hand on his chest. Rose went to him and gently patted his back. When he recovered, he glanced at me and brightened. "This is my boy! All ready? Doesn't he look good, Rosey? Like a real man. I remember when you held that jacket tight around your neck. We watched the sun rise over the water."

On the way out of the condo, I dropped the tape recorder into my suitcase. For the rest of the weekend, it lay where it had fallen. At dinner, to my grandfather's delight, I ate three salads and seven breadsticks and agreed to take home the remains of my lasagna for a late-night snack.

IN ANOTHER FOUR MONTHS, HE WOULD BE DEAD AND I'D BE floating through Europe, long past the time I was supposed to have begun working for the ad agency in Morristown. My mother begged me to come home for the funeral, but I refused. My grandfather wouldn't have wanted me to give up my travels, I argued. This was a once in a lifetime opportunity, and if I came home, I'd have to stay. What I didn't want to tell her was that I'd sold my return ticket and couldn't possibly buy a new one. Not with the seventeen dollars in Hungarian forints stuffed into the toe of a putrid sock, my entire stash at the time. Instead I spent a night alone in a tiny hotel room, bawling into a cardboard-thin pillow whose starched cover scratched my face as roughly as my grandfather's beard.

A month and a half before this, I finally graduated with a degree in history. I didn't write an honors thesis, and my grades would get me into only the most mediocre of graduate schools. Because it was summer, there was no commencement ceremony, and on the day of my last exam, my brother's wife gave birth to a baby girl. Nobody came to visit or called to congratulate me. I didn't expect my grandfather to remember, but I dialed him, hoping to tell someone what I'd accomplished, even if he didn't understand me at all. Rose answered. "That's wonderful, Daniel," she said. "Good for you. I'll be sure to tell Grandpa. He's lying down now. Doesn't feel so hot." The next morning, my mother left four messages on my answering machine, the first apologetic, the second condescending, the third annoyed, the fourth indignant: how could I ruin such a happy time for the whole family? How could I be so selfish? The entire morning I sat in a low chair staring bitterly at the machine's blinking red light. Forget this family, I thought. I'd never be like my brother, my mother, or her father. On purpose, I decided, I'd never do a thing in my life to make them proud.

But on the day before I was to leave Florida for the last time, I sat with my grandfather beside his condo's pool, more relaxed than I'd felt since first dropping my courses in marketing. The shadow of a huge umbrella kept us cool, though there was rarely a breeze. We both held hands of gin, but neither of us had played a card for nearly an hour. Rose was asleep on a lounge chair beside us, close enough for my grandfather to rest his knuckles on her shoulder. In the pool, an obese, white-haired man was doing laps, breaststroke toward us, backstroke away. Two old ladies in bathing caps sat on the steps with their feet in the water, and by the diving board, a young woman, somebody's granddaughter, lay in a bikini on the bare concrete, her slim feet, pale an hour earlier, already noticeably red.

My grandfather was speaking leisurely, without any prompting. From one minute to the next he mistook me for somebody different, but I wasn't bothered. I'd worn his checkered jacket in public. I'd eaten all the food he'd placed in front of me, and now I sat with my shorts unbuttoned, the zipper halfway down, perfectly calm. I'd been broken, I guess, or else had nothing left to prove. And maybe neither did my grandfather, though this wouldn't have occurred to me at the time. Maybe, for the first time, he felt in my presence the ease I'd never thought to seek out in his.

For a while he talked about his grandchildren. "Jared," he said, lighting on my brother. "A very sensitive boy. So serious, so shy, but so smart. One day he'll sprout wings, you wait."

"I wonder what he'll be like as a father," I said.

"A father? Too far away to tell."

"They're expecting the baby in August."

"Jared can't have a baby," my grandfather said. "He's too young."

"He's twenty-eight."

"Twenty-eight?"

"He will be some day," I said.

My grandfather sighed heavily. "Yes, a smart boy. But that Daniel. Him I worry about. He doesn't know who he wants to be." Soon he was talking about his own children, with puzzlement and a hint of sadness. "I tried hard with Virgil. Too hard, maybe so. He loves me, his wife, his children, I know this. But from fifteen miles away when he's standing face to face. And Carol. Everything for her. Going to the bank, taking a vacation, always a struggle, a fight. Not enough like her mother. Of them all, Hannah. Hannah turned out the best, I think." He paused a moment and caught my glance. It was the surprise of recognition, I imagine, that made him flinch. "You know that. Of course you know. She's your mother. A wonderful mother."

I nodded, stretched my arms above my head, and turned away. What did I know about anything? "Yes," I said. "She is."

Across the pool, the young woman in the bikini sat up, gingerly testing the burn on her belly with a finger. She took off her sunglasses, unclasped her ponytail, and shook her hair free. Then, in one motion, she swiveled her body and slipped feet first into the pool. When I turned back to my grandfather, he was smiling mischievously, all silver fillings and yellowed caps. "Why talk to an old man all day?" he said, and winked. I shrugged, and without a word or a single thought, without a moment's hesitation, I stood and walked to the pool's edge. With a confidence more natural, more effortless than any I'd felt in my entire life, I plunged into the mild water. Chlorine stung my eyes and burned inside my nose. I came up coughing, less than three feet from the young woman whose wet hair clung to her sore, glowing neck. Her eyes were opened wide in horror. Splashing furiously, she backed away toward the pool's shallow end, and though I wouldn't allow myself to look, I heard – I swear I heard – the slow creak of my grandfather's neck as he sadly shook his head.

# Why Not?

AT ONE TIME, IT'S TRUE, ARTHUR BRICKMAN CONSIDERED himself adventurous. He even liked to think of himself as impulsive. Hadn't he followed a friend from Brooklyn to his university upstate, without any research or much thought at all? Hadn't he, on a whim, joined the Army ROTC and then just as quickly dropped out, saving himself, wholly by accident, from a terrible death in a Southeast Asian jungle? Hadn't he changed majors – from chemical engineering to pure chemistry – just one semester short of graduating? Hadn't he proposed marriage to his girlfriend, now his wife, after only four months of dating and one night of tortured indecision?

As a young man Arthur was undeniably slight, standing no taller than five-feet-seven. His chest was narrow, his wrists bony, his arms hairless. He knew his shoulders tended to sag, and in public made a conscious effort to square them and straighten his back; when he lapsed, his upper body seemed not only small but sunken, in the midst of shriveling. To his credit, he had a full head of wavy black hair and dense, bushy eyebrows. During his last year of graduate school, six months after his wedding, he grew a full beard. Nothing unique at the time – this was 1966 – but unlike those of other young men on campus, Arthur's beard stayed neatly trimmed. He didn't march in protests or participate in sit-ins. He sympathized with demonstrators and their causes, but he was a scientist, a man of knowledge: he had vague dreams of saving the world through advances a hippie could never hope to imagine. His beard was less a concession to radicalism than a mark of his sincerity, and in combination with his hair and eyebrows it made his face look dark, mysterious, almost fearsome. Shuffling across campus with his hands thrust deep into his pockets, brows knit in an intense, even furious concentration, he had the appearance of someone to be reckoned with, someone to be taken quite seriously – an appearance he was aware of and worked hard to cultivate.

When his Ph.D. was finally completed, he applied for positions in the most exotic places he could think of and was accepted for a dream job, a two-year postdoctoral stint in Switzerland. The institute was run by Walter Mulberry, a renowned American researcher, a true genius by most accounts, who'd already shared a Nobel Prize for his synthesis of complex natural products and was rumored to be in the running for another. Mulberry himself hand-picked each year's new fellows; to be chosen was an unquestionable sign of prestige. But to his friends, his family, his colleagues, Arthur made light of it. "I turned up the corner of my application," he'd say humbly. "A trick I learned playing poker." Not that he believed a word of this himself. No life, he felt, was simply charmed, nothing gained without merit or influence. He didn't for a moment doubt that he deserved the position. But to talk about luck gave the whole enterprise an airy, magical feel: he had no expectations for the job, the country, the people. Whatever followed would be utter surprise and welcome happenstance.

Not yet twenty-seven, he was ready to pack everything he owned into a single trunk and lead his wife of less than two years across the ocean. Hannah was just twenty-three. In Arthur's mind she still lingered on the threshold of girlhood. She was pretty and soft, slightly plump, subject to wild swings in mood. Her father, a Russian immigrant with a heavily accented voice always booming about independence and self-reliance, had been an overprotective parent with a tendency to spoil his children. This left Hannah a curious mix of confident and naïve, helpless and decisive – a mix Arthur was occasionally amused by, but often found annoying. Bouts of hysteria broke his concentration while he studied for exams or prepared his dissertation. They happened mostly in the kitchen. Once when Hannah had forgotten to buy tomatoes for a salad, another time when she'd burned a roast and filled the apartment with a menacing, sulfuric smell. When Arthur offered to help prepare dinner, she shouted at him for using a serrated knife to cut vegetables, for not pivoting the blade from the tip. "Aren't you supposed to be a scientist?" she cried. A month after their wedding she'd sworn she didn't need him, didn't need anybody, and had run out the door while a pot of spaghetti simmered on the stove. What exactly had provoked her, Arthur was never sure. He found her fifteen minutes later, a block and a half from the apartment, face down in the snow. He helped her to her feet, scolded her jokingly about not wearing gloves to play outside, but she didn't smile. She stared at her shoes and said, "I don't know if you love me."

He lifted her chin so she had to look him in the eye. "Of course I do," he said.

"It doesn't matter what you say. I just don't know."

Each of these episodes was followed by a brief period in which Hannah was unable or unwilling to face the world. She wouldn't leave the apartment alone after dark, wouldn't ride in Arthur's rusty Chrysler. She taught French at the public high school in the center of town, and suddenly her students began to leer at her and make threatening gestures. She spoke fearfully of the protests on campus, worrying they might turn into riots; she imagined that the wiring in their building was old and faulty and would start a fire in the middle of the night. It was at these times she most needed Arthur's comfort, and he did what he could. But as he reassured her, stroking her hair, whispering whatever words filtered through his distraction – "Everything's fine. Nobody's going to hurt you. That's why I'm here." – he felt less like her husband than a stand-in for her father, who lived only sixty miles away. More than just irritating, this made him uneasy; he couldn't yet imagine being a father to anyone. Leaning on his shoulder, she rocked her head back and forth until it began to grind against the bone. Instead of comforting her, he wanted to pass on what his own mother had often muttered during the most unreasonable moments of Arthur's adolescence: Stop acting like a child.

For the past two years, Hannah's teaching had been supporting them both while Arthur finished school. She'd complained the entire time about the lazy kids, the gossipy, disgruntled teachers who smoked so much in the lounge she had to eat her lunch in the parking lot. She'd be only too glad, Arthur thought, to drop everything and follow wherever he led. But it was precisely this, dropping everything, that made her worry about Switzerland. Her friends, her family, everyone she knew would be too far away even to call on the telephone. The streets would be strange and disorienting. How would she know what to buy in grocery stores if labels weren't printed in English? Arthur was sure Europe would be the perfect place for her. Yes, everything would be new and unfamiliar, and she would rely heavily on her husband's support. But after a few triumphs with language, with haggling over prices, she'd stop doubting herself and her abilities. Two years away from her father would give her the chance to grow up. Of course he didn't put it to her in these terms. Instead he said, with honest feeling, "This is a once in a lifetime chance, but I can't do it on my own. I need your help. If you don't want to go, we won't go."

AND WASN'T IT EVEN MORE PERFECT THAN HE COULD HAVE imagined? They were living just across the Rhine from Basel's ancient center, treated the entire time as honored guests, though they rented a Swiss apartment and owned a German car. People they barely knew escorted them to cocktail parties, took them skiing beneath the Matterhorn, arranged a boating trip on Lago Maggiore, a shimmering lake straddling the Italian border. Always on the spur of the moment they sped off on trips to Austria, to Bavaria, to Dijon. In his mind—both at the time and years later—Arthur saw it all as jagged white crags set against a blaring blue sky, though in their photographs, which he always developed the moment they returned to Basel, the mountain peaks were rarely distinguishable from an unwavering backdrop of pale clouds.

There were times, too, when he lost himself entirely in chemistry. Not in the lab, where beakers and test tubes often slipped from his fingers to shatter on the floor, where several times a perfectly commonplace reaction unexpectedly burst into bright orange flames, but in his tiny, windowless office, where, squinting into his logbook for hours, he rearranged carbons and bonds until he no longer knew or cared why he was doing so, or for what purpose. He was able to see reactions in their pure state, the way chemicals would combine if freed from his clumsy, human intervention. More than hunger or fatigue, it was his contentment that always shook him from these reveries, that frightened him from his office back into the world. In those moments when he achieved the greatest peace, when he needed nothing else but a quiet room and a head full of chemical structures, without fail, Hannah's lonely figure appeared before him, wandering helplessly through a maze of peculiar, foreign streets. Then he left work an hour early and picked up flowers on his way home, his guilt somewhat allayed by Hannah's surprised cry and grateful kisses.

As perfect as it all was, they did, of course, have their difficulties. Hannah fared well with her French and rarely got lost. It was Arthur who couldn't manage to pick up more than a handful of words in either French or German, and more than once found himself being shouted at in public – the bus drivers were particularly ruthless, more so because Arthur never seemed to have correct change. He never learned to read the schedules either, and once accidentally boarded a bus for Liestal, a town twenty miles away. He'd just left the lab and was still thinking about chemistry. Daydreaming, really: specific chemical structures slowly expanded into the abstract notion of great scientific achievement and the praise of distinguished peers. Only when, outside the bus window, stone houses and narrow lanes gave way to staggered industrial buildings, then farm houses and open countryside, did he realize what he'd done. Panic set in at the thought of Hannah all alone in the apartment, cooking dinner, waiting for his return. During the first year of their marriage, she'd once been in tears when he'd come home fifteen minutes late from a lecture, and his explanation – disputing an exam question with an inflexible professor – had not been enough to console her. Now he hurried to the front of the bus and begged the driver to let him off, trying to explain in gestures that from here he might still be able to walk back. Already it would take an hour, and his feet, so comfortable in the soft brown loafers he'd bought during a weekend in Rome, began to throb at the thought. But the driver, a lanky man with a red, beaky face, driving with only two fingers on the steering wheel, barked without taking his eyes from the road, "*Setzen Sie sich hin!*" Arthur backed away quietly and sat toward the rear of the bus. He'd only been four years old when the war had ended, but he'd heard enough stories and seen enough photographs and movies – a Jew ordered in German stirred some collective memory of terror he'd never before noticed in himself. He huddled low in his seat, but it wasn't only his own peril he thought of now. He pictured Hannah at their bedroom window, crouched on the floor, peering fearfully onto the street below.

In Liestal he searched half an hour for a phone. Dusk was falling quickly, and the spires and curved cornices of the strange town threw elongated, overlapping shadows wherever he turned. He ducked into a small hotel and at the front desk mimed spinning a dial and speaking into his hand.

The clerk was a young man but completely bald, with long feminine eyelashes. His chair was tilted against the wall, his feet on the desk. He laughed roughly at Arthur's efforts and said, "Again, please." Finally he pointed to an unmarked door just over Arthur's shoulder.

The phone rang two, three, four times. His imagination was growing frenzied – he now saw Hannah cowering in a closet, listening to boots pounding on the front door.

"Hello?" Her voice was steady and clear, but for Arthur this was somehow worse than if she'd been screaming into the receiver: if she was in danger, she didn't yet have any idea.

"I'm sorry," he said. "I'm so sorry."

"For what? Are you still in the lab?"

"This reaction. It's taking forever. I'll be here at least another hour."

Away from the phone Hannah said, "No, sit, sit." Then to Arthur, "I invited Rhea for dinner. Do you mind if we start eating without you?"

"Of course not," he said. "Go ahead. I'm glad you're not alone."

The bald clerk was still laughing as he crossed the lobby. Outside the street had grown completely dark. He started walking in one direction, then changed his mind and headed the opposite way. He couldn't remember which street led back to the bus station. Footsteps sounded loudly on cobbles, but he saw no one. Each breath he took was shallower than the last. This was ridiculous; he'd grown up in Brooklyn, had walked the streets of Manhattan as a toddler, had ridden the subway by himself at ten years old. Here he was in a small city in one of the safest countries in the world. What could he possibly be afraid of? Now he was nearly panting. He walked, and then ran, up one street after another, past identical rows of stone houses broken only by an occasional church or beer hall, the shop windows all blackened for the night.

By the time he found the station, he'd promised himself this would be the last bus he'd ever ride. The next morning he took Hannah shopping for a car and gleefully signed the papers for a black Mercedes-Benz, more than a decade old, with a missing taillight and a dent in the grill the size and shape of a small fist.

LATER, AFTER IT WAS ALL OVER, ARTHUR WOULDN'T REMEMBER having worked much at all. But he must have done something right. Six months before his contract was set to expire, Walter Mulberry called him into his office. Mulberry was then only in his late forties but could easily have been taken for sixty. His skin was pocked on both cheeks and grizzled below his chin, his complexion ashen and waxy. His pink, bleary eyes blinked constantly against the smoke rising from his cigarette. His hair clumped strangely, sticking up in back and smoothed flat over both temples. Only his lab coat showed any sign of tidiness – it was, in fact, immaculate, starch white and pressed, unmarred by a single stain or cigarette burn, though Mulberry never took it off to eat or smoke. Everything else in the office was specked with mustard. Butts, bread crusts, and bits of lettuce littered the desk and floor.

From the age of four, Mulberry had never lived a day as an ordinary person. Nobody, not his parents, not his teachers, not his classmates, had treated him like a normal boy. Before he was tall enough to sit at a table without being propped on cushions, he joined in roundtable discussions with groups of serious adults who wanted to discuss his future plans. In his presence people constantly whispered about his "gifts," casually tossing about the word "brilliant," and even "genius." But then it had had nothing to do with chemistry. Mulberry had been a painter, a prodigy, who at ten years old completed a series of canvases – based on Monet's *Rouen Cathedral* – of his grandparents' house in different seasons and at different times of day. Only in high school did he discover an aptitude for science. At Harvard he split his time between art studios and labs. When it came time to decide what to pursue in graduate school, he spent months deliberating. Chemistry departments all over the world courted him; he received a letter from the great Irving Langmuir on behalf of Princeton.

His painting mentor was an old realist who'd lost his right hand in World War I, and with it his technical skill. But he wasn't bitter or angry about his fate. In fact, he spoke nostalgically about the war, claiming that breathing mustard gas had given him a heightened sense for colors. He refused to give Mulberry advice about his future. The day Mulberry had to make his final decision, the old man said simply, "Some things are more important than others." Since then Mulberry had never picked up a brush or painted another stroke.

All this Arthur had learned from magazine articles long before he'd arrived in Basel. What remained now of Mulberry's artistic beginnings was an unmatched ability for drawing chemical structures accurately, precisely, almost beautifully. His syntheses, too, had an aesthetic quality, always simple and direct with no material wasted. The scope of his talents should have further intimidated Arthur – as if a Nobel Prize were not enough? – but instead it made his boss seem flawed, more human. Wouldn't a perfect person have been born for one thing only? Why should he have had to sacrifice something he cared about so deeply? Mulberry's all-consuming drive seemed to have its source in a profound and painful loss, and to Arthur – who was also driven, but only part of the time – this was somehow comforting.

Today wasn't the first time Mulberry had called Arthur into his office, but usually their conversations lasted no more than thirty seconds. Mulberry, one hand gripping the thin hair over his forehead, would pound on his blackboard with a piece of chalk and point to a string of structures representing the synthesis of strychnine or vitamin B12. "What's wrong with this?" he'd cry. "Why can't I see it? Is this bond single or double?"

It wasn't a difficult question, and Arthur knew the answer, or he would have, given a moment to think. But he was flustered, distracted by the shards of chalk spitting into the air, by Mulberry's impatiently tapping foot. For Mulberry there was no such thing as time: there was either now or too late. Tentatively, Arthur suggested, "Double?"

Mulberry stared at him a full two seconds, the chalk held to his lips, mistaken, maybe, for his cigarette. "Double? That's crazy. That makes no sense. Double." And then he was tapping away again on the blackboard, not another word for Arthur who was already creeping toward the hallway. By the time Mulberry discovered whether his suggestion was crazy or not, he'd be safely back in his lab.

But today the blackboard was empty. Mulberry sat at his desk, smoking. "I don't want to take a lot of time with this," he said as Arthur was walking in. "So let's just get right to it. You like it here?" Arthur didn't know what to make of the question. Was he being fired? Put on probation? He stood before the desk, unsure whether or not to take the only other seat in the office, a metal stool piled high with journals and unopened mail. He gave a nod, so slight it might have been a twitch. Mulberry squinted. "You like it enough to stay?" Now he was talking quickly. In two gruff sentences he offered Arthur a permanent position, his own lab, complete scientific freedom. Arthur was stunned and speechless. He still didn't know whether or not to sit, though now he desperately wanted to. Would it be rude to clear the papers from the stool? He started to ask, but Mulberry waved a hand. "No," he said. "Don't tell me today. It's a big decision. Talk to your wife. Think it over."

He couldn't go back to the lab. Instead he headed straight for the stairs and was nearly running by the time he hit the walkway outside the institute. His car started on the third try, and before he knew what he was planning, he'd crossed the river and pulled up in front of the house whose top floor he rented from the young widow of a stonemason buried in an avalanche two years ago while repairing an alpine road. Arthur didn't expect Hannah to be here – she usually spent her days shopping, browsing the museums, lunching with new friends, taking cooking lessons from their landlady, teaching English to neighbors' children. But maybe this was why he'd come here: he'd have the apartment to himself, hours to prepare for Hannah's return. He would spring the news the moment she walked through the door. He'd catch the surprise in her face, the admiration, even pride – who among her friends had a husband offered a job by the winner of a Nobel Prize? – before she calmed herself and said rationally, inevitably, "Of course, you'll have to turn it down."

But Hannah was home, standing at the open window in their bedroom, staring out across the river, absently fingering the lace curtain. She turned slowly, as if she'd been expecting him, though it was only two in the afternoon. The curtain came with her. She was gripping it now to her chest. "You're finally home," she said.

"I'm early," he said. "I've got a surprise."

Her expression was comically thoughtful, lower lip between her teeth, brows bunched and straining. She nodded with difficulty. Only now did he realize she was holding back tears. "I've got one, too," she said. "I bet yours doesn't involve diapers."

When her first sob came, his arms were mostly around her – the curtain kept him from closing his embrace around her back. Over her shoulder he could see the slow-moving Rhine, no more than two hundred yards away. Ferries were floating from one side of the river to the other, and cars inched across the Middle Bridge. Beyond were the pastel faces of the old city, topped by the baroque tower of the Rathaus and the gothic spire of St. Peter's Church. A thought that had come to him often during the last year and a half struck him again: *Am I, Arthur Brickman, from Brooklyn, New York, really living on a bank of the Rhine?* But the city had never looked so foreign, so exotic until this moment. Why now, when he knew for sure they'd be leaving it all behind? A child had not been in their immediate plans – they'd agreed it would be best to wait until they were back in the States before trying. "Hannah," he said. "This is wonderful news. We're going to be parents. Why are you so upset?"

His lab coat muffled her moan. "I don't want to go home!"

It was the surprise, he guessed, that brought on the sudden feeling of lightheadedness – this was the last thing he'd expected her to say. As he caressed her back and gazed out the window, the world slowly turned on edge, the apartment impossibly high in the air, the spires of the city waiting below. A breeze through the window tugged at him gently. His knees buckled, and he teetered slightly before recovering his balance. He held Hannah tighter and said, "So we won't go." Only as he spoke the words did he begin to believe them. Was this really possible? Could they actually spend their lives thousands of miles from where they'd grown up, surrounded by people who spoke three languages other than their own? To assure himself, he repeated, "We won't go."

Hannah leaned away, sniffling. Her eyes were still watery, but her stare was skeptical. "What do you mean?"

"I mean we'll stay. Why shouldn't we?"

"That's not funny," she said. "You're just teasing me now. We can't stay. You've only got six months left. What would you do for a living?"

"You haven't let me tell my surprise yet."

She was weeping again, this time joyfully, alternating with nearly hysterical laughter. Arthur tried to catch her excitement. Their child would be lucky, he agreed, growing up here with so much culture, with such broad opportunities. They would give the baby a European name. "As long as it's not German," Hannah said. "Our parents would never forgive us."

Their parents. Arthur would have to write them letters. What could he possibly say? To Hannah's father: *I've taken your daughter far away and am never bringing her back.* To his own mother: *You won't see your grandchild more than once a year.*

"It'll have to be French," Hannah said. "Monique. What do you think of Monique?"

"It's beautiful," Arthur said.

"And what if it's a boy? Marcel? I like Marcel. I guess I like names that start with M." She patted her stomach and cooed in a high voice that Arthur barely recognized as his wife's, her accent flawless. "Marcel, Monique, *comment allez-vous?*"

How could he be anything but thrilled? The day couldn't have worked out more in his favor. But the view outside the window, the river's steady current, the lazy ferries, the ornate façades of the ancient buildings, all of it still partially filled him with anxiety. Along with Hannah's voice, he couldn't help hearing the voice of her father, booming, cursing in Russian and Yiddish, accusing him of betrayal. And then his mother's exasperated Brooklyn whine, "What did we do so bad to him? How did we chase him across the ocean? Are we such terrible people?"

"Do we have any champagne?" Hannah asked. "We have to celebrate. I think we have some wine. Stay here. I'll get some."

Arthur sat on the edge of the bed. He bounced up and down, testing the springs. Did he like this mattress? He'd never wondered about it before, the way he never wondered about beds in hotel rooms, knowing he would sleep in them only a night or two. Did he feel comfortable in this apartment? Did he like this city, this country, now that it was to be home?

Hannah came back with a pair of wine glasses. "I poured in some seltzer so there'd be bubbles," she said. "Regular wine doesn't seem important enough."

They raised the glasses and clinked their rims. "*Prost*," Arthur said. "*Salut*," Hannah answered.

Arthur took a small sip and watched his wife drink deeply.

TO CELEBRATE THE PREGNANCY AND THE NEW JOB — WHICH he hadn't yet officially accepted – they hastily planned a trip, and Arthur took a two-week leave from the institute. It was mid-summer, 1968. They packed a tiny bag with two changes of clothes, bathing suits, a single toothbrush to share between them, hopped into the Mercedes, and drove – arbitrarily, as he still intended to do many things in his life – southwest. They spent a night in Lausanne, charged through Geneva, glimpsed Mont Blanc on the way to Grenoble. They made love on a beach near Marseilles, suffering the hard, pebbly ground with only a towel beneath them; how could they tell their friends at home they'd lived in Europe nearly two years and had never done it on the Riviera? He thought they would drive across southern France until hitting the ocean, but somewhere along the way he got turned around and was heading south. Once again, mountains towered all around. The road signs changed abruptly from French to Spanish. "Spain?" Hannah asked.

Arthur shrugged. "Why not?"

As they wound out of the Pyrenees, slate-colored slopes gave way to a dense forest of beech and occasional pine. Only narrow, scattered beams of sunlight penetrated all the way to the ground. Hannah pointed to the side of the road. There, in the underbrush, appeared to be a small column of mossy stones, one stacked upon another, the smallest on top. Even when they pulled close, Arthur only half-believed it to be a man crouching in the shrubbery. His sandy hair fell in ringlets to his shoulders, their ends nearly impossible to distinguish from the surrounding confusion of leaves and twigs. His beard hung far down his neck, and he wore rubber sandals beneath frayed olive trousers and an olive canvas vest with no shirt underneath. From his shoulders hung an olive duffel bag. When the car was nearly alongside him, he stood and waved. Now a beam of sunlight struck the windshield, making Arthur squint. Again, he couldn't help wondering if it wasn't a man at all in front of him, just a tree limb waving in the breeze. Nevertheless he pulled over without hesitating. Hannah didn't seem to object. The man approached, and even with all his hair and his ragged clothes it was easy to see how young he was, younger than Arthur by five years at least. There'd been plenty of young men like this on the highways in upstate New York before he'd left, but Arthur had never once considered picking them up. That this one was a Spaniard somehow made a difference. It didn't occur to him the man might just as easily have been French or German or even American. He'd never heard the word Basque, and wouldn't for another year. He thought only: Spaniard.

As if in confirmation, the young man leaned into Arthur's window and said, "*Grácias.*" When both Arthur and Hannah only nodded, he tried again, "*Danke? Merci?*"

Hannah lit up at the sound of French. "*Parlez-vous anglais?*" she said.

Now the young man smiled broadly. His mouth seemed too large for its teeth to be so crowded. "Ah," he said. "Subjects of the majesty. Your Queen, I don't like her."

"He thinks we're English," Hannah said.

"Close enough," Arthur said.

"Go to San Sebastián?" the young man asked.

Arthur glanced at Hannah, who only raised her eyebrows. "Why not?" he said, and reached behind him to unlock the back door.

Hannah rode backward down the hill, knees on the seat, arms hugging the headrest. Arthur drove more carefully than usual, both hands on the wheel. In the rearview mirror he could glimpse only a shock of the young Spaniard's hair and his bare arm leaning against the duffel, the canvas and his skin only slightly different in shade. From the back seat came the smell of damp soil, reminding Arthur of the one time he'd gone fishing with cousins in the Catskills and had refused to pluck worms from their pail of slimy earth. Hannah was speaking French, slowly enough for him to catch a few words – hotel, restaurant, museum. The Spaniard's answers were too swift for Arthur to understand anything.

But after one question, the young man said, "*Non, non.*" When Hannah repeated herself, he sat up and shook his head vehemently. "*Non, non, non, non.*"

"What's the matter?" Arthur asked.

"He says we shouldn't stay in Madrid."

The young man let out a long, angry burst of Spanish – it rushed out with such force that Arthur wondered whether holding it back had been painful. Then, in English, the young man said, "Very bad, Madrid. Bad, bad."

"Ask him why it's bad," Arthur said, but when Hannah questioned him again in French, he said only, "Barçelona." He told her about the delicious seafood there and taught her a few Spanish phrases to use with waiters – they charged higher prices to tourists who couldn't speak the language. Then, without another word, he laid his head against the duffel and closed his eyes.

Hannah still sat backward, staring. In astonishment, Arthur guessed, and maybe admiration. He felt the faintest twinge of jealousy: he might have brought his wife to live in Europe, but never would he be as exotic as this. He would never stand in ragged clothes on the side of a mountain road waiting for a ride. Maybe he should have let his beard grow out after all. Hannah put a hand on his arm. "We have to go to Madrid anyway," she said. "I don't care what he thinks."

Her words were decisive, emphatic, and when he glanced sideways, he saw in her expression something new and striking – what it was he couldn't put his finger on. At most he sensed in her entire composure some sort of forward motion, or at least momentum. He noticed for the first time that though she was pregnant her face was not so round as it had been when he'd married her.

"Whatever you want," he said. "We can be in Madrid by tomorrow, I think."

He followed signs for San Sebastián, and soon the road began to flatten. The forest tapered away. On the plain far ahead, a small city fanned out around a glimmering blue bay. Just as suddenly as he'd gone to sleep, the young Spaniard came alive and stuck his head over the front seat. He spoke to Hannah in French. "He wants you to let him off here," she told Arthur.

"Here?" Arthur asked. To the rearview mirror he said, "I can take you all the way into town. It's no problem."

Now the young man seemed wide awake and agitated, already hooking the straps of the duffel over his shoulders. "*Sí, sí,*" he said. "Here."

Arthur pulled over beside a vast meadow circled by a rickety log fence and grazed by a handful of emaciated cows. A gray barn leaned at one end, but he could see no house or building of any other kind. The nearest village was still a mile off, marked by a hilltop church and a small smokestack soiling the cloudless sky. The Spaniard was already out of the car, scrambling up the steep, crumbling road bank. He didn't thank them or wish them well. He vaulted the fence and made his way past the cows to a clump of stout trees near the center of the field. Only then did Arthur notice it, what he'd been missing all along: from the top of the Spaniard's duffel stuck a thin black cylinder, nearly hidden in his hair. For a moment Arthur thought it might have been another ringlet, or the shadow of one, but now he could see it clearly, even as the young man disappeared from view – the tip of a rifle. He'd read Hemingway; he knew Spain had once been a country torn by civil strife. He read the papers enough to know it was a country still ruled by a dictator. Had he and his wife harbored a revolutionary in their German car? The truth of it chilled him: he had no idea. He didn't know which places were safe and which weren't. He just drove blindly from one to another, blindly leading Hannah, who had willingly put her life in his hands. She was smiling dreamily, still staring after the Spaniard, though he was no longer in sight. "They're so different from us," she said.

Arthur nodded. The steering wheel had grown slick under his palms. He had to clamp his teeth to keep them from chattering. The young man's smell lingered in the car, earthy, wormy, and again Arthur experienced the mild stab of envy. What type of courage did it take to become a rebel, to sneak off across a field with a rifle on your back? What type of dedication? Yes, Arthur worked for a man whose research had changed the face of science, and maybe the world. But now science struck him as dishearteningly ordinary. He suddenly regretted quitting the ROTC and avoiding Vietnam. He regretted shunning the campus protests. How could he have never raised his voice – to say nothing of taking up arms – against a government he didn't trust?

Hannah took his arm in both her hands, kissed his ear. "I'm so glad you took me here," she said. "This has been so wonderful."

He observed her face closely, the eager brown eyes, the curious raised brows, the open forehead, the soft, innocent cheeks. The same face he pictured on the child growing in her belly. She hadn't seen the rifle in the man's pack – she didn't know how dangerous the world could be. But he wouldn't tell her. This, he thought with distress and a swell of purpose, was his true adventure, however modest: to protect his wife, and soon his child, from whatever might harm or even frighten them. He pecked Hannah quickly on the forehead, the nose, once on each cheek, then put the car in gear and slid quietly past the meadow.

A mile short of San Sebastián, they came to a checkpoint of some sort, a makeshift gate comprised of a wooden pole thrown across overturned metal buckets. On either side of the road stood soldiers in full gear, carrying rifles and wearing helmets. They searched the Mercedes' trunk and back seat, emptied their bag, examined their passports. Arthur worried that the scent of their passenger still clung to the leather seat. But all he could smell now was his own sweat, his breath soured with fear. Hannah smiled and tried out the few Spanish phrases the young man had taught her. The soldiers laughed and waved them on their way.

"What do you suppose they were looking for?" Hannah asked after they passed through the gate. Her voice was still cheerful. If it trembled at all, it did so only with excitement.

"Who knows?"

"Maybe they thought we took exotic plants from the mountains."

"Maybe," Arthur said hoarsely. "I guess so. Yes."

IN MADRID, ARTHUR WAS ILL. FOOD POISONING, HE FIGURED, though Hannah had eaten the same watery, undercooked fish baked with the skin, tail, and head intact and wasn't sick at all. They'd made it to the city after dark and settled for the only café with an empty table, open air on a wide avenue choked with traffic. Half the cars that went by seemed to have lost their mufflers, coughing out huge clouds of black exhaust. Not five minutes passed without someone blaring a horn. After dessert and a last glass of wine, they tried to walk to the Prado, but the crowds on the sidewalk slowed them, and less than halfway there Arthur was doubled with pain. By the time they got back to the hotel – dim, creaky, filled with cigarette smoke though no one was smoking in the lobby or stairwell – both his own and Hannah's shoes were splattered.

He spent all night in the filthy bathroom shared by the entire floor, head hung over the rim of a toilet as Hannah brought him cups of water and mopped his forehead with a damp shirt; the housekeeper hadn't left them towels. All around the bowl, dust was clumped with wiry black hairs. Other hotel guests – all fat men, it seemed, with furry chests and receding hairlines – came in carrying soap and razors, exclaimed at the smell, and went shouting down the hall. For a time he thought the spasms would never end: he would vomit what was in his stomach, then the stomach itself, his heart and liver, his lungs, his blood, his bones, until all of him swirled through the rushing water and rattled down the rusting pipes. What didn't come out his mouth exited through his pores, which hadn't stopped sweating since they'd come through the soldiers' checkpoint outside San Sebastián. The thought of the young hitchhiker, the rifle in his pack, brought on a new round of shivering. No longer from fear, the dread of what might have happened; that had passed hours ago. Now it was simply awe, the overwhelming scope of what he did not – might never – know, that shook his frame and blurred his vision.

Finally there came a pause. Arthur wiped his mouth and gasped for air. Hannah said with confidence, "The worst of it's over, I think."

Arthur's throat burned, and his lips were swollen, but he forced himself to speak. "We can't stay here."

"It's too late to find another place now," Hannah said. "It's only one night. Tomorrow –"

"No." He shook his head and took a deep, rasping breath. "Here. Europe. We have to go home."

"We don't have to talk about this now."

He managed to sit up on his own but wasn't sure whether to lean against the sticky toilet or the grimy steel partition of the stall. He wrapped both arms around his knees and pulled them close to his chest. "I'd love to stay," he said. "You know I would." His voice came out weak and shaky, and he didn't try to change it. "But we can't think only about ourselves." Their child, he reasoned, should grow up surrounded by grandparents, aunts, uncles, cousins. Family was more important than whatever wonderful experiences they might have living overseas. It was time to stop being selfish. "If I kept you here, your father would never forgive me."

Hannah opened her mouth to answer, but before she could say a word, Arthur was wracked with another wave of nausea. He jerked toward the bowl but caught the side of the porcelain, drenching his hands, the sleeves of his shirt. Hannah was busy again, wiping his mouth and the floor, rubbing his back. And an hour or so before dawn, when he finally managed to crawl into bed, she seemed resigned. "Not every girl from New Haven can say she lived in Switzerland for two years," she mumbled as she pulled the blanket to her chin. "Not every girl conceives her baby in the Alps."

Two days later they were in Barçelona. Arthur's stomach had recovered completely. They ate seafood at a patio restaurant with an expansive view of the harbor. Not a word passed between them about leaving or staying, but Hannah didn't bother to use the Spanish phrases the young rebel had taught her—nor did she bother speaking French. They were charged an extravagant price for their meal, and Arthur couldn't have felt more relieved as he handed over a thick stack of bills.

THE SECOND DAY BACK IN BASEL, HE WAS IN WALTER MULBERRY'S office. Mulberry was more haggard than ever, pacing behind his desk. His cigarette dove dangerously close to piles of paper, and, rising, nearly singed his hair. "Are you out of your mind?" he said.

"You told me to think it over," Arthur said. "I did."

"That was just something to say. My God, what's to think over?"

"I decided it's not the best thing for me. For my family."

"What could be better for you?" Mulberry cried. "Aren't you supposed to be a chemist?"

"I can be a chemist at home," Arthur said.

"A nobody. Working nowhere for nothing." Mulberry fell into his chair and stubbed out his cigarette. He took his head in both hands. "Look, Arthur. I don't make this offer to just anyone. There's a reason I asked you to stay. You could make a real difference here. To the institute, to the field.

You might really do something. I'm telling you this now, so if you walk away, you'll know it for the rest of your life."

"That sounds like a threat."

"It's a warning."

"I've got responsibilities."

"I thought you had balls, too," Mulberry said. "Did Hannah forget them in Spain?"

Arthur leaned forward with both fists on Mulberry's desk. For the first time he raised his voice. "Leave my wife out of it."

Mulberry waved a nervous hand. "Forgive me. I think the world of Hannah. I do. But she doesn't know what this means. She doesn't know how important this is. For both of you. For all of us."

"This has nothing to do with her," Arthur said.

Now Mulberry was reduced to pleading. He spoke of a higher salary, greater responsibility, a provisional vote on the institute's board of directors. Arthur listened in silence and took in the office, dark, musty, crowded with hundreds of books and journals and a handful of empty wine bottles – a model portrait of scholarly gloom. Mulberry spent ten, twelve, fifteen hours a day in here, taking cat naps on the desk, eating partial meals only when hunger shook his concentration. He'd once been married but had no children. Was this what he wanted for Arthur? There was a time when such a lifestyle had appealed to him, at least as an ideal: the thrill of utter devotion. Wasn't this why he'd spent seven years working toward a degree? He tried to imagine Mulberry's expression the day he'd first managed a complex synthesis from various simple parts. Or the day he'd stood on a stage in Stockholm to accept his prize. But he couldn't picture Mulberry's face any way other than it was now, drawn and smoke-stained, eyes blinking uncontrollably. Would it look any different if he'd given up science long ago to pursue a career in painting? Or if he'd dropped everything to raise a family? Still Arthur saw only the miserable, driven face before him. Even more clearly he saw Hannah's face, the face of his unborn child – round, wide-eyed, trusting, indifferent to whether he was a scientist, a salesman, a plumber, so long as he was husband and father.

"Please," Mulberry said. He reached for another cigarette and held it unlit between his lips. He took a match from a box but didn't strike it. A single word from Arthur, his desperate eyes seemed to imply, and he would toss them both, match and cigarette, out the window and never smoke again. "Please. You've got to stay." He gestured at the stacks of journals crowding his desk, the precisely drawn structures on his blackboard. "Don't you see how important this is?"

"Some things are more important than others," Arthur said, and immediately regretted it as Mulberry's head lowered. "I'm sorry. I've made up my mind."

HE FINISHED HIS WORK IN THE LAB MECHANICALLY AND CAME home early in the evening. He should have felt lighthearted – all that had been troubling him was now over with, his immediate future set. But instead he saw new and cumbersome burdens wherever he turned. Here, in the living room, the sofa with the agreeable pattern of blue and gold flowers, the black leather armchair he could fall asleep in so easily, the huge, unframed canvas of a quiet city lane hung with drying laundry, not very skillful, but pleasant and comforting, bought from a street painter in Salzburg. In the kitchen were hand-crafted bowls and pitchers, crocheted potholders, a fondue set given by friends who couldn't believe Hannah had lived without one for so long. All these things spoke of a life, a real life, built slowly and steadily over the past year and a half. Not one tenth of them would fit in the trunk they'd come with, not half would return to the States. The Mercedes that had carried them across the borders of so many countries he would have to sell quickly, for a pittance. Only now did he begin to consider what recrossing the ocean would mean – finding a new home, new furniture, a new job, a new car, new friends.

In the bedroom the window was thrown wide open. Hannah sat on the sill, her feet in the apartment, the rest of her leaning far out over the street. Only two fingers reached back to hold the sash. On either side of her the lace curtains fluttered rhythmically. The sun was setting, and the river, the bridge, the spires of the old city were touched with soft pink flames. He wasn't afraid she was going to jump, but her posture, the ease of her manner, suggested something entirely more troubling: that she believed she might fly or simply float to the ground. He rushed to her, wrapped his arms around her waist, rested his chin on her lap. He braced his knees against the wall to keep them both from plunging.

"It's beautiful, isn't it?" Hannah said.

"What is?" Arthur asked. The river burned slowly, the ferries crossing through fire. How could he agree with her? He only knew the facts of what he saw, the water, the buildings, the mysterious color that filled him with fretting and wonder – he wasn't able to judge them.

"What's beautiful?" he repeated.

Maybe it was easier for Hannah to see beauty here, or anywhere, she who hadn't seen the dark cylinder against the young Spaniard's light hair, though it had stood out plainly before her. He wondered if he should have pointed it out after all, if that somehow might have been safer for both of them.

"It's gorgeous," Hannah said, firmly.

He waited for more words: *I wish we were staying.* Or, *I think you should reconsider.* But she didn't say anything else, and for that he could have thanked her. Instead she kissed the top of his head and swiveled her body as he held her, swinging her legs out over the street. Only the edge of her backside touched the sill. Her hands rested in her lap. Arthur gripped her tighter; only his arms would keep a sudden breeze from carrying her off. Beneath the knobs of his wrists, beneath the thin cloth of Hannah's dress, he couldn't yet feel the first bulge of her belly, though he tried to convince himself he could. He tried to imagine a growing child, a person that resembled him in some way. He wanted to believe that through his fingers, through his wife's stomach, he was passing something on, a message of great significance.

But no matter how hard he tried to imagine, it was only Hannah's flesh he felt beneath his hands. It was Hannah and no one else kicking her feet against a ledge two stories above a cobbled street, letting Arthur keep her from falling. Hannah and no one else. The same one he'd married, the same he'd taken away with him less than two years ago, though it was so hard to believe. He might never have loved her then – or believed it was love he felt – if he'd known how much he would love her now. At home, their friends and family would remark on how much she'd changed, how thoroughly she'd grown up. What would they say about Arthur?

# Hannah of Troy

NOVEMBER 1965. MY MOTHER, TWENTY-ONE AND MARRIED A month, was giving up. She'd go home to her mother and father, would walk all the way from Troy to New Haven if she had to. She'd get the first divorce in the history of her family, the first among her friends from high school and college, half of whom were already pregnant. Hannah, formerly Collins (from her father, formerly Kollachelnik), now Brickman, would be Hannah Collins once again.

Of course she wouldn't have to walk. Troy had a bus depot. From there she could ride to Albany, fifteen minutes at most, though who knew how frequently the service ran. From Albany to Manhattan in a straight shot, and then it was only a matter of puzzling out which subway line would take her to Grand Central, which train would follow the Connecticut shoreline. All she had to do now was hurry from the apartment – where Arthur, my father, would soon be struggling into his coat to chase after her – into the center of town and inquire about buses and the location of the depot. These things she could do on her own.

"EVERYTHING NOW," MY MOTHER SAID, MORE THAN THIRTY YEARS later at the kitchen table in the house where I'd grown up. "It's all so much easier." We were sitting close together, my mother sipping from a steaming cup of herbal tea so clear it couldn't possibly have had any flavor. I clutched a bottle of beer. Across the hall, in the family room, my father sat reading the newspaper, and every minute or so I could hear a faint rustling as he turned a page. My mother's smile was tight and teacherly, and each time she made a point, she tapped the glass table with a fingernail. "Really," she said. "You're lucky."

I didn't feel lucky, though I should have. I was engaged to Julie, a woman I was sure I loved deeply. "We complement each other perfectly," I told everyone I knew. She couldn't have been more of a change from my family, or from the girls I'd dated in college. She spoke with a syrupy North Carolina mountain accent, which she swore was a mistake, or else a cruel joke. The South, with its reserve and polite indirectness, made no sense to her.

She was convinced she should have been raised at least north of Virginia. The next best thing, I gathered later, was to marry a guy from New Jersey, especially a Jewish one. Somehow my Jewishness lifted me several degrees in latitude.

We'd met in the most ordinary way: I was supposed to give Julie money I didn't have. For more than a year before this, I'd been living in Chicago, writing mundane copy for an ad agency, watching stacks of rented movies in the evenings, and working hard to convince myself I wasn't lonely. But when the agency offered a promotion – from account coordinator to junior account manager – I had a terrible vision of my future: stable, comfortable, unendurable. To the shock of my boss and colleagues, to the despair of my parents, I turned down the position, quit the job, moved to North Carolina, and entered a master's program in journalism, a subject in which I'd never before taken a course and a career I'd never even considered until now.

At the time, Julie was working as a university cashier, taking classes at night; she'd already transferred from four different colleges and had no intention of ever getting a degree. I knew right away she wasn't meant to be a teller – she was far too alert and cheerful behind her window, when, during my first week of graduate school, I begged her to take the hold off my registration even though I couldn't afford to pay more than one-third of my tuition. "My loan should come through any day," I said. In truth, I hadn't yet filled out a loan application or so much as visited the financial aid office.

"And why should I trust you?" she asked, not sternly, but not mockingly either. She was pretty in an almost typically southern way, with high cheekbones, straight brown hair clipped back to reveal delicate, childlike ears, a smile abundant in teeth and gums. What didn't fit was her clownish pair of glasses, steel-rimmed and lightly tinted, far too big for her face. They sat on her nose awkwardly, a hasty disguise that didn't seem to hide anything.

It was the glasses that somehow put me at ease, made me lean against the counter, and say, "I can't give you a reason. It'll have to be a pure leap of faith." Who was this person speaking? I'd suddenly become one of the suave, overconfident figures from the movies – or at least a sincere if pathetic imitation – the ones who always got their way when they didn't deserve it, the ones I loved to scorn out loud but secretly admired. I think I even winked. She returned my gaze for a full three seconds and then with one click on her keyboard turned me into a legitimate student. "That's great," I said. "That's really terrific. I'm in your debt. Let me do something for you. Let me buy you dinner."

I was surprised again at my own boldness – never before had I asked a girl out without first stammering in front of a mirror for twenty minutes and feeling sweat sprout on my back. But even more surprising was the way she stared straight at my chest, adjusting her absurd glasses as if to get a better view into my soul. "That sounds nice," she said. "But, sweetheart, you can't even afford your tuition. How were you planning to pay for dinner?"

"That's a good question," I said. "How about coffee?"

"Maybe you'd better go on and register first."

"I guess I should. Where do I do that?"

"Aren't you a mess," she said. "Come on." She closed her window, came around the counter, and led me from the building. She took me to the registrar, then showed me the library, the student union, the main quad. We had coffee and shared a chocolate-chip cookie. Close to four o'clock, I asked if she shouldn't be getting back to work. "Oh Lord, no," she said. "They must have fired me by now." She leaned forward with her chin in her hands and again fixed me with that penetrating stare, disconcerting and at the same time entirely welcome. "I reckon it was worth it," she said.

Julie turned out to be thrillingly, maddeningly carefree. She'd ask me to ride with her down the road to the 7-11 – "I gotta get a Dr. Pepper right now, Danny. I never needed anything so bad" – and halfway there she'd decide she needed to go to Atlanta. She'd tell me, "You worry too much," and then go skipping off into heavy traffic. Most people, including me, felt compelled to look after her, though she claimed protection was the last thing she wanted. Occasionally I was able to match her with brief bursts of impulse – midnight drives to the beach when we both had to work at eight the next morning, skinny dipping in our apartment's overly chlorinated, very public pool – but mostly she appreciated me as an anchor, or as she put it, "the person who reminds me not everybody's as happy as I am."

Not once during our first two years together did I question the depth of my love. Even now, just thinking about it, the feeling I had for Julie fills me completely; I find myself sinking low in my chair trying not to breath, and I swear, the hair stands straight up on my arms. Marriage for us was, more than anything, a formality. For two years we'd been living together in Raleigh – Julie claimed to hate the South but couldn't bring herself to move far from her family; and anyway, I never could stand the cold – as committed, we felt, as any couple who'd exchanged rings before the justice of the peace. The only reasons for a ceremony were to please both our families, to rake in a haul of gifts, and to let me leech off the university's generous health plan – she'd lost her cashier's job but had found another in the campus bookstore. In no significant way was the wedding supposed to change our lives. But two months before the scheduled date, I stopped sleeping. I'd never been much of a sleeper, but this was miserable, hours and hours of staring at the darkened ceiling, the first dreams of the night interrupted by the morning alarm. For the first time, I really began to notice Julie's presence in the bed. The bristling of two-day stubble against my shin suddenly became an offense. The slightest hiss of her breath produced in me an almost physical revulsion. I was disgusted by her coughing, the smacking of her lips, the unconscious gurgling of her stomach. Late most nights, propped on an elbow, I stared in near horror at this strange creature I'd invited to share my bed for the rest of my life.

I told myself she was pulling away from me. There were times when we'd be sitting together on the couch, reading or watching TV, and I could see in her face that she wanted something, that she was waiting for me to say the exact words she needed to hear. I'd lean forward, brush my lips across her ear, and say, "I love you so much it scares me. You know that, don't you?" She'd nod, but still her eyes were stuck on my mouth, waiting. What else was there to say? After a while she'd yawn and get up to go to bed. I'd ask if she wanted me to join her. She'd hesitate a moment, and then say, "No, I'm pretty sleepy. You come in when you're ready." If there was something missing from our relationship, if there was some hole in her life I might be able to fill, couldn't she just tell me what it was? In another hour I'd drag myself into the bedroom, knowing I wouldn't sleep. This was punishment, I felt sure, for some shortcoming in the love which, until now, I'd believed was all-encompassing and complete.

Still, I never seriously considered calling off the wedding. Even to think it brought on immediate, crippling headaches. When Julie was away from the apartment, running errands or seeing friends, I paced, terrified of answering the phone. I imagined her calling from Tennessee, telling me in her soft, southern voice that she was heading west with a mountain-biker named Andreas, who could make her feel loved in three different languages; or worse, a state trooper calling to tell me a tanker full of nuclear waste had jackknifed on I-40 and sizzled my fiancée from the face of the earth.

Three weeks before the ceremony, on a whim, I told Julie I was driving up to my parents' house, just for the weekend. Just to pick up some things we could use in the kitchen, I told her, and to talk to the old man about some possible investments. She always laughed when I called my father "old man" – it sounded wonderfully northern to her, urban and somehow tough – and didn't question me any further. Neither did my mother when I called, though she knew I hated the long drive and never came home without a good reason, and even then reluctantly. For half an hour I let my father read to me from the stock pages, and then took my mother aside as she finished brewing her tea. I explained as much as I could. She didn't show any surprise. She threw away her tea bag, gave me a chocolate-chip cookie from a fresh batch I knew she'd baked only when she heard I was driving up – a doctor had advised my father to lower his cholesterol, so my mother usually kept the house clear of junk food – then went to the fridge and handed me a beer. I was sure she'd set me straight. She liked Julie, I thought, and had mostly gotten over her not being Jewish. "Religion is personal," I'd argued over the last two years. "How could Julie's possibly affect mine?" It helped that Julie hadn't been to church since she was eleven. We both ignored the fact that I hadn't been anywhere near a synagogue since high school. "I worry, that's all," my mother would say. "You're both so different." But now that she'd resigned herself to having a shiksa for a daughter-in-law, I expected her to tell me everyone had jitters like mine before a wedding, that I just needed to ride out the next three weeks and everything would be fine.

Instead she lowered her voice and glanced toward the family room. Her smile disappeared. Her hands went to her lap, searching, it seemed, for our cat Stanley, who'd been gone now for years – after recovering from a long illness my senior year of high school, he'd died in his sleep, without warning, eight months later. She seemed startled not to find him there, and equally startled by her words, as if she'd never before spoken – or even thought – of the things she was now telling me. The bottle was cold in my hands, but I couldn't let it go. "You and Julie, you've got such an advantage. Two years. I envy you. Two years you've had to figure everything out. Can you stand to be around each other every day? If so, good, get married. Your father and I. You think we got to be friends first? One day I woke up next to a stranger. My God, that first year." She shook her head and took a long sip of tea, and I began to pick at the label on my beer bottle. Then, in barely more than a whisper, she said, "You've never heard the story. No one has. Once, I walked out. I walked right out on him."

MY FATHER, COMPLETING RESEARCH FOR HIS PH.D., SPENT every weeknight in his lab at Rensselaer, the polytech university. Whenever my mother asked, he told her he'd be finished in six months, no more than seven, and then he'd start writing the dissertation. "That's not such a long time, is it?" he'd say. The spring before, my mother had graduated from a local women's college and now taught French at the overcrowded high school on the river. Her classes were packed full with the unmotivated children of waitresses and truck drivers. Whether she spoke French or English, they stared at her blankly; sometimes, when boys nodded to each other across the room, she was gripped by brief bouts of fear, convinced they were planning to attack her. She longed for the children of professors and businessmen, but they all went to the school near the university, which never hired teachers straight out of college.

Every afternoon she rushed home from work to meet my father in the cramped apartment on the second floor of what once must have been a comfortable one-family townhouse. The apartment had only two rooms, a combined kitchen–living room and a bedroom. The bedroom was a constant mess, no matter how often she tried to clean. Everywhere my father piled his books and records, and ridiculous things he never used but wouldn't let her throw away: tennis rackets, golf clubs, bulky, woolen army blankets given to him by an uncle who'd been a fighter pilot and had supposedly survived the terrors of Pearl Harbor. Without complaining, she set up her wardrobe in a corner of the living room and stuffed an empty kitchen cupboard with bras, underwear, and sweat socks.

Of course my mother didn't tell me what went on when she met my father in the afternoons. I can only imagine that they must have spent an hour or two in bed, taking all necessary precautions – my older brother wasn't born for another four years. Then she cooked his dinner, kissed him wildly until he laughed and pried her fingers from around his neck, and stood on the street waving as he trudged uphill toward the drab brick building, which, instead of having ordinary windows, received its meager sunlight through a grid of thick, smoky, glass squares. Often she begged him to stay home. Not because she so desperately needed him there – she had papers to grade, a lesson to plan, a book to help her fall asleep – but because it seemed a new bride should beg her husband to stay home, should wish for him to spend every possible moment by her side. No, she didn't need him there, though as a young girl, when she'd dreamed of marriage, never did her fantasies include such long, solitary nights.

This afternoon, once they'd crawled from bed and dressed, she searched through the refrigerator and pantry but could find nothing interesting to make for dinner. The truth was she didn't want to make dinner. She'd felt cold all day today, and more tired than usual. For hours a pressure had been threatening in her temples and now began to throb. Half the kids in her classes coughed and sneezed their way through recitation, but these Troy parents didn't have the sense to keep their sick children home. They lined up at her desk with red eyes and runny noses and – purposely, she was certain – let soggy handkerchiefs slip from their pockets and brush against her arm. She would have liked nothing more than to lie in bed propped on pillows and have a tray of hot food placed in her lap. Her mother, my grandmother, would have scolded her for being lazy, for neglecting her wifely privilege. "Nothing tastes so good as what you stir with your own spoon," she would say, though everything my mother had stirred so far tasted bland and pasty. And anyway my grandmother couldn't even sit still in restaurants. She'd once excused herself to go to the ladies' room, only to sneak into the kitchen, peering over shoulders and criticizing – "I was only giving advice," she said later – until the chef stormed into the dining room and ordered my grandfather to take his family elsewhere.

My father stood by the sink, stuffing his thumb into the bowl of his curved wooden pipe. Only after their engagement had he begun smoking, and my mother had made the mistake of telling him he looked sophisticated. By the time she discovered how the smoke clung to his hair and clothes, it was too late to object – the pipe had become a part of him. Now he would puff and puff and when he finished would expect something to be boiling or baking. My mother wasn't my grandmother, and didn't intend to be. She would cook him dinner tonight. Because he'd be leaving for the lab in an hour she'd do what she had to, but she'd at least make clear her preference. "Wouldn't it be wonderful," she said. "Wouldn't it be wonderful to spend the whole evening in bed? We could order Chinese and forget everything until morning."

She didn't expect him to say, "Why not? Let's." She only wanted him to agree it would be wonderful. But instead, he slipped the end of the pipe between his teeth and spoke from the corner of his mouth. "Stay home? You know I can't do that."

She stood on her toes, kissed his neck and ear. "It's just one night. The lab won't miss you."

He searched the kitchen drawers for a match, struck one, and sucked the end of his pipe with a snapping sound. The smoke drifted into his eyes, and he had to shut them a moment. Then, squinting, he said, "You want me to get my degree, don't you? You don't want to support me forever."

The pressure in her temples was spreading to the back of her head, and she tried to calm a sudden surge of anger. She curled two fingers over the waist of his pants and said, "If you stay home tonight, I'll gladly support you forever. I promise."

He laughed and then coughed. Billows of bluish smoke hit her square in the face, tasting like wet wood. Why anyone would want the taste of wood between his teeth was beyond her. This was the first thing she would never understand about him. "Don't you think," he said. "Don't you think, maybe, you're being a bit childish?"

She pushed away. The kitchen lights grew brighter. She glanced at the refrigerator and pantry, picturing all the food she'd bought to cook for him tumbling and crashing to the floor at his feet. Childish! She was the one who'd graduated. She was the one who had a job, the one responsible for educating hundreds of hopeless teenagers. Every month she paid two-thirds of their rent. "You're just a student!" she cried, as surprised at her own words as my father seemed to be. The pipe sagged; only a pencil-line of smoke twisted toward the ceiling. She went for the hall closet, grabbed the first coat she could find, not the warmest. She thought he would stop her before she could open the door. Or else he'd stand there numbly until its slam startled him, and he'd catch her arm before she was halfway to the bottom landing. But now the wooden stairs were passing quickly, and already here was the door to the street. She took a deep breath of the stair-well's musty air before pushing into the cold dusk to find her way home.

I LAUGHED UNEASILY. WHEN I WAS A KID, MY MOTHER'S ANGER had always seemed precise, controlled, frustratingly justified. No matter how strongly I might have believed I'd done something for the right reasons, a single hard look and long silence from my mother made me stoop and shuffle around the house with the weight of my wrong. A shout would drop me to my knees. Never could I bring myself to argue when she placed blame on my actions. But instead of trying to reform, or accepting this punishment as inevitable, I became a sneak. I adopted an expression of such absurd innocence that I still can't believe people didn't immediately see through to my deepest faults.

Once, when I was nine or ten, I'd crept with a friend into a neighbor's flower garden, where among the beds were scattered decorative pieces of driftwood, smooth logs with twisted silver roots. We lifted them over our heads and smashed them against large rocks. I held some grudge against the neighbor's kid, who later became my friend again and helped me destroy another neighbor's bird feeder. As we were running away, the boy's mother came out of the house hollering after us. She may or may not have seen who we were. I came home prepared to cry at the sight of my mother's crossed arms and darkened face. She wouldn't yell or threaten to spank me. She'd simply say, "I just received a very, very disappointing phone call," and I'd burst into a hysterical fit of denial and repentance. But she only kissed me and asked about my day. I forced myself to breathe normally and made up some story about how my teacher said I was getting better at math. I set the table and helped make a salad, then went to my room and lay on the bed. My breathing slowed, the knocking in my chest began to fade, and I waited to feel the terrible guilt. But after a few minutes the feeling didn't come, and I went to the closet to shuffle through my baseball cards. If my mother wasn't angry, I'd done nothing wrong. I could be exactly as innocent as she believed me to be.

So now, hearing about her shouting at my father in a blind, unreasonable fury, I couldn't help but laugh. Still, a twitching in my stomach grew worse with each sip of beer, and my armpits were sticky. She was supposed to be telling me how fortunate Julie and I were. I wanted her to say, "For your father and me it was hard. For you it'll be easy." But what she said was, "It's not funny," and rested her hands in her lap. "I was serious. That was the worst thing he could have said to me."

"But you forgave him," I said. "You stayed with him for thirty-five years." She sat far back in her chair and said nothing. "Because you loved each other so much."

Now it was her turn to laugh and shake her head. "You can't live with every person you love. Don't you think we had to work at it? You can't imagine the sacrifices. Mostly we were lucky."

I didn't want to hear the word luck again. It sounded too much like fate, in which Julie swore she believed. "Not in a flaky sort of way," she'd explain. "But if two people are really meant to be together – or not be together – there's nothing you can do about it."

Of course, I hated this idea. It left me and the strength of my love powerless. "What if it's our fate to end up hating each other?" I'd ask. "What if fate says our apartment's going to burn down? Should we chuck our smoke detector in the trash?"

She'd only shrug and say, "You've just got to enjoy what you have." All this was an elaborate excuse for her to be reckless. If her fate was already sealed, why should she bother being safe? In a few hours she'd be going to sleep, kicking around in our big bed, hissing and gasping and snoring all she wanted without me to hear. But even alone in my childhood room, I knew I wouldn't sleep. Julie would forget to lock the door. She'd leave the blinds raised. Our neighborhood wasn't the safest in Raleigh. Any number of dangerous men could sneak into our bedroom unobserved. All night I would stare at the ceiling, picturing knives and ropes and mysterious blunt objects, hating myself for coming here, where I'd have no control over what might happen.

My mother leaned forward again. "If I'd made it home, I might have left him for good," she said. "It was really just luck I didn't get to the bus depot."

AN INSTANT ON THE STREET AND HER NECK WAS FREEZING. Poor circulation, a doctor had once told her. She had to wear gloves to take a tub of ice cream from the freezer, but now she'd left them behind. Also her scarf, her hat, her boots. All my father's fault, and again her anger flared. It was getting late and would soon be dark. The sky was already the same soiled gray as snow lingering on the sidewalk from a storm three days earlier. In spots slush had turned to uneven ridges of ice.

I'd been to Troy once, when I was sixteen and visiting college campuses. It was a shabby city built on a hill, the university at its peak, the city center at its base along the Hudson. My parents pointed out their first apartment on a street as steep as any I'd seen in films set in San Francisco. At the time, of course, I couldn't have pictured my mother storming out the front door. But now it was easy to see her there, bracing against the cold, staring down the long slope. Below was her college, the school where she taught, and, somewhere, the bus depot. Whenever she'd left town before it had been in her father's car, or in my father's. She could call her father now. Across the street was a drugstore and lunch counter, inside a payphone. She could reverse the charges and listen to her father, my grandfather, curse first in Yiddish, then in Russian, and finally groping for the right language, whisper, "Chachkala, he slapped you? Don't lie to me. What I'll do to him. My own hands." I'm assuming there were payphones in 1965, and collect calls. This part my mother didn't tell me, but I'm certain she must have imagined my grandfather charging over the ice, getting lost in Pennsylvania or New Jersey, but eventually finding her and bringing her safely home. He'd come without question, no matter how early he had to work in the morning.

But she wouldn't call her father. Arthur had called her a child, but she was an adult, she could find her own way home. She waited a moment, maybe two or three, for my father to reach the sidewalk. She'd let him come all the way to her, let him put his hand on her shoulder, and then she'd shake it off and make him watch as she walked away. She waited, but no shoes clunked down the stairs, no fingers fumbled with the doorknob. Up the hill a car sped through an intersection, and from around the corner came the jumbled laughter of college boys hurrying somewhere – joking, probably, about a girl. Even now the light was fading, but the streetlamps hadn't yet come on. Her shoes were flat, no heels, but no treads either. She took one step and immediately slid, the shock a fist against her chest. She slid three feet and kept from falling only by grabbing for a telephone pole and hugging it in both arms. Across the street, in the drugstore window, an old man sat staring. His face, round and yellowed, hovered above a steaming cup of coffee. A newspaper was spread on the counter before him, but he was looking right at her, had watched her, she was certain, but made not the slightest move to help. She didn't dare glance up toward her own window. What if Arthur had seen as well? What if he was laughing at the way his wife's arms thrashed above her head and grasped desperately for the telephone pole?

The cold cut through her stockings. Her feet and ankles were bricks, her hands cramping in pain. The throb she'd felt earlier was a full headache now, worsened by a ripple of chills. The old man in the drugstore took a sip from his cup but didn't look away. His eyes were too small for his face, his nose and ears drooped. He was the trouble. He, my mother decided, was what had gone wrong with everything. Not only because he didn't come to her aid, but because he, too, was surely married, and at this very moment his wife was bent over a hot stove preparing his dinner. She could picture this woman, stout and cheerful, a wonderful cook. Cheerful except occasionally, when she remembered – had she been twenty? twenty-one? – the day she'd decided to walk out on the husband who didn't appreciate her and then changed her mind. More than anything, my mother would have liked to talk to this old man's wife. To ask how she could have given her life to another person. Given everything she had and only then discovered that he answered every question with a question, that he didn't know how to replace a burnt fuse, that he'd leave her willingly every night to work in a gloomy, cluttered lab.

She pushed away from the pole and took two steps on crunchy snow. Just ahead, the sidewalk had been shoveled and seemed clear for the next block. She hopped gingerly, and only when her toe touched did she see the ice, transparent, no more than a glossy film. This time there was nothing to grab onto, and she swept past one townhouse and half another. A wind gathered in her face. When the speed became frightening the only thing she could do was drop to her backside. The blow rattled from her spine to her teeth, and her head pounded. Between two parked cars, she could see the old man, moon-faced and empty, not concerned, not laughing, not anything but staring and sipping his coffee. To be fair, I don't believe the man saw my mother. It was dark on the street, light inside the drugstore. Most likely, he was grimacing at his own reflection. I understand that now, though I didn't listening at the kitchen table. Thirty-five years later, there was still a pressing bitterness in my mother's voice when she mentioned him, which was really only in passing: "There was an old guy in the drugstore across the street. He saw me fall and wouldn't help. Wouldn't even check to see if I was okay." In just three sentences I could tell she hated him, even then, and I hated him too, blamed him for everything. But hating him on the street, she momentarily forgot my father. Not until she rolled to her belly and pushed up onto her hands and knees – out of the corner of her eye, she thought she saw movement up the hill, near her apartment. But when she looked directly it was gone. The light in the kitchen was still burning, the window empty. Arthur would simply let her leave. This was what he'd wanted all along. Her head thumped, and tears began to freeze on her cheeks.

She scrambled to her feet, slipped, fell hard on her knees. And she was sliding again, down, down toward the city and river. The apartment was drifting away. All anger and pain crystallized as panic. With her elbows, her wrists, her fingers, frantically, she flailed for a grip. Ice flaked under her fingernails. She pictured my father, still standing in the kitchen, stunned, the pipe, nearly the size of his entire face, bobbing from his lips. He was no more than a boy. The pipe was a lollipop, a pacifier. She'd promised to spend eternity with a twenty-four-year-old boy. How was she supposed to take care of him? She couldn't even find her own way to the bus depot. She swiveled her body sideways, and slid toward the street. Her leg caught the tire of a parked car. She lay hanging over the edge of the curb, her hands and legs numb. Tears blurred her view as she stared up the hill, at the length of the slope she'd survived so far. Even if she wanted to, she didn't see how she could ever make it back.

"AFTER I FELL, YOU KNOW THE FIRST THING I THOUGHT OF?" my mother asked. Her voice had taken on a solemn, almost mystical hush. With my thumb I scraped at the label on my beer bottle, and when it was gone, flaked away the brittle glue. From the next room I no longer heard the rustle of newspaper. Was my father straining to listen? "Our honeymoon," she said. "You remember that story, don't you? You've heard part of it, at least."

I knew they'd gone to Bermuda. On the second day there, they'd ridden a catamaran across a bright blue bay. The sun and wind burned my mother's face, arms, belly, and thighs redder than coral. She spent the rest of the week in bed, howling at the slightest breeze from the air conditioner.

But now I was having trouble concentrating on her words. Julie and I, too, had taken a honeymoon, when we'd first moved in together. So what if we weren't married, we'd both agreed. We loved each other. Why shouldn't we celebrate it? I'd just finished journalism school, and neither of us could afford a cruise or a flight to the Bahamas, so we packed her car full of camping gear, drove up to the Blue Ridge, and wandered until we found a secluded spot. I propped the tent on a slab of granite jutting out a thousand feet above a narrow gorge streaked with mist. It seems absurd now, but if you had asked me at the time what I pictured when I closed my eyes and imagined the life Julie and I would have together, this was it: breathtaking and strangely serene. I would have been perfectly happy to spend all day sitting on the rocks, staring out over the hills in the distance, or walking the steep trails winding into the gorge. But Julie couldn't focus on anything other than the sheer, crumbling cliffs. She lay with her head hanging over the rim and said, "There's plenty to hang onto. It's only about thirty feet down to the next ledge. I bet we could make it, easy."

I knew by then not to tell her there was something she couldn't or shouldn't do. The minute I said, "That's too dangerous," or "You're nuts," she'd be halfway down the cliff. So I said, "I'm not saying you couldn't do it. But you know me. I'm so clumsy I'd probably drop with the first step. You'd have to carry me up on your shoulders."

"You're right," she said. "You're right." But still her head hung over the edge, judging possible finger grips in the rock's slight crevices and cracks, picturing her feet dangling in the air beside a hawk's nest, already telling me in her mind, "I told you I could do it. I told you."

For an hour we walked safely in the woods and then went back to the tent to make love. We slept, and I woke sweating. The sun had come out, and the tent's thin nylon was a cone of blue flame. Julie was gone, as I knew she would be, but I didn't move. She wasn't far away, somewhere on the cliff just outside the tent – I could hear her grunts, the trickle of dislodged pebbles, a brief, startled cry of "Oh, shit!" Her first call was tentative, apologetic. "Danny? Are you awake? Can you come help me?" But soon she was shouting, "Daniel! Help!" I tried to raise myself, I swear I tried, but the strength went out of my arms. They weren't simply asleep, but utterly useless. I closed my eyes and tried to convince myself I hadn't yet woken, breathing heavily, even feigning a snore. I knew what she wanted. She'd ask me to grab onto a root and swing myself into the abyss. "I'll just hang onto your ankle," she'd say. "You can pull us both up." The root would break and I'd topple head-first onto the next ledge. Only thirty feet down, but I'd be just unlucky enough to land on my neck and suffer terribly, lingering for days before fading off into a world of blind pain. Somehow, Julie would manage to clamber to the top, would stare down at my mangled body, shake her head, and say, "Fate."

She called once more, "Daniel! I need your help." Then the only sound was the rustling of a tree branch and a frantic scraping. Sweat was dripping over my eyelids, but I couldn't open them. Any second I expected the echoing scream. Hadn't I told her not to do it? Hadn't I done what I could? Later, when a policeman or forest ranger appeared at the scene of the tragedy, I'd explain, "She was always unpredictable, officer. I never knew what she'd do next."

In a few minutes, she unzipped the tent flap and dropped beside me. I let my eyes flutter open and stretched my arms. Part of me hoped her glasses had dropped into the gorge, so she wouldn't get a good look at my theatrical yawn. But there they were, specked and sweaty, her T-shirt smeared with black soil. "Didn't you hear me?" she said. "I was calling you." In an excited rush, she told me how the lower ledge was narrower than she'd first thought, how she'd had to stand with her chest to the cliff and still her heels hung over the gorge. "The only way I could get back up was by grabbing onto the littlest tree branch you ever saw. It was hardly more than a twig. If that had snapped, I'd be gone."

My strength came back in a rush, and I sprang up. All the disgust I felt for myself exploded in anger. "That was a fucking stupid thing to do," I said. "What would I do if you fell? Did you think about me at all?"

She rubbed at her fingers caked with dirt. "You're right," she said. "It was selfish. This is our honeymoon. I'm sorry."

She hugged me, and I mumbled into the soft skin of her neck, "If I lost you, it would kill me." To myself I kept whispering, I told her not to do it, I did what I could. If she even suspected I'd been awake, I would have been torn apart by shame. But that she didn't know was almost worse – what good were those ridiculous glasses if they couldn't see into my heart? She kept her head lowered, and between clumps of her hair I glimpsed tears collecting on her chin.

"I know it would," she said, and hid her face in her hands.

At the kitchen table, I felt suddenly lightheaded and drained. My mother didn't seem to notice if my face went pale or flushed. She was saying, "I was freezing under that car, but all I could think about was sunburn. The feeling wasn't so different, really. Bermuda. You know your father. He kept pacing in that tiny hotel room, asking every five minutes, 'Is there anything I can do? Is there anything that would make you feel better?'"

She snapped at him. "I don't know. Just do something!"

In the lobby store he found a tube of ointment and brought it back to the room, smiling. "Look what I've got," he said and held it up, triumphant, as if it were the first thing he'd ever bought on his own. He squirted a white blob onto two fingers and touched it to her shoulder. The cream went through her skin, through bone, to the center of all pain. She cried out, tore at the sheets, bounced her heels against the mattress.

"It was supposed to hurt like that," she told me and shuddered visibly, lifting the teacup to her lips. "You know what your grandfather would have said. 'It don't hurt, it don't work.' I knew it was true, I only needed to hear it from Arthur. But he just apologized and capped the tube. When he started pacing again, I told him he was stirring a breeze and sent him out of the room. The rest of the afternoon, I listened to him pacing in the hallway. The housekeepers must have thought he was crazy. So why should he come after me now? I'd driven him away. I'd gotten exactly what I'd asked for."

NOT THIRTY SECONDS AFTER SHE GRABBED THE TIRE, MY MOTHER heard the rumble of a car engine and a heavy crunching of snow. My father's car, enormous, maroon, a Chrysler from late in the last decade, backed from their driveway onto the street. If he turned uphill, toward the lab, their marriage was over for sure. But only the bulbous trunk rose up the slope. The headlights shone directly at her. For a moment she could see the passenger door, crumpled in an accident a year before they'd met. My father had used the insurance money to buy a record player. "Who needs four doors?" he'd asked, when, on their first blind date, my mother had had to climb in on the driver's side and crawl across the worn leather bench. She hadn't been offended. Here was a Jewish boy unlike any she'd ever gone out with. Not bohemian, exactly, but secure in his own set of expectations, oblivious to those of others. He spoke to her in an immediately familiar way, as if she were a cousin, or even a sister. She was careful to lift the hem of her dress as she slid into the seat, and glancing behind, was pleased to see my father watching, not glancing politely away. It was a thrill she felt, a sense of adventure.

Now the car – its door still damaged – rolled only a few feet down the hill before twisting sideways. It didn't stop or even slow as it neared her. She pulled herself to her knees and watched it pass, backwards now, my father tiny behind the high ridge of the dashboard. The trunk of the next parked car blocked her view of the drugstore, but she knew the old man was staring at this new disaster in silence. Her husband, a little boy in a giant Chrysler, was sliding all the way to the base of the hill, would drop straight into the Hudson. Her tears came faster now, grieving for my father, whom she'd driven to his death, for herself, a widow at twenty-one.

She forgot her headache, her numb hands and feet. None of it, nothing about herself mattered at all. She ran after the car, no longer worried about falling, her smooth-soled shoes slapping the ice in challenge. When she did fall, it was face forward only a few feet from where my father's car had backed into a telephone pole, cushioned by a high bank of snow. Her arms were stretched straight above her head, her cheek pressed against pavement, but nothing hurt. Still, she groaned as my father knelt over her, asking, "God, Hannah. Are you all right? Can you move?" She lifted her head, nodded, tasted tears. He helped her up, led her around the Chrysler's long hood and in the driver's door. "Warm up," he said. "Your hands must be ice. I'll get us out of here." She was sobbing, embarrassed by her wet cheeks but unable to wipe them. Part of her still believed my father's car was sinking into the river, and that she was alone forever. From the vents in the dashboard hot air spilled onto her lap, and she heard my father open the trunk. She tried to close her hands but couldn't. This was pain, real pain, vibrating from her elbows to her fingertips and back.

My father stood in front of the car now, holding a brown sack under one arm. He stuck a hand inside and shook sand under the tires and along the road for half a block. When he dropped behind the steering wheel and slammed the door, she forced herself to stop crying and asked, "Since when do you keep sand in the trunk?"

"Always," he said. "You never know. Give me your hands." He rubbed her fingers between his gloves until she cried out and then dropped them, bright red now, back to her lap. "Next time you run out on me, make sure you dress properly, please?"

She wanted to smile but feared her lips would betray her, breaking again into sobs. "I will," she said. "I promise." Chills splashed over her back and neck in waves. Out the window, the row of parked cars stretched the length of each block, but she had no idea which had sheltered her.

The engine whined high before the car jerked forward. My father stroked the steering wheel as if it were a dog or pony, and they climbed slowly. Soon they were passing the drugstore. There was the old man, still in the window, now puffing an enormous cigar. They came to the driveway, but my father didn't pull in. "You're coming with me to the lab," he said before she could ask.

MY FATHER WASN'T TRYING TO LISTEN FROM THE FAMILY ROOM. He was snoring now, softly. The newspaper would have slumped to his lap, his chin quivering against his chest. Over the next fifteen minutes, the snoring would grow louder, then sputter, and eventually choke off altogether. He'd wake with a start, gasping for breath. When I was five or six, I used to sit in the family room while my father read the paper, running my toy cars along the hardwood floor at the edge of the carpet. I'd watch him fall asleep, listen for the stages of his breathing, and make a loud noise just as the air stopped passing through his nose. It was my job, I believed, to keep my father from dying in his sleep. Once, I'd played in my bedroom longer than usual. When I came downstairs my father's head was already hanging. The newspaper had fallen to the floor. I approached slowly and heard no noise, no snoring or wheezing. I'd been lecturing to a crowd of stuffed animals and had let my father slip away. My wailing brought my mother running from the kitchen. My father stood up so fast he knocked the chair over backward. It hit the wall and cracked one of the wood-colored panels hiding the sheetrock. In my mother's arms I moaned, and nothing she or my father said could make me tell what was wrong.

Now, my mother swept her hand along the table, collecting crumbs into a small pile. "I must already have been pretty sick by the time I got in the car," she said. "I ended up in bed for the next four days. You know how it is when you've got a fever. Everything is hazy, and a hundred confused thoughts go through your head, but you believe every one of them."

She'd pressed against the passenger door, as far away from my father as possible. His face was smooth though she hadn't seen him shave in a week. When the tires began to spin, he bit his lower lip, and she saw something very clearly. It wasn't a premonition so much as a certainty. Of its cause she couldn't yet be sure – illness, maybe, troubled children, financial worries, there were so many possibilities. But this was what she knew without a doubt: one day, without warning, my father would take her hand and hold it to his lowered forehead. Maybe it was the face of the old man in the drugstore she pictured, hanging in defeat. In a soft, wavering voice, he would say, "Hannah, I have no idea what to do." He spoke from far off, across the limits of despair. "Hannah, please. What should I do?"

"It's ridiculous," my mother said, and laughed. "To think this was the big turning point in my life? I was convinced. I thought I had to decide right then what to do. I had to know whether I could trust myself to answer him when the time came. By then it would be too late to run away. As soon as I was well enough, I went into town and found the bus depot. I did all the research into prices and times and connections."

"But you stayed," I said. This was what I'd been waiting to hear. She'd tell me how everything had worked out in the end. I held my breath, ready for a long exhale of relief.

"I stayed."

"So what was it?"

"What was what?"

"The big crisis," I said. "The thing you had to answer."

She crossed her arms, hugging herself tightly. "I don't know," she said. "I'm still waiting. Every day."

INSIDE MY FATHER'S LAB, A SOUR STINGING SMELL FILLED her nose and mouth. The warmth here was even more startling than inside the car. Her hands had loosened enough for her to clench them into fists. My father led her into a room crossed with wires and packed with elaborate instruments and glass containers of various shapes. He set her on a stool before a high counter and held a match over a stout metal tube until it spouted a blue flame. Over it he placed a three-legged stand and a glass cylinder full of water. "You'll drink some tea?" he said.

She nodded. "Why did you take the car? To follow me. Why didn't you just run?"

He rubbed his chin, confused, or maybe hurt. "I didn't know which way you'd go," he said. Then after a pause, "I don't really know."

"It took you long enough. I could have been halfway to town."

He shrugged and stared at the floor. "I couldn't find the keys."

"I didn't think you were coming at all," she said. "I thought you'd just let me go."

His smile was slight and pained. Gently, he lifted her hand from the counter. "I'm your husband. You should have faith in me."

Faith. She repeated the word silently, several times, until it sounded senseless. "I know," she said. "I know."

She let him put his arms around her. "I'm sorry I didn't come faster," he said.

When her tea was ready, my father slipped into a long white coat and draped over his ears a pair of comical plastic goggles that stuck out an inch from either side of his face. "I didn't make you dinner," my mother said.

"Are you hungry?"

"No."

"Neither am I. I'll get us some take-out later. Are you warm enough?"

She nodded and took another sip of tea. The cold was leaving her hands, but it was taking something with it. Her very center was weakening. My father clicked on a radio, and the lab filled with steel drums and calypso voices, occasionally scratched by bursts of unexpected static. He shuffled between two arrangements of metal clamps, yellow rubber tubes, and glass bottles filled with colored and clear liquids, making marks in a notebook. Sometimes he leaned into a small alcove with a fan that sucked away dangerous fumes. He called it a "hood," and she immediately smelled motor oil and pictured a car engine. She would quickly concede, her husband understood certain secret workings of the world. But he was so blind to the obvious. Already he believed that everything that had happened tonight was resolved. He was swinging his hips to the wrong rhythm, occasionally glancing at her over his shoulder, smiling. Why couldn't she so easily put it all behind her? She still saw herself on the bus from Troy to Albany, the train to New Haven, arriving wearily into the arms of her mother and father. It wasn't so difficult to imagine herself teaching in the high school she'd graduated from, growing fat on her mother's cooking. But her parents were already getting old. Soon enough they would need to be cared for. Some day, her father would forget all his old advice, and her mother's arthritis would keep her from stirring soup. My mother would have to drive to doctors' offices and hospitals. She'd have to sort through complicated medical bills. There was nowhere she could go to simply worry about herself; nowhere would her life suddenly become simpler.

My father bent close to a scale, trying to balance a bottle with tiny brass weights. "This is never going to work," he said. "I just hope they'll give me a degree for it."

High on the walls were the grids of thick glass. When I visited Troy the summer I was researching colleges, my father took me into the dark lab where he'd spent half of his twenties. Gradually, I came to understand what these windows were for – in an explosion, ordinary glass would shatter and maim, but these would hold firm. Sitting there drinking her tea, with a fever rushing on, did my mother suddenly grasp this? Or maybe she knew already, but only now allowed herself to realize what it really meant. In those glass bottles my father examined and adjusted, a pressure might be lurking, ready to force its way out one night while she was home quietly grading papers or reading a book. The tanks full of gas – the same gas feeding the tube that heated her tea – could ignite and singe all life from the building. My father might be found face down inside his hood, strangled by the fumes of his research.

He snapped his notebook shut and came to her. "Another cup?" he asked. "Hannah, what is it?"

As soon as he stepped within reach, she lunged. One fist cracked against his chest, the other sunk into the soft flesh of his side. "I'm not a child!" she cried. "Tell me I'm not a child." She closed her eyes and punched blindly. Her knuckles struck skin, hair, cloth, and once, the plastic of his goggles. She couldn't stop her arms from swinging, driving him backward, worried most that her fists would soon find nothing in front of her. She opened her eyes and swung again, but now grabbed onto the collar of his lab coat. "Say I'm an adult."

His arms went around her neck. She breathed the wooden smell of his pipe. "You're wonderful," he said. "You're the best thing that ever happened to me." His lips pressed against her forehead. "My God. You're on fire."

"I feel like I'm dying." Her own father would have been quick with instructions and remedies. "You feel bad now, sure," he'd say. "A week, you won't even remember." Arthur wasn't her father. He would have nothing to tell her. But she knew these things for herself. "Do we have any aspirin at home?"

"I don't know," he said. "If not, I'll get some."

"I'll have to call in sick tomorrow."

"I'll call for you. You can stay in bed."

"You'll stay with me, won't you?" she said. "You don't need to be here tomorrow, do you?"

He pulled her close, pressed her cheek to his chest, and held her more firmly than he ever had before. She slipped a button of his coat between her teeth and bit hard. "Of course I will," he said. "Of course."


MY FATHER WALKED INTO THE KITCHEN, YAWNING. HE OBVIOUSLY hadn't heard a word we'd said. My mother leaned back in her chair, holding the empty teacup in her lap. I took a long swallow of warm beer. He opened the refrigerator door, bent low, rustled something wrapped in cellophane. Without glancing at us, he said, "So. What are we going to be eating at this wedding?"

If I'd known then how little it was going to matter, I would have made something up. If I could have said for certain there would be a wedding in three weeks. As it turns out, there was. The caterers served some sort of chicken in a creamy sauce, but I was too drunk and too busy chatting with guests to taste it. My father never mentioned it, but since he didn't complain, I assume it wasn't bad. My mother danced with me stiffly, reminding me to take plenty of suntan lotion on our honeymoon to St. Thomas. "And don't forget you're still a Jewish boy," she said, sniffling. Three weeks after I sat in the kitchen listening to her story, I was legally bound to Julie, the woman I loved. For the next two years I slept no more than four hours a night. Julie's thrashing in bed grew almost violent, and occasionally I woke with bruises. In the mornings, she complained of not being able to breathe. We divorced. If I'd even had the faintest notion of how much I still had to learn, I would have told my father, "Shrimp scampi."

But at the time, his question pinned me to my chair and nearly brought me to tears. My mother covered my hand with hers and squeezed. "I don't know," I said. "I have absolutely no idea."

My father shrugged and said, "The hors d'œuvres are usually good. People always fill up on those. We have any pears?"

"Bottom drawer," my mother said.

He picked up a brown pear, turned it around in his fingers, and put it back. I suddenly imagined Julie dancing across a crowded freeway, begging me to make her stop. What about me? I wanted to call from the guardrail, but couldn't. Who'll take care of me?

My father closed the refrigerator door and said, "Any bananas?"

"On the counter. I'm not sure if they're ripe yet."

He lifted a banana, still somewhat green, and dropped it back into the basket. Then, quietly, he popped the lid from the tin he wasn't supposed to touch, stuck one cookie in his mouth, two or three more in his pocket, and strolled into the hallway. My mother stared after him, mystified, I think, and I glanced from one to the other, nearly choking with envy.

# Titles available from Hawthorne Books

AT YOUR LOCAL BOOKSELLER OR FROM OUR WEBSITE: *hawthornebooks.com*

## Saving Stanley: The Brickman Stories
### BY SCOTT NADELSON

Scott Nadelson's interrelated short stories are graceful, vivid narratives that bring into sudden focus the spirit and the stubborn resilience of the Brickmans, a Jewish family of four living in suburban New Jersey. The central character, Daniel Brickman, forges obstinately through his own plots and desires as he struggles to balance his sense of identity with his longing to gain acceptance from his family and peers. This fierce collection provides an unblinking examination of family life and the human instinct for attachment.

SCOTT NADELSON PLAYFULLY INTRODUCES *us to a fascinating family of characters with sharp and entertaining psychological observations in gracefully beautiful language, reminiscent of young Updike. I wish I could write such sentences. There is a lot of eros and humor here – a perfectly enjoyable book.* —JOSIP NOVAKOVICH
author of *Salvation and Other Disasters*

## So Late, So Soon
### BY D'ARCY FALLON

This memoir offers an irreverent, fly-on-the-wall view of the Lighthouse Ranch, the Christian commune D'Arcy Fallon called home for three years in the mid-1970s. At eighteen years old, when life's questions overwhelmed her and reconciling her family past with her future seemed impossible, she accidentally came upon the Ranch during a hitchhike gone awry. Perched on a windswept bluff in Loleta, a dozen miles from anywhere in Northern California, this community of lost and found twenty-somethings lured her in with promises of abounding love, spiritual serenity, and a hardy, pioneer existence. What she didn't count on was the fog.

I FOUND FALLON'S STORY *fascinating, as will anyone who has ever wondered about the role women play in fundamental religious sects. What would draw an otherwise independent woman to a life of menial labor and subservience? Fallon's answer is this story, both an inside look at 70s commune life and a funny, irreverent, poignant coming of age.* —JUDY BLUNT
author of *Breaking Clean*

HAWTHORNE BOOKS & LITERARY ARTS ∷ Portland, Oregon

## God Clobbers Us All
BY POE BALLANTINE

Set against the dilapidated halls of a San Diego rest home in the 1970s, *God Clobbers Us All* is the shimmering, hysterical, and melancholy story of eighteen-year-old surfer-boy orderly Edgar Donahoe's struggles with friendship, death, and an ill-advised affair with the wife of a maladjusted war veteran. All of Edgar's problems become mundane, however, when he and his lesbian Blackfoot nurse's aide best friend, Pat Fillmore, become responsible for the disappearance of their fellow worker after an LSD party gone awry. *God Clobbers Us All* is guaranteed to satisfy longtime Ballantine fans as well as convert those lucky enough to be discovering his work for the first time.

## Things I Like About America
BY POE BALLANTINE

These risky, personal essays are populated with odd jobs, eccentric characters, boarding houses, buses, and beer. Ballantine takes us along on his Greyhound journey through small-town America, exploring what it means to be human. Written with piercing intimacy and self-effacing humor, Ballantine's writings provide entertainment, social commentary, and completely compelling slices of life.

IN HIS SEARCH *for the real America, Poe Ballantine reminds me of the legendary musk deer, who wanders from valley to valley and hilltop to hilltop searching for the source of the intoxicating musk fragrance that actually comes from him. Along the way, he writes some of the best prose I've ever read.* —SY SAFRANSKY
Editor, *The Sun*

## September 11:
## West Coast Writers Approach Ground Zero
EDITED BY JEFF MEYERS

The myriad repercussions and varied and often contradictory responses to the acts of terrorism perpetuated on September 11, 2001 have inspired thirty-four West Coast writers to come together in their attempts to make meaning from chaos. By virtue of history and geography, the West Coast has developed a community different from that of the East, but ultimately shared experiences bridge the distinctions in provocative and heartening ways. Jeff Meyers anthologizes the voices of American writers as history unfolds and the country braces, mourns, and rebuilds.

CONTRIBUTORS INCLUDE: *Diana Abu-Jaber, T. C. Boyle, Michael Byers, Tom Clark, Joshua Clover, Peter Coyote, John Daniel, Harlan Ellison, Lawrence Ferlinghetti, Amy Gerstler, Lawrence Grobel, Ehud Havazelet, Ken Kesey, Maxine Hong Kingston, Stacey Levine, Tom Spanbauer, Primus St. John, Sallie Tisdale, Alice Walker, and many others.*

 HAWTHORNE BOOKS & LITERARY ARTS :: *Portland, Oregon*

## A Walkabout Home

### BY STEPHANIE ROSE BIRD

The American mystical practice of Hoodoo seeped into Stephanie Rose Bird's consciousness before she even knew its name. During her childhood, she took long walks amidst the lush green landscape of Southern New Jersey – a landscape bounded by the wetlands, the Pine Barrens, the Atlantic Ocean, and a rich tradition of folklore. The power of this walking – of these human foot tracks – has been the subject of many incantations, chants, and songs. The folkloric tradition pays careful attention to the cleansing of pathways, especially the pathway home. Steeped in these worlds, A Walkabout Home tells the story of an African American writer and artist raised in the Pine Barrens of New Jersey who has traveled the globe in search of art and home.

*In the end, Bird is not one to shy away from the harder questions in life. On nearly every page her words here seem to ask, indirectly and in just so many words: Who am I? Why am I as I am? What has formed me? But because of Bird's travel across cultures and continents, the book's ultimate subject is the way these questions provide a connection between people. A Walkabout Home is an eloquent bridge across the span of human experience.*

—MICHAEL FALLON
Annuals Editor, Llewellyn Publications

## Dastgah: Diary of a Headtrip

### BY MARK MORDUE

From India to Paris, Iran to New York, Australian award-winning journalist Mark Mordue chronicles his year long world trip with his girlfriend, Lisa Nicol. Mordue explores countries most Americans never see as well as issues of world citizenship in the 21st century.

*I just took a trip around the world in one go, first zigzagging my way through this incredible book, and finally, almost feverishly, making sure I hadn't missed out on a chapter along the way. I'm not sure what I'd call it now: A road movie of the mind, a diary, a love story, a new version of the subterranean homesick and wanderlust blues – anyway, it's a great ride. Paul Bowles and Kerouac are in the back, and Mark Mordue has taken over the wheel of that pickup truck from Bruce Chatwin, who's dozing in the passenger seat.* —WIM WENDERS
Director of *Paris, Texas; Wings of Desire;*
and *The Buena Vista Social Club*